Benefits of Friendship

by

Theresa Stillwagon

Just Like Sisters, Book One

Cover Art by *The Wild Rose Press, Inc.*

The Wild Rose Press, Inc.
PO Box 708
Adams Basin, NY 14410-0708
Visit us at www.thewildrosepress.com

Publishing History
First Edition, 2025
Trade Paperback ISBN 978-1-5092-5975-5
Digital ISBN 978-1-5092-5976-2

Just Like Sisters, Book One
Published in the United States of America

Dedication

To my husband, Mike, who has always been there for me.

Chapter One

Cass needed to get her anger under control before she did something crazy. Like hit that lawyer.

"Maybe you should talk to the owner of the building." The blonde server settled the hot coffee pot on the edge of the table before sliding her model-thin body into the booth. "Getting upset won't solve anything, Cass."

She shook her head, refusing to look toward Angie. Right now, she wished her other, more distrusting friend were here. She needed Maddie Thomas's hotheadedness a bit more than Angie Ferguson's comforting attitude. She wanted to stay angry. "Why would Mr. Brown change our deal? Mr. Martinson promised I could lease the building month to month. And now his lawyer is saying I need to pay six months' rent upfront." She waved the offending letter in the air. "I just don't understand why."

"You need to calm down."

"I don't want to calm down." She glared hard at Angie. "I want to be mad. I want to yell and scream. Don't tell me to calm down. You're not the one looking at a major expense due before the end of the month."

"Stop it, Cassandra Rogers," Angie said. "I didn't do anything to deserve your anger."

She was right; yet, Cass still wanted to punch something. Or someone.

"Maybe you just misunderstood the letter." Angie slid her closed hand across the smooth table, stopping an inch from the envelope. "I've known Mr. Martinson all my life, and he's always been true to his word. Maybe you should talk to him, instead of his lawyer."

"I didn't misunderstand it." Placing her empty coffee cup on the table between them, she looked out the window. People milled in and out of the stores along the main road—mothers with their children, couples with arms wrapped around each other's waists, dusty cowboys, and flirty women. She turned her head slightly and scanned the area on the opposite side of the street. Where once stood a row of older businesses, now a park filled with young birch trees and white, pink, and purple flowery bushes eased her mind a bit.

Simple, wholesome townsfolk spending a warm afternoon mixing with the influx of cowboys arriving to participate in the crowd-pleasing Friday night activity of a small Texas town. She'd always looked forward to the end of winter.

Just your typical early spring afternoon in Greenfield, Texas.

"Cass?"

She shook her observation away and returned her attention to Angie. "Why would he need that much money now?"

"Do you have it?" Angie crossed her arms.

She sighed, nodding. "But I don't want to use it."

"Why?" Angie lifted her arms, and then dropped them. "Oh, never mind. You still refuse to use any of the money your dad left you."

The day of his funeral came to mind. She pushed it aside. "Leaving it to me wasn't his first choice."

"That's not true."

Cass sighed. "Please, I love you like a sister, but I'm not in the mood to explain my reasoning."

"I'll let it go for now." Angie studied her, and then nodded. "If what you told me earlier turns out to be true, you will need that money."

"I don't even want to think about that," she said. "All I want to worry about now is The Horse and Bridle Bookstore."

Angie shrugged.

"Everything would be fine, if I'd left the bookstore the way Dad had it." She shook her head. Pain sliced through her temple at the slight movement. "Why did I ever think I needed to expand in the first place?"

"The Monday night lecture series, possibly." A bright smile moved across her tanned face. "It's gotten so fashionable with all the folks around the area, you needed to find a bigger place. Half the bookstore just wasn't kicking it anymore."

"Who would've thought listening to a bunch of long-winded cowboys would be so popular. All these people grew up around horses, farms, and rodeos." Cass glanced out the window again; pride at the accomplishment of the last year warmed her before the letter came back to mind. "And now Mr. Martinson wants to change all that."

"You'll fix it."

"I've been thinking about turning the front area of the new building into a café-type place and selling coffee, tea, and soda. Maybe some nutritious snacks, vegetables, and fruits."

"I remember you mentioning something like that." Angie nodded. "It's a great idea."

"Yes, and I'm hoping my mother will help me out." She breathed out. "Unfortunately, what I'm thinking about doing with the rest of the building will cost even more money."

Silence followed her statement, and for once she wished this friend would speak out. She wouldn't have time to begrudge her choices if Maddie was the one sitting in the booth with her now. She wouldn't have the silence to second-guess the bad decisions she'd made in the last few months. Placing a hand on her flat belly, she swallowed her regret and focused on the swaying limb of a baby tree across the main road.

"You okay, Cass?"

A small child pulled away from her mother's hand and raced into the park. Young joyful laughter seized her.

A bittersweet ache filled her heart as a young man moved behind the woman and circled his arms around her waist. Such love filled the scene with such peace.

"Cass?"

Concern echoed in that single word; yet, she couldn't move her gaze from the family unit. "Some people are so lucky."

A soft hand settled against her chilled skin. "You need to have faith."

"Yes."

"If I were you, I'd go and speak with Mr. Martinson's lawyer."

Thankfully, she moved back to their original subject.

The couple disappeared behind a set of trees. The boy's laughter faded in the gentle wind.

She sighed and twisted toward her friend. "I don't

think it would do any good. I got the impression he might have had another offer…a better one."

"Probably from that new vet in town," Angie offered. "I heard he doesn't want to use the old vet clinic."

"I heard the same thing. That building did get damaged badly in the fire, so I don't blame him. But why does he want the same building as me? There are better choices for him." A feeling of heaviness sank her into the seat. "Oh, why did I have to change things?"

"Change is good."

"Even when it's not necessary," she added. "The bookstore was doing fine the way my father ran it. Now…everything is so messed up."

"Things will work out." Angie slid from the booth and stepped toward the counter. "Believe me."

Gratefulness lifted her unease. "I hope so."

"They will." Angie patted her arm and backed a few feet from the booth. "But I still think you should reconsider using some of the money from your father. He would want you to use it. Or you could apply for one of those special government-sponsored loans. You should qualify easy because of the damage the fire did to your building."

"You're probably right." Bitterness edged in her voice. "After Billy left, the business was all Dad cared about."

"Your father loved you." Angie moved back to the table. "Think about this, if he didn't care about you, why did he leave you the bookstore?"

"Why?" Her chest tightened. "Because Billy is dead, and I'm the only person left. Just like Mom, Dad had always expected his son to return home. Even after

I showed him the proof of his death, he still wouldn't accept it."

"Well, he's gone and so is your father. The bookstore is your business." The tall server smashed her hands against her narrow hips. "If you want to change things, then change them."

Cass jerked in her booth at the harsh words, fighting an unexpected smile. Angie stood strong and straight in front of her—a fierce and determined friend, willing to go to battle for the one she loved. "Wow, I think Maddie is rubbing off on you."

She shrugged, relaxing her arms to her sides. "Talk to the lawyer."

"Okay, I will." She raised her hands toward Angie. "I'll call him as soon as I get back to the store today or tomorrow. I might go to the bank after I leave here to ask them about that loan."

"You wouldn't need to do that if you weren't so stubborn."

"I'm not using my father's money."

Angie shook her head and turned away, wandering through the half empty tables to the long counter. She twisted her head and waved before disappearing into the kitchen, a gentle grin fighting with her frown.

Could Angie be right? Her father may have started the business, but it was hers now. Even before her father's death, she'd been responsible for the day-to-day activity.

When she'd taken over running the bookstore alone a year ago, it'd been a thriving enterprise. Regular customers came in, and new ones arrived most weekends. The county fair and Memorial Day rodeo brought in people from towns all around the area, enough for all the businesses along the main drag to get their fill of profits during the warmer months. And the new lecture series brought in business all year long. Things were tight, and she could use some extra space; yet, she had no real need to change anything.

"If you had to use your savings, would you have enough to pay the old man?"

Cass jumped in her seat, twisting around to face Angie. She'd been so wrapped up in her thoughts she hadn't even noticed her return. She grabbed her long hair and flipped it behind her. Soft strands flowed down her back to her waist. "Yes, but my account balance will drop to less than a thousand dollars."

"And how much did your father leave you?" She shook her head. "I think you're making a mistake not using that money to expand the bookstore. And Maddie agrees."

Now, Maddie's input comes up. "So, what's one more mistake?"

"Hey," a gruff male voice rang out, "You have other customers, you know?"

The bell chimed over the entranceway door a second later, sending the server scurrying away from the table. "Settle down, Fred. Let me get this new customer first."

Angie raced to the counter and picked up a laminated menu before greeting a dusty cowboy with a beaming grin. Her laughter filled the room, followed by a deep-throated grunt.

Another cowboy arriving for Ladies Night at The Corral, hoping to catch a little filly to ride for the duration of time in town. And damn the consequences. The one Lady's Night Maddie and Angie had dragged her to six weeks ago had turned into a week-late period and a colossal headache. The one and only time she'd allowed a stranger to spend the night left her feeling like a complete fool, with a possible lifetime problem.

"You can take a seat over there." Angie spoke to the new arrival. "I'll go get you some coffee."

"Thanks."

Cass looked up at the same time the cowboy approached her table and swallowed her breath. A tall, lean man slowed near her, dark beard hiding his face. His jaw tightened under the low brim of a dusty cowboy hat before he nodded and moved toward the booth behind her. The seat groaned under his lanky weight.

An odd sensation slid up her back…like a pair of gentle hands moving over the top of her head, scorching her with delicious heat. Half of her wanted to turn her head, to meet the man's gaze; yet, the other half kept her stiff in her seat.

She'd made one mistake with a cowboy recently. Cass didn't plan on making another one.

Chapter Two

Billy's sister.

Jack Fontaine placed his cowboy hat on the seat beside him.

It had to be.

No other woman could have that shade of black-on-black hair, gleaming with hints of blue in the afternoon sun and falling down her slim back like black silk. No one could have those deep, intense green eyes the shade of fresh summer grass after a rainstorm. Billy had had the same eye color as his sister except sadness and pain never shined from his eyes. Sureness and aggressiveness, but none of his sister's pain and sorrow.

Three years? Had three years really passed since his friend's car accident? Two years since his own father's death?

An incomplete DVD, a confusing movie of misplaced scenes and blurry focus, tore through his mind. He gazed out the window at the sights of the town. A decade ago, he'd been a part of this area, an up-and-coming cowboy with a great chance of making the Professional Bull Riders.

But now? What was he now?

Jack wasn't sure.

Not much about the people roaming around had changed; yet, the town itself was different. He'd heard about the fire that had devastated the west end of the main road. The same remembered businesses lined the east side of the street, with the same signs over the doorways and the same displays in their windows. Yet, the opposite end was different. Instead of the long line of old buildings sat a newly planted town park, baby trees and colorful bushes filling out the bareness of the area, interspaced with rough wooden benches and swing sets. A large, covered gazebo sat in the center of the cleared land. Both parents and grandparents sat in the scant shadows falling from the young trees. Groups of children raced around the area, laughing joyous sounds rising into the afternoon air. A few teens hung around the gazebo, leaning together with conspiratorial whispers. A swift stream roared beyond the park on its way toward San Antonio.

"Hey, cowboy, here's your coffee."

The tall, blonde server poured hot, black liquid into his cup. A tag pinned to the upper portion of her dress uniform showed her name.

"Angie?"

Throaty laughter flowed from her. "Have you decided what *else* you'd like?"

If he thought he was being discreet about his interest in the other woman, then this lady's attitude silenced that belief. "Ah, sort of."

She raised the pad and placed her pencil next to it. "If you need a few more minutes, I'll come back."

"No." He picked the first thing he read when he looked at the menu clamped in his hand. "I'll take the chicken special."

She grinned. "Are you sure about that?"

"Why?" He kidded. "Is there something wrong with it?"

"No." Her voice lowered, grin deepening the lines around her thin mouth. "Just seems like you made the decision pretty fast."

"I like chicken."

"Okay, then." Her mouth twitched downward a bit. "No skin off my butt."

Soft laughter echoed from the booth in front of him, sensuous and warm, whispering over him like a soft feather on naked skin. He remembered her laugh, bright and warm, filled with life.

Angie tapped his shoulder with her pencil. "Her name is Cassandra Rogers. Cass, for short."

He half-rose from his chair. "What?"

"You've been staring at the back of her head since you settled in the booth," She leaned nearer. "I figured you'd like to know her name."

"Cassandra," he said.

The woman's back stiffened, head turning slightly to her left.

He settled back in his seat. "That's an unusual name."

"Fits her, though," she said softly. "So, have you changed your mind, or do you still want the chicken special? I was joshing with you before; everything here is good."

"Haven't changed my mind."

"Okay, I'll be back in a few minutes."

She moved a couple of steps toward Cass's table and jerked her head backward with a nod and a wink.

"Knock it off," her sweet voice whispered. "I'm not interested."

"Yeah, right."

Seems your friend doesn't believe you.

11

"I would love some more coffee, honey."

Jack glanced toward the bar where a gray-haired stick of a man waved his cup around his head. He focused back on the sitting woman, just in time to watch her shoulders sag low.

"Hold your horses, Fred," Angie said. "I'll be back in a few minutes, Cass."

"Thanks for the warning."

A smile warmed her voice now, one he wished he could see. Pathetic, wishing to see the smile of the sister of the man he'd given up on when Billy had needed him the most. He forced his gaze to the window again and studied the people wandering past the diner.

"Here you go, cowboy." The server placed a steamy plate of fried chicken, mashed potatoes, and green beans in front of him. A second later, fresh coffee warmed the old, dark liquid sitting unremembered in his cup. "Will that be all?"

"Yeah." He grinned. "Thanks."

"You're welcome." She turned toward Cass's booth.

He reached out his hand and grabbed the edge of her bright blue apron, stopping her near his table. Maybe he could get this woman to introduce him to Cass. "The name is Jack, Jack Fontaine. Dr. Jack Fontaine, the new veterinarian. Will you tell her that?"

She stood tall. "So, you're the new vet?"

"Yes."

"You want to meet her, do you?"

No, I'm not ready for her to remember me. Soon, but not yet. "Just tell her my name."

"Sure thing, cowboy. Oh, by the way, everyone calls me Angie." She studied him before shaking her head. "But you're not interested in my name, are you?"

"Angie's a nice name."

She grinned. "I'll tell Cass your name, but I doubt she'll do anything about it."

"Why?"

She glanced over toward her. "Let's just say she's not interested in anything but her bookstore now."

"The Horse and Bridle?"

"Yes." She studied him for another few seconds. "I need to get back to work."

Jack watched her walk away.

She stopped and refilled Cass's cup, whispering something low.

"Why would he think I wanted to know his name?"

Angie laughed. "He's hot."

"So was Johnny," Cass answered. "And look what that got me."

Silence lingered for so long at the other table he glanced through half-closed lids at the dark-haired woman.

Angie settled in the booth, staring with widened eyes. "Johnny was selfish." The server leaned into the table, words lowering to almost a whisper. "Jack doesn't seem that way."

Who is Johnny?

"No offense," Cass said. "But you're not the best judge of character."

Anger leaped into the thin server's face. "When I was young and stupid, I might have made some bad choices. But I'm not young and stupid anymore. He seems like a good guy."

"Then you go out with him."

I don't want to go out with either of them. He'd just

wanted to see if his name registered with the Comanche beauty. She didn't seem to remember him. To be truthful, he couldn't remember if she'd known his name then or not. All he remembered was how she used to flush and look away whenever he glanced in her direction.

"I'd go out with him in a second." The server glanced over Billy's sister's head, raising her eyebrows. "If he asked me."

At one time, two women talking about him wouldn't be unusual. Now was a different story. *Nice, though.* Jack grinned.

She grinned back. "But I think he *wants* you."

Might be nice, but he didn't want her.

Or did he?

****

Jack exited the diner twenty minutes later, only a minute after Billy's sister. His cell phone vibrated as the reason for his confusion wandered down the street and disappeared into a building at the end, The Horse and Bridle Bookstore. He knew that building well. His mother had dragged him to that store time and time again before she got too ill to travel around, trying to raise his knowing level beyond horses and farming. He'd complained about it then, but now it was one of his more pleasant memories.

"Dr. Fontaine?"

He jerked up at the unexpected voice. Jack had been so wrapped up in his thoughts he'd forgotten about the call. "Yes, this is Jack Fontaine."

"Good afternoon, Jack," a cultured voice said. "This is Gary Brown."

Gary Brown? He didn't remember meeting anyone

by that name since his arrival in town a week ago. "How can I help you?"

"I think I can help you."

His cryptic statement froze him at the driver's side door of his truck. "I don't even know you, so how can you help me?"

Silence followed his question.

"Or do I know you?" Jack asked. "I don't remember meeting any men named Gary. Are you someone looking for a vet? Do you have a sick animal I can help you with?"

"You probably don't remember me," the man said. "But I knew your mother and father when you lived in Greenfield years ago."

"Really?" A hint of sadness raced through him. "My father passed away last year."

"I'm so sorry about your father, Jack."

Real sorrow lowered his voice.

"And I remember when your mother died. Very sad time. She was a wonderful woman. Her illness brought you here, and her death forced both you and your father away."

A sudden image of a lean, slightly bald man flashed in Jack's mind.

"The three of you lived near me back then." A moment of silence passed. "I was your father's friend as well as his lawyer."

"Wait." He stood straight. "I remember you now." Recollections pushed past his lingering grief. "You and my dad were friends. The two of you used to go fishing together almost every weekend. Even after we left town, he talked of you."

"I'm glad."

"What can I do for you, Mr. Brown?"

"Like I said," Gary said. "I have something I can do for you."

"What?"

"Are you in Greenfield now?"

He nodded. "At the diner. Why?"

"Could you meet me at the corner building at the north end of the street?"

"The one next to the bookstore, you mean?" His heart raced at the prospect of maybe seeing Cass again. Like it had when their eyes met thirty or so minutes ago, like the few times he'd studied her a decade ago. She'd been a beauty at sixteen, and that beauty had only intensified over the years. "Cass's store."

"Yes, that's the one." Deep laughter flowed from the line. "And sweet Cassandra Rogers is running it all by herself now."

"Yes."

Laughter erupted. "You took a great liking to the woman, if I'm remembering correctly."

"She was my best friend's sister." He pushed away the broiling guilt. "And she was only sixteen the last time I saw her."

Gary didn't say anything for a long moment. "That Billy was a good kid. Maybe a bit cocky, but respectful enough. His parents never got over him leaving town, especially his mother."

Way more than just a bit cocky, Jack almost said. His attitude had gotten him into trouble. If he'd listened to him and his other friends, and stayed away from the booze, Billy might still be around today. The ribbing he'd received after his last disastrous ride caused him to get into the car in the first place. He was way too drunk to drive that night.

"So can I expect to see you in a few minutes?"

Jack forced back the memory and focused on the present. "I don't have a lot of time now. I'm scheduled to go to the Williams' ranch to check out a sick horse."

"I won't keep you long, Jack." His voice lowered suddenly. "What if I told you that building your mom loved is for sale? Would that interest you enough to give me a few minutes of your time?"

"Really?" His head shot up. "Every time Mom and I went into town, she would stop at the corner building. She had a dream of opening her own thrift shop and even started buying things for it."

"I remember."

He looked down the street, remembering how happy that dream had made her. Even after the doctor's diagnosis of cancer, her dream had never faded. She continued to buy little collectibles and old-fashioned clothing, storing them all away in units in Dallas. What harm would it do to look at the building? "Sure, Mr. Brown. I'll be there in a minute."

"Good," he said. "Just come on inside. I'm there now."

"Oh?"

Gary laughed. "Hope springs eternal, Jack."

"I guess so."

"Someone else is interested in the building," he said. "The owner is partial to that person. That's why I wanted you to see it as soon as possible."

A loud motor roared past. He gazed at a beat-up, rusty old truck. "Who?"

"That's not important," Gary said. "She's only leasing it now. According to Mr. Martinson, she made an offer. He hasn't decided whether to accept or reject it yet, however. The building could be yours by the end of the week, if you're interested."

An older model SUV drove by as he thought over the lawyer's words. What harm would it do him to check out the building? Wasn't his mother's dream worth a few minutes of his time? "I'll talk about it, but I'm not promising anything, Mr. Brown."

"I'll be waiting," he said. "And the name is Gary."

"Okay, Gary." A breeze ruffled his hair. "See you in a minute." He disconnected the call and looked down the street again. If he leased the Martinson building, he'd be close to the bookstore. Did he really want to be that close to Billy's sister?

Oh, what harm would it do?

Chapter Three

Should I apply for that loan or not?

"Cass, you here?"

"Maddie, I'm in the back." Cass let go of the question. Typing the necessary information onto her tablet database, she placed the last book into the box near her. She set the device on her desk and picked up the heavy box, storing it near three other boxes. Done. Tomorrow, her teenage workers would be here to stock the books in her storage room before filling out her new online orders.

"Hey, you busy?"

"Just finished updating my database." She glanced at the door. A small ball of energy burst through it. "I was stopping for coffee. Want some?"

"Sure, sounds good." Maddie flipped her brown hair to her back and flopped into one of the visitor chairs. "The place is looking and smelling so much better."

"Finally, yes." She wandered to the coffeemaker, pulling two cups from the lower shelf. "I didn't think the smoky smell would ever leave."

"So, does that mean you've changed your mind about Mr. Paine?"

"He didn't mean for the fire to spread the way it did." Cass poured the coffee. "He only wanted to destroy his realty business, not half of Main Street."

"Yeah, yeah, so he says." She huffed out a deep breath. "Too bad the weather wasn't being cooperative when he decided to do it."

Cass agreed, but still, she'd always been the one able to see both sides of any story.

"If you still think Paine cared if he destroyed the whole town"—she leaned forward—"then you're more charitable than I am."

Handing Maddie one of the cups, she sat into the second chair. "Well, everyone knows that."

Her eyes widened. "What?"

"That I'm the charitable one." The small moment brightened her mood. "But isn't that why you love me so much."

"Oh, you're hilarious." Maddie groaned. "Over the years, you and Angie have been both friends and enemies."

"Someone has to keep you in line," Cass said easily. "Otherwise, that temper of yours might get you into even worse trouble."

Her brows arched upward. "Well, if people would stop doing and saying stupid things, then I wouldn't have to get angry."

Cass took a sip of the rich liquid, letting the hot bitterness linger on her tongue for a moment. She swallowed it and sighed. *Perfect.* "You know, everyone has the right to believe what they want."

Maddie only huffed again and sat back into her chair. It toppled an inch off its front legs, startling her forward. "Oops, almost broke your chair."

"Don't worry about it." Cass glanced at the loan application. "If I decide to try for this loan, and get it, I'll have the money to buy a whole new set of office furniture."

"Same old Cassandra," Maddie whispered. "Always finding the good in every situation."

Cass tore her gaze off the application and studied her coffee. "No, that's how Angie is, not me. The state promised loan money to businesses damaged by the fire for rebuilding, so why not take advantage of it?"

"Maybe, because it's from the *government*." Maddie shook her head. "I haven't checked on it, but I'm guessing a few tough stipulations will be added before anyone qualifies for one of *those* loans. I'd rather use up all my savings."

"I did that."

"Oh, I didn't know that." Maddie leaped from her seat and leaned onto the desk. "Are you telling me you used all your money?"

Cass refused to look away from the blank tablet. "Yes, most of it."

"Then what do you plan on doing with your dad's?" Maddie pulled the tablet from her hands.

Forced to look at her friend, Cass dragged in a deep breath, letting it out slowly.

"You told me last week you'd ordered tables and chairs for your proposed café and upgraded your Internet and phone package, and you didn't use any of the money your dad left you. That's crazy."

"I'm not using my father's money." Bitterness heightened in her system, sharpening in her voice. She sensed Maddie's reaction, yet she didn't care. "I'm only using what the store earns."

"Why are you doing that?"

"I'm not touching my *father's* money." Her nails bit hard into her palms. "Money was all he cared about, but it's not all I am."

Maddie stayed silent, and then she crashed into her seat. "That's not true."

"It is true." Sadness fought past the bitter anger, an emotion she refused to accept. Her father never wanted her. He never loved her, so why should she feel any sadness at his death? "My brother was the person Dad expected to take over the bookstore. He never even tried to hide that fact." She glanced beyond her. "Billy left town over ten years ago, without a word of goodbye. His leaving tore Mom apart."

"Yes, I remember that time."

"I loved my brother." Cass placed her full cup on the desk. "I know he would've returned home if he could have. Yet, Dad's obsessive need to control him stopped him from doing it."

Maddie reached across the desk and touched her arm.

"Mom's talking about him again." Pain tore at her heart, a pain so overwhelming no tears could ease it. "She wants to start looking for him."

"He's gone."

When Cass had kept the news of his death from her, she thought she'd been doing the right thing. Except for her and her father, Maddie, and Angie, everyone thought he was bronco riding in the rodeo. She'd never found the right time or words to tell Mom, and now, it was too late. Between her parents and her, she had suffered the most when Billy had left Greenfield.

Maddie gripped her arm lightly. "Cass?"

She glanced toward Maddie. "More and more, I'm wishing I'd told her the same time I told Dad, you, and

Angie. If I'd shown her the newspaper articles I found about his accident, then she wouldn't be acting this way. Now I don't have the heart to do it. How do you explain hiding a loved one's death? My mother will never forgive me."

Maddie still didn't speak.

Say something. Why are you being so silent? Rarely did her outspoken friend have nothing to say.

Maddie released her arm and grabbed her cup, settling back into her seat. "So, why didn't you tell her?"

Right to the heart of the issue, right to the one question Cass wasn't sure how to answer. In her senior year of college, someone had mentioned knowing a Native American man by the name of Billy Rogers, and that person wondered if he could be related to her.

Another image rose in her mind, of a man she shouldn't remember—yet had a hard time forgetting. "Billy's friend."

Maddie sat up and looked behind her. Then she faced forward. "There's no one standing at the door."

"I know." Those few years when she'd followed Billy and his new friend around like a breathless little puppy made all the other not-so-happy ones bearable. She'd been eleven when she'd first seen him and a slightly less-innocent sixteen when he and his father had left town a few months after his mother passed away. Her tender heart had ached for him. "I was just thinking about one of Billy's friends."

"He must have made a good impression." Maddie picked up her cup and took a sip. "Billy left Greenfield over a decade ago."

"Yes, he did. Billy's friend was my first crush."

Warm memories flooded her. "I doubt he even noticed I existed, though."

"Hey, how come I don't remember this guy?" Soft lines wrinkled around her eyes and over her forehead. "Angie and I used to harass your brother left and right when we were younger, but I don't remember you ever acting weird around any of his friends."

"I was just a girl." Cass looked at the forgotten loan application. "His dad was attached to the rodeo in some way." Her chest ached. "My crush used to be a rodeo clown. My brother started getting interested in it. That guy was the reason he'd left town."

"Not ringing any bells." Maddie shrugged. "I went to the rodeo a few times when I was younger." She grinned. "We got Angie to go with us one time, remember that?"

Yes, Cass remembered. She'd been surprised when her prissy, high-maintenance friend decided to meet them there.

"Angie used to be so…girly."

Cass shook the memory away and glanced up. "Well, she was a girl."

"She still is," Maddie said. "A prissy, little pain-in-the-butt girl." She huffed. "It didn't surprise me at all when she went into modeling."

"Me, either." The phone rang, and she shot upward. Papers flipped around her desk. Grinning at her reaction, she covered the surface with both hands and glanced at the display screen. "Wholesome Natural Products?"

"What?" Maddie peered at the phone's display. "Wonder why the company is calling you? I gave them both my shop phone number and my cell." She pointed at her purse. "And the cell has been with me all day."

"You gave them the bookstore's number too, as a back-up." Only a dial tone sounded when she accepted the call. "They hung up."

"Well, if it was important, they'll call me again." Maddie looked away from the phone. "Or you."

"Yes, you're right." She replaced the phone. A slight breeze lifted the edge of her loan application. "So, you think I shouldn't send in this application?"

Maddie shrugged. "It's up to you."

"But you think it would be a mistake?"

She didn't answer for a moment, and then leaned toward her. "For someone who just inherited a wad of money from her father, yes."

Cass tried to ignore her comment. Unfortunately, doing so was beginning to make less and less sense. Stubbornness can go too far.

"Why pay it back plus interest when you have money just waiting to be spent in your business bank account?" Maddie took a sip of her forgotten coffee. "Why not ask your mother about the money?"

Yes, why not? The money belonged to her and Mom now, so why not use it for something that would give them both pleasure? Fixing up the bookstore and finishing the negotiation to lease and potentially buy the empty store next door would be a good start.

"Maybe you should see what she wants to do," Maddie said. "She should have some say, don't you think?"

Yes, she did have a say in what happened with the business. "I'll talk to her."

Her eyebrows rose. "You will?"

Cass nodded, picked up the loan application, and

tore it into pieces. "Dad never let Mom have any say in the business. I'm changing that."

"Great."

The phone rang again, and Cass looked at the display. "Wow, speaking of the devil. It's Mom."

"You always were close to your mother." Maddie jumped from her seat. "Oh, don't forget. We're meeting Angie at The Corral tomorrow night." She winked. "I know Wednesday is Ladies' Night there, but Angie and I promise to keep you from leaving with another hunky cowboy."

"I would rather not go there again, for a while."

"Look, Cass, we go there together," Maddie said. "We leave there together."

"Promise?"

"I promise," Maddie said. "Only positive thoughts allowed now."

"Well, okay." Yet Cass still hoped to find a way out of going. Maybe Mom would help her.

"I'll order the first drinks." Maddie leaped toward the door and raced out of the office without a backward glance.

The phone rang a second time, and she answered before noticing the caller.

Her mom's sweet voice filled her with peace. A peace she rarely felt since her father's funeral. Mom might not want to get involved with the business, but Cass planned on changing her mind. "I'm glad you called, Mom. I want to talk about the bookstore."

"Oh, honey," Mom said. "I can't really talk right now. I'm just calling to let you know I'm heading out the door to catch my plane for Oklahoma."

She stood from her seat. "You're leaving today?"

"Yes."

Her voice lowered. Cass heard the conflict in her tone.

"Didn't I mention it the last time we talked? I'm spending the week with my family and friends on the reservation. We've had this scheduled for a few months."

Cass shrugged. "You probably mentioned the trip, but I've had so much on my mind the last couple of weeks." Silence followed her confession. Then a soft sigh rang out on the line. "Mom, are you okay?"

"If you really need to talk with me, I can get a later flight."

"No, don't do that, Mom." The last thing Cass wanted to do was deprive her of a trip to see the family. She needed to get away from Greenfield. "We'll talk when you return."

"Do you still like Chinese take-out?"

She fought a smile. "You're the one who likes Chinese, Mom."

"Oh?"

"But I'd love to share it with you." Bright laughter filled the phone line.

"Good. I'll pick it up on the way home from the airport. I'll call you when I get back to Greenfield. Will that be all right?"

"Sounds good," Cass agreed. "As long as you promise to talk about the business."

Dead silence.

"Mom?" She still didn't respond. "Dad might not have wanted your input, but I do. The only way I'll feel free to use that money he left me...left us...is on the bookstore."

A loud sigh broke through the silence.

"I'm not sure what I could add to the conversation, but I'll discuss it with you."

"As soon as you get back?"

"Yes," she said. "While we eat."

Cass disconnected the call five minutes later, fighting to keep her temper in check. Not anger at Mom, but at Dad for making this beautiful, wonderful woman believe she didn't have anything to offer beyond the ability to cook his meals, clean his house, and share his bed.

The sudden ringing of the phone sent her heart racing. She let out a laugh at her reaction and glanced at the screen. *Wholesome Natural Products?* "The Horse and Bridle Bookstore," she said. "How may I help you?"

"Oh, I'm sorry," a female voice said. "I must have dialed the wrong number again." The woman on the other end laughed. "I meant to call All Things Western Women's Clothing Store." Laughter rang out again. "That's a mouthful, isn't it?"

Cass had to agree. "That's my friend Maddie's shop."

"I'm so sorry."

"That's no problem." Cass shook her head as she replaced the phone. Before she shut off her computer for the night, she checked her emails. "Now, why would Mr. Martinson's shyster lawyer be contacting me now?"

She read the short message. Disbelief fought with a rush of anger at the words. "I don't believe this." Why would the owner need six months more rent by the end of April? Was another person interested in her building? The building sat empty for over five years, and now, two people wanted it.

Unbelievable.

She grabbed the phone and dialed the lawyer's number.

A female voice answered, saying he wasn't in the office now.

Cass left a terse message and number and hung up. "No one is getting my building."

Chapter Four

The store phone rang the second she stood from her seat. Cass fell back down and picked it up. "The Horse and Bridle Bookstore. How may I help you?"

"You can help me by sharing my food."

She settled back into her chair. "Oh, it's good to hear from you, Mom. You've been gone more than a week."

"I'm sorry I didn't call you."

She shook her head. "Don't worry about it. I've been so busy here I barely missed you."

All Mom did was laugh. "The food is getting cold, so you need to leave the shop now."

She jumped off the chair and grabbed her purse. "I'm on my way."

"See you, honey."

Cass arrived at her old home twenty minutes later. She shut off her engine and settled into her seat, looking at the front door of the one-story house. Except for sleeping and one Wednesday Ladies' Night, she had spent the rest of the last week cleaning and reviewing her father's inventory and reworking the website with her expanded list of guest lecturers.

Thinking about the expansion of their bookstore had kept her new potential problem at bay.

Just because her period came about the same time every month didn't mean anything. Stress could affect her, right? Cass released the thought and exited her vehicle.

Droplets of cool rainwater splashed into her face, followed quickly by heavier beads. Soon, rain slid from the top of her head, caressing like damp fingers down her cheekbones and onto hunched shoulders. She lifted her hand to knock at the same time the front door swung open, backing her into a pool of water.

Mom reached toward her. "What are you doing standing out in this rain, honey? Get into this house before you catch your death."

The delicate hint of spring flowers flowed toward her. Mom's signature perfume. Contentment rose at her mom's concern. As far back as Cass could remember, she had always made things better...without even trying. Yes, she needed to be here.

"Didn't you bring an umbrella? You should keep one in your car.

A soft, warm hand pulled her into the living room. The door slammed behind her.

"I was hoping you would get here before the rain started."

"I'm always amazed how quickly the weather changes around here." She pulled her plastered blouse away from her breasts and grinned. "I'm soaked."

"That you are." Mom directed her toward the narrow hallway to the downstairs bathroom. "Go and take off those wet things. I'll get you a robe or something to wear."

"I'd appreciate that."

"I'll be right back."

Cass entered the bathroom and started peeling off her wet clothes, wiping her body dry with one of the big fluffy towels hanging on the rack by the shower before wrapping it around her damp hair. She settled on the edge of the tub. The door opened slightly a second later, and a long white robe poked through the small opening. "Thanks, Mom."

"Give me your wet things, and I'll put them in the dryer."

"I know where the dryer is." She slid her arms into the warm robe, securing it around her waist. "You don't need to do that."

"Are you covered up?" Not waiting for an answer, Mom pushed at the door and walked into the small bathroom. She picked up the wet things from the tub and stepped back out. "While I'm doing this, why don't you go and start eating?" She eyed her up and down. "You look like you've lost some weight since I last saw you."

"No."

"Well, it looks like it, and you're already skinny enough." She raised the pile of wet garments. "Go and dish out the stuff for us then. I'll be there in a few minutes."

"Let me comb out my hair first."

"I'll wait."

Mom didn't move from her spot by the doorway while she dried her hair and finger combed it into a ponytail. "That looks better now."

"Thanks, Mom." Cass followed her out and turned toward the front of the house while Mom went into the laundry room in the back. A mouthwatering aroma of spicy chicken and mixed vegetables hit her a few seconds later, causing her stomach to growl. She hadn't eaten anything since breakfast around seven that morning.

Maybe she was right. Because Cass had been blessed with a high metabolic level like her father and brother, she could afford to eat a bit more than other women. Unlike Mom, she never had to worry about gaining too much weight.

Guess she'd inherited something she liked from her father, after all.

She shook her head and moved through the kitchen door. Five minutes later, two plates were filled with spicy chicken, saucy crab, vegetable-flavored rice, and a crispy egg roll. She set a glass of sweet tea in front of Mom's plate and black coffee in front of her own before settling into her seat. Cass picked up her cup and blew into it, releasing the sweet vanilla scent of the creamer.

"Oh, you remembered my sweet tea."

She grinned. "Sit and eat before everything gets cold."

Neither of them said another word as they dug into the meal. As usual, Cass attacked the spicy chicken first while Mom reached for the crab. Both placed a forkful of rice in their mouth next. Just enough spice and heat, with a lovely crunch. It was delicious.

"So, you mentioned something about the bookstore?"

She shot up her head. "Well, that's a surprise? I thought I would have to plead and beg before you would even say anything about the business."

"That was my plan at first." Mom looked at her half-filled plate. "But my family and friends reminded me of who I am."

Cass studied her mom. "You had a nice time

visiting?"

"Of course, I did. But don't change the subject."

Determination widened her eyes.

"I've never regretted giving up my old dreams for new ones with your father, Billy, and you, but now I want to be a part of the bookstore."

Cass had never been as proud of her. "I'm glad, Mom. I'd really like your input and thoughts on the café."

"Yes, your brother would have wanted me to be a part of it."

Soft wispiness sounded clear in her voice. And Cass froze in her chair. Bad enough she mentioned her brother, but it was the way she did it that had her reeling.

"We need to keep it going for his return."

Her heart sank into her chest. "Mom?"

"And he will come home, honey." Mom set her fork with a soft clink to the table. "I know he will now that your father is gone." Tight fingers clamped around the fork once again. "That man was the reason your brother left. He was the reason he never returned. If your father had allowed him to join the rodeo with that friend of his, he wouldn't have needed to run away. If he'd accepted his phone call that day…" She glanced down at her plate. "He would have gotten that outrageousness out of his system a long time ago. Things would've been the way they were meant to be."

"Dad's been dead for almost a year. If Billy planned on returning home, he'd be here by now." She swallowed a few times, folding her arms around her stomach. *Even Mom doesn't think I'm capable of running the bookstore.* "What if he…can't…because he's—"

"I know Billy will return," she said. "I know once he finds out your father is gone, he'll come home."

She took a deep breath, fighting to stay calm. "And take over running the business?"

"No, honey. Why would you ask that?" She laid her hand lightly on her arm. "You weren't your father's first choice—"

"No kidding."

"But he soon changed his mind about that." She sipped her iced tea. "He loved some of your ideas for The Horse and Bridle, honey."

Oh, if only she could believe her mom. "He did?"

"Yes, he was proud of you." Mom grabbed both of her hands and held on tight. "Your brother's leaving the way he did hurt your father more than you'll ever know. He was afraid you would leave, too."

Mom entangled their fingers together, like she used to do when Cass was young and afraid. She wasn't young anymore or fearful, but the familiar gesture still touched her heart.

"He told me of a few of your ideas about updating the business."

Cass shook her head. "Wow, I didn't even think he was listening."

"Oh, honey. Just because your father had a hard time showing his feelings didn't mean he didn't have any. He loved you."

"It would've been nice if he could've said it at least once."

"Yes," she agreed. "But he might have been waiting for you to say it first. Did you ever think of that?"

Why would he expect that? He's the parent, so he shouldn't have been waiting to hear the words. He should've been yelling it out to the world, like Cass's Mom did every day. "No."

"Well, you should have." A frown deepened the sharp lines around Mom's mouth. "I know you don't want to hear this, but you and your father were more alike than different."

"No, I'm nothing like Dad was." Her body tensed. "Nothing."

All Mom did was grin.

"I don't want to talk about him anymore." She raised her hand. "I want to talk about The Horse and Bridle."

Mom's grin only diminished slightly.

Then she nodded. "Did you make an offer on the store next door?"

"Dad told you about that?"

"Yes," Mom said. "He wasn't sure if he liked expanding, though."

Cass shrugged. "I got that impression."

"But I think it's a good thing."

A peaceful surprise lightened her mood a bit. "You do?"

"You need a bigger place for those lectures." The older woman grabbed her tea and sat back in her seat. "They are so popular."

Cass grinned, relaxing back in the hardbacked chair. She picked up her coffee and took a drink. "I'm still surprised by that."

"Have you ever thought of adding other types of speakers to the list?" Mom glanced over her glass. "Like the tribe's elders? Professors or writers? Or maybe renting out the new café-lecture room for club meetings? Like book clubs or women's meetings?"

"Expanding the lectures, yes." She nodded, warming up to the subject. "I've added a few new ones. That's what I planned to do once…if I get that building."

Her eyes widened. "If?"

Cass sighed. "I got a phone call followed up by a letter from the owner's lawyer, Gary Brown, explaining Mr. Martinson wants an entire year of rent before the end of the month. That's not the deal I tentatively had."

"Will you have rights to the building? To do with it as you please?"

"I'll sign a contract for that, yes."

She settled into her seat. "Well, then give it to him."

She sighed and glanced at her cooling coffee. "That will use up a third of the store's income."

"So?"

"I'm not sure if I'm ready to do that now."

Mom stood from the table and moved toward the refrigerator. She refilled her sweet tea before placing the pitcher back into the fridge and grabbing the coffee pot. "Need a refill, honey?"

"Yes, thanks."

She poured the coffee and then set the pot back in its cradle. Settling down into her seat, she sipped her tea while studying her.

Cass fought the urge to look at her plate.

"Tell me something, what do you plan on doing with the money your father left you?" She set her glass on the table and leaned toward her. "I might not be all that familiar with running a business, but I do know that money sitting in a bank account untouched won't help you expand." Mom's eyes narrowed. "And neither is allowing your unresolved feelings for your father to affect your decisions. He is gone."

She tightened her fingers around her warm cup. "I know that."

"You and I are here," she added. "Alive and well."

"So, you think I'm being stubborn about using that money?"

"Yes."

"And you want us to use it?"

She nodded.

"Okay, I'll do it." Her throat burned, easing only slightly at Mom's nod. Yes, she wanted to expand the bookstore, and the money was just sitting in the business bank account. Not to use it would be dumb. "I'll call Mr. Brown's office tomorrow and tell his paralegal my…our decision. Maybe then he'll finally call me back."

"And I will call Wayne and Gray," Mom said.

Cass tensed in her chair. "Who?"

"Wayne and Gray Investigations."

Oh, please, no. "Investigations?"

"Private detectives," she clarified.

"Why would you need to talk with one of those?" Hoping against hope it wasn't for the reason she feared. "We don't have any one we need to investigate."

"Yes, we do." Mom sat up high in her seat, eyes widening. "I'm hiring them to find Billy."

****

Pete Morgan glanced around the unfamiliar ranch, taking in the large front porch of the white two-story house. Planters filled with green plants and brilliant-colored flowers swung around weathered outdoor furniture. The soft Texas breeze blew the sweet scent in his direction. He twisted around, studying the area leading toward a rustic barn and corral. The rustling of a few horses echoed in the quietness around him.

Peace filled him.

No memory of the place came, however. Since he'd left the hospital and got involved with Wholesome Natural Products, he'd called this place home. A home he desperately wanted to remember,

He clamped his fingers around his cowboy hat, flattening the brim around the edge.

Why can't I remember this ranch?

"I love this place." Daniel White stepped out of the two-story ranch house. His shorter friend stopped at the steps and glanced at him. "I do admit I don't like horses or ranches much, but this one is quiet and peaceful. Beautiful."

"No matter how hard I try, I still don't remember it." Pete twisted toward his friend. He watched him adjust his paisley tie and smooth his hand down his jacket. Only Daniel would come to a ranch in a three-piece suit. "But, yes, you're right. It is a fine place. *Billy Rogers* did a good job buying the farm. At least he did something right."

"You *got* it, Pete." Daniel sighed. "You might want to separate who you were to who you are now, but you can't. Not really."

"I guess I wasn't such a bad guy then." He slammed his cowboy hat against his thigh. "No family or friends from the rodeo bothered to show up at the hospital except for that one man. I was in a coma for days, and yet, no one came to visit me. That tells you much about who I *used* to be."

Daniel didn't say anything.

"Even you have nothing to say to that, do you?" He gazed at him and then looked away. "At least *Billy* left me this ranch and money in the bank to use for Sarah's Intimate Marriage Collection. I'm glad I could help make her wish come true before the cancer took her."

"My sister loved you, Pete."

"Her sweet face was my first memory after waking up in that hospital bed." Pete set his hip against the porch rail. "Meeting Sarah, Ed, and you gave me back my life. Billy Rogers is gone. I'm Pete now."

"Yes, legally changing your name was the right thing. You can't stop searching for your past, though."

"Can't I?" A fleeting image of that girl who looked so much like him floated into his mind, only to disappear. He sighed. "Frustrating."

"See that girl again?"

He nodded. "I just wish I could remember more about her."

"You will, Pete."

"But why?" He stepped toward the barn. "I have a new family now. I have a new life. Maybe it'll be better to focus on Sarah's dream and let the past go."

"Sarah didn't want you to give up, Pete." Daniel placed his hands on his shoulders. "You promised my sister you would keep searching for your family."

Pain burned him. Sarah? Oh, why did she have to leave us? "Yes."

"You need to honor that promise."

Would the pain ever get better? Sarah had been his lifeline and support in the hospital. Since his arrival after his car accident, she'd been with him. He'd never known it until he saw her warm grin that day. Soon Sarah and her husband, Ed Davidson, and her brother, Daniel White, became his new family. Her cancer, that had been in remission for a decade, came back only a month after he'd left the hospital in the middle of the night against doctor's orders. Six months later, she was gone.

"Yes, Daniel, I plan on doing that." Pete faced the quiet man. "You and Ed are my family now." He tightened his fingers around the brim of his hat again. "But I do miss Sarah. I do miss my angel."

"So do I." His shoulders sagged. "Believe me, so do I."

That girl's face flickered into his mind, holding for an elusive few seconds before once again dissipating. *Oh, why is this vision coming to me? Who is she?*

Pete might tell his friend he didn't want to find out about his past, but he couldn't lie to himself.

The girl, who looked so much like him, could be a sister or cousin. Someone he was frantic to find.

That girl could be the best part of the man he used to be. Someone worth remembering.

Chapter Five

Coffee-logged and jittery from staying up most of the night and half the day relieving the colic symptoms of a sick horse, all Jack wanted now was his warm, comfortable bed.

His entire body sagged into the car seat, his eyes closing slowly. He shook his head and tightened his hands around the truck's steering wheel. The road to his home appeared on his right, and he turned with a tired sigh.

Home. His parents would've been proud of him. Things were still tight with his business, but he was glad he had enough money to move back to Greenfield. No other town spoke like home.

New-growth trees lined both sides of the curvy road. A stream flowed gently along the path of the dirt lane, disappearing around the bend on the opposite side of the enormous farmhouse. He parked in front of the front porch and glanced around. The old barn he planned on using as his vet clinic sat a few feet to the right, a corral stretching around the building. The rustling sound of the stream echoed in the quiet, easing his tiredness a bit.

"Home." His whisper echoed in the silent air. He closed and locked the truck out of habit and then stepped onto the porch. "I wish you could be here, Dad."

So many memories rushed him now—his mother's soft laughter, his father's gruff words, the scents and smells and sounds of a well-loved and well-worked farm. He'd learned so many things from the elderly owners of the place, things that had made him a better rodeo clown than his father, and things that made him an even better vet.

"The past is the past, Fontaine." His rough words pulled him back into the present. He quickened his steps and unlocked the front door. Early morning sunlight beamed warm light into the front room, catching the dust particles in the slight breeze. He batted his hat against the microscopic specks and moved toward the sturdy stairs at the far end of the room, leaping up them with his last burst of energy toward the furnished bedroom.

Furnished, he almost said aloud, if a person liked their bed surrounded by half-emptied boxes lying in every free space on the floor. Yes, then it was furnished. Much like Cassandra Rogers's store had been every time he'd walked past it in the last few weeks, looking for nerves to go inside and say hello.

"Let it go, Fontaine." He shook the image away and wandered into his bathroom. Lemon-scented cleaner invaded his senses, reminding him of his mother. "I miss you, Mom." Less than a minute later, a naked Jack sank into the pillow-soft comfort of the bed.

The sun sitting high in the sky, burning a bright glare through his uncovered windows, woke him from a deep sleep. He turned away from the heat and brightness and drifted back to sleep. The blaring sound of the phone downstairs jerked him out of bed. He raced down the steps and picked up his cell phone.

"Fontaine."

"Are you Jack Fontaine?"

"Guilty." He wiped the sleep from his eyes. "And you are?"

"My name is Henry Wayne," the caller said. "I'm a private investigator with Wayne and Gray Investigations."

He stood straighter. "Why would a PI be calling me?"

"Do you know a man named William Rogers?" the Investigator asked. "My research says you were his friend at one time."

"Billy, yeah." *How did he know that? And why was it so important?* He silenced those questions. "You know he's dead, don't you?"

"That's what the daughter of my client told me," the hearty voice said. "Died in a car accident, about three years ago."

He clutched the phone hard. Why should he feel this way? Billy's cocky, sure attitude brought on his death, but not anything he had done. "Yeah, it was a car accident."

"My client believes he's still alive."

How could that be? The hospital had notified Dad a few days after the accident. Billy's family should have been called at the same time. Or rather Cass should've been. He swept a hand through his longish hair and sank into the cool recliner, the only piece of furniture decorating the large living room. "I'm not sure what to tell you." Silence followed his words.

Then the detective took a deep breath. "Are you sure he's dead?"

"Yes." He swallowed, staring at his bare feet. "I

read about it in the newspaper."

"He died instantly?"

Why is this man making me live through this again? At one time, Billy had been his best friend until he started drinking and acting the fool. Refusing to listen to people because he thought he was better than more seasoned cowboys.

"Were you with him when he died?"

"No, I wasn't." He swallowed. "I was in college at the time."

"What about your father?"

"Not when he died, no." Jack leaned forward in his seat and placed his elbows on his bare knees. "Dad did go see him a few days before. Billy had just come out of his coma, according to my dad, and had no memory of his past."

"Really?"

"Strange, isn't it? He must have had internal injuries the doctors missed." He clutched the phone hard. "He was doing better until he had that surgery."

The PI stayed silent.

"I just don't understand it." More silence answered his more controlled comment.

"That is odd. What is odder is Mrs. Rogers didn't know about it," Mr. Wayne said. "Her daughter knew about his death, but not Janessa. How could that have happened?"

"I'm not sure why." He sat back and looked at the ceiling. Cobwebs hung low in the corners, blowing in the slight breeze from the opened side windows. "She should've been notified. The next-of-kin form the rodeo doctor demanded everyone fill out listed Cass's information. I know because I was there when Billy filled it out. He put my father's name as an emergency contact. My father was notified, so his sister should've been notified, too. And she would've told her parents."

"Why didn't he use his parents as his next-of-kin contact?"

He shrugged. "I'm not really sure."

"Could you hold for a second?"

"Yes." The faint clicking of a keyboard broke through the quietness, followed by the crinkling sound of papers.

"Wow, this is interesting."

Jack jolted straight at the intensity in the PI's voice. "What?" The rustling sound moved through the phone line. "Mr. Wayne?"

"Name's Hank," he said. "My dad was Henry and my granddad Mr. Wayne."

Jack grinned. "Okay, Hank. Mine's Jack."

Two or three silent minutes went by before Hank asked again. "Are you sure it was your friend who died that day?"

This question jerked him out of his chair. "Yes, I'm sure. Why are you asking?"

"What about your father?" Hank asked. "Was your father at the hospital at the time?"

"No, he could only visit with Billy for a few hours. He had to get to a rodeo early the next day." Jack glanced at the phone for a second. "Why are you asking me these questions?"

Instead of answering, he read the name of the hospital in Montana Billy had been rushed to after his accident. "Is this the information you were given?"

"Yes."

"Man, I think there might have been a major

mistake here."

Excitement sounded in the man's voice.

"Your friend might not be dead."

He stiffened. "What? Not be dead?" What had this private investigator found out? "He's dead, Wayne. My father told me he went to his funeral. Well, to the graveyard."

"Did he mention if his parents and sister were there?"

Man, what is going on? Is Hank claiming there is a mistake? A slight shiver chilled his naked body. "No, he told me they weren't there."

"Why?"

Yes, why wouldn't they have been there? Wouldn't Cass have shown up at her only brother's funeral, and at least his mother? Sure, Jack got the impression his father wasn't too thrilled about him running off and following the rodeo, but that wouldn't have stopped him from attending. The father and son were like night and day, disagreeing about everything. Deep down they'd loved each other. If possible, his father would have been at that funeral.

"Jack?"

He shook his thoughts away. "That always bothered me."

"No family members were there?"

"My father didn't recognize anyone," he said. "But he didn't arrive until the funeral was almost over and stood way in the back, so he might have missed them. My parents and the Rogerses were close when we lived in Greenfield. He hadn't seen Billy's family in years, but he would've known them."

"And you didn't find it odd your father didn't

recognize anyone?

Jack swallowed down an unexpected rush of excitement. "Yeah, now that you mention it, it does seem a bit odd."

"I might have found out the reason why."

Barely contained enthusiasm deepened the detective's voice. Jack stepped toward the front window, optimism filling him.

"Another man named William Rodgers—spelled R o *d* g e r s—was in the hospital at the same time. He'd been involved in a three-way car pileup on the freeway a few days after your friend's accident. That man died in the operating room three hours later."

"You're kidding me." Jack stood straight, back rigid against the rough window frame. "Are you saying that nurse might have given me and my dad the wrong information that day?"

"Maybe," he offered. "Five or six others were sent to the ER during that same accident, and two were in bad shape. So, I can understand the possible confusion."

"Damn!" What a pleasant mix-up if that were the case? Shouldn't he be more upset at this turn of events? "Have you told Cass or Janessa this yet?"

"No, not yet," Hank said. "I'm not telling them anything until I know for sure."

"That's probably for the best." Boisterous laughter rang from the phone line.

"What I'd like to do is find this guy and show up with him at their door? That would be a great change of pace."

Jack couldn't agree more.

Chapter Six

Cass had gone out with Angie and Maddie the last two Wednesdays, so she hoped by meeting them in the parking lot she could talk her way out of going again. No way. As soon as she arrived, her two friends led her toward the entrance to the noisy dance hall. Music echoed in the air the closer she got to the double doors, drowning out all thoughts.

Why had she ever thought she'd *not* be going dancing with them again tonight? She could never talk them out of anything.

"Hey, beautiful."

Maddie waved the cowboy away and stepped into the milling fray of males and females.

He shrugged and moved onto the next group of ladies following them into the overflowing room.

Wednesday night always brought out all the females in the general area—young and old, both married and single—as well as every male living within a fifty-mile radius of Greenfield.

"Wow, look at all these men," Maddie said.

Cass grinned. Maddie might speak outrageously at times, but she didn't follow through on her words. Even after a few drinks, her morals stayed intact. Unlike hers had been the time she'd gone to The Corral two months ago, and she'd met that foolish cowboy. Johnny had a sweet way about him, causing her to let her guard down enough for him to take advantage. Great kisses and a fun time could never make up for him not being next to her when she woke up early the next afternoon. Or any time after that. If she was pregnant and wanted him to know about it, she wouldn't have a clue how to find him. She didn't even know his last name.

"I'll get us our drinks," Maddie said. "White wine for the two of you and a draft beer for me."

"That'll be fine." Angie settled in the seat beside hers. "But Cass shouldn't be drinking."

"Oh, that's right."

"One glass won't hurt me, but Angie's probably right." Her body had been signaling a hint of the beginnings of her period for the last few days, but she figured it was only wishful thinking. *I really need to get one of those home pregnancy tests. Enough time has passed since that night to know one way or the other, right?*

"Are you sure?" Angie leaned toward her. "Cass? Do you want a glass of wine or not?"

She buried her thoughts and nodded. "Why should I have to suffer? I doubt Johnny is."

"Well, of course he isn't." Maddie clamped her hands to her hips. "He's not the one pregnant."

"Cass doesn't know if she is yet. She only missed one period." Angie glanced around and lowered her voice. "And I'm praying she isn't."

"You and me both," Maddie agreed. "Stupid men."

Cass had a bit of a say in her situation, but she wanted to agree with Maddie now. They'd used protection, but that didn't mean anything. No birth control method was one hundred percent foolproof.

"Speaking of men," Maddie said. "Will you look at

him? I've never seen that one before."

Cass glanced behind her and swallowed her breath. "Billy's friend."

"No, that's Jack." Angie grinned. "He's the new vet in town. You met him a couple of weeks ago at the diner, remember?"

"I don't believe this. How could I not have remembered him?" Haunting blue eyes lingered for so long, she grimaced and looked away. "My...first big crush."

Maddie sighed. "Oh, boy, looks like your first big crush is heading this way."

Oh, no, not now, not when my life is in such a bad place.

"Ladies?"

When she glanced up, she spied a way too intense gaze. "Hello, Jack."

His head jerked back. "Cass."

Maddie arched her eyebrows, silly grin lingering around her smooth mouth, while her other suave friend floated like a graceful lioness out of her seat. "Well, hello there, cowboy."

"Angie, right?"

And he was grinning like a fool. Sometimes, Cass had a hard time remembering why she called this blonde bombshell a friend.

"You remembered."

His gaze skimmed over Angie, fell on Maddie briefly, then once again settled like warm sunlight on her. Tingling heat flowed slowly up her body, sending her breath racing out of her lungs. No man had ever had this sort of power over her emotions and physiological reaction with just a single look.

Maddie glanced at her, eyes wide and grin even wider.

Don't you dare, Maddie?

"Want to join us?"

No, say no, please say no.

"Sure." Jack hooked his foot under the lower rail of the chair nearest her. "I'd love to."

"Welcome to the table." Maddie grinned. "The more, the merrier."

He settled into the chair and nodded at Maddie before fixing that penetrating regard back onto her. His look warmed her to the core.

"How have you been, Drea?"

"Drea?" A peaceful memory, from a time long before her father had chased Billy away teased inside her. Without wanting to, barely knowing it was happening, Cass relaxed. "My brother was the only person I allowed to call me that silly name."

"I know." A slow grin arched the left side of his mouth. "One time I accidently called you that in front of him, and he set me straight real fast."

She relaxed against the back of her chair. "He did?"

"If you had the same look in your eyes than as you have now," Maddie butted in, "Billy probably got angry for a totally different reason."

A hint of embarrassment darkened his eyes into the shade of the sky before the rain. The brighter color returned with a nod and a boisterous laugh. Cass remembered his laugh, slightly sadder and a bit rustier. The sound still managed to touch her senses, somehow. "You should ignore Maddie."

"So that's your name?"

"Yes, Maddie Thomas." She turned to Angie. "And this is Angie Ferguson." She winked at Cass. "And now the two of us are getting something to drink."

"Maddie?" Cass raised her hand. "A barmaid will come to our table."

She winked again. "Would you like something, Jack? I'm buying this round."

"Sure, a beer would be nice." He stood and dug his wallet out of his back pocket. "But I'll be paying."

Cass sighed. "You don't need to do—"

"If the man wants to pay for our drinks, we're letting him." Maddie grabbed the money from the cowboy's hand. "We'll be back as soon as we can."

If she knew those two at all, that would be when the band just now starting to play went on their first break.

"Wow, that friend of yours is something."

"You could say that."

"I just did."

The beat of her heart spiked at his teasing words, leaping along with the booming bass of the upbeat music. Laughing, joyous couples raced to the dance floor, a swirl of cotton and lace clouding her vision. The suffocating scents of overpowering perfume and aftershave whiffed past her. She gazed at the quiet man as the scents dissipated a bit and the music faded. *Say something, Cass.* "So, you're the new town vet? Did you take over old Dr. Morgan's practice?"

"Not really." Jack leaned back, placing one ankle over his leg. "He did sell me his client list, but I'm not working out of that old building."

"Oh, why is that?"

"Not worth fixing," he said. "The fire did a lot of

damage to that place. Not worth the cost to rebuild."

Cass nodded. "The firefighters thought they had everything contained to the other side of the street, but then the wind shifted, sending sparks flying into the buildings directly across from the realty office. Dr. Morgan's clinic got the worst of it. It reached all the way to my bookstore."

"It started at the realty office?" His eyes widened. "That must have been frightening for everyone."

"Yes, for a bit." Cass glanced toward the bar and spied her two friends talking with a group of cowboys. The up-tempo tune turned into a slow ballad, leaving her afraid to look at Jack.

Two of the cowboys grabbed Maddie and Angie and pulled them to the dance floor.

Didn't look like they were in any hurry to return with the drinks.

"The newspaper articles I read online said he'd set it himself."

"He did." Cass swallowed and pulled her gaze from the dancers. "It didn't take the arson investigator long to figure that out. No one was really all that surprised, either."

Jack stiffened. "Small towns, right?"

Cass grinned back. "Everyone knows everything." Intense quietness surrounded her. "And you still want to move back here? You still want to live in Greenfield?"

"I prefer smaller towns," he said. "I heard about the fire from Mr. Speyer and checked out how the town fared afterward online. When I heard that the old vet was thinking of retiring, I called him. And the rest…" He waved his hands upward. "Well, I'm here."

"Why here?"

"Why are you asking?"

"You could've set up your practice anywhere in the state or in the country," she said. "You and your father followed the rodeo from one town to another. I'm sure you've had better offers than Greenfield."

He glanced at his cupped hands. "I like Greenfield."

Cass should just let this be, but she couldn't. Was it wrong to wish his memory of her younger self was part of his reason for returning? "This small town is much the same as others in Texas. Why did you decide to come and practice veterinarian medicine here?"

"My mother."

"Oh, I forgot." How unthinking not to remember about his mother? "You were living here with your mother and father when she passed away."

His shoulders slumped.

Oh, why did she have to bring that up? "I'm sorry."

"You don't need to be sorry, Cass."

She set her hand lightly on his raised knee before snatching it away. "It made you sad."

"Been over ten years." He glanced beyond her head. "Mom liked you and…your brother."

"I didn't know her all that well."

Jack focused back on her.

A more damaging emotion to her peace-of-mind roared hot from him. "Yet she seemed like a good woman. She always had a kind word for me and Billy."

"Yes."

A hint of uneasiness slipped into the atmosphere around them. Whether from talking about his mom or Billy, Cass wasn't quite sure. The discomfort increased when the memory of that conversation with Mom came to mind. Was it because the PI would bring the bad news of Billy's death three years late, giving her an easy way out of her cover-up of the truth? Or was it because she'd allowed Mom to believe he was still alive for all these years? "I'm a horrible person," she whispered.

He jerked forward. "What?"

Cass took a long breath and let it out slowly, glancing toward the bar once again.

Another grouping of cowboys jockeyed for Maddie's and Angie's attendance. One very interested cowboy, Ethan, stood close to her smaller friend while Andrew, Angie's ex-husband, lingered at the edge of the crowd.

Maddie glared at Ethan before moving closer to the blonde. All the cowboy did was smirk. "I was just wondering when my friends would be back with our drinks."

His narrow-eyed look studied her for a long second before he glanced toward the bar. "Looks like they're a bit distracted right now."

"Same thing happened to them another time I was at The Corral."

"Oh?"

Cass shook her head. "But that's not happening this time." Old crush or not, hot or not, Cass was not leaving with this man. And it didn't matter if everything inside her screamed, *it wasn't the same at all*. This man was nothing like the one who'd spent the night with her and left before she woke up.

Chapter Seven

Wow, what had Jack done? What had he said to get Cass to put the brakes on their conversation? One moment she was warm and giving, making him feel so good to be a man; the next, she was stiff in her seat, looking at everyone and everything except him.

And why did she just say she was a horrible person?

Horrible was the last word he'd used for Cassandra Rogers. Sweet and beautiful, warm, and friendly, sexy as all get out, were the adjectives he would use. A little shy, a bit thoughtful, caring, and loyal, but never horrible.

"Jack?"

He pushed his frustrating feelings aside and glanced over at her. "Want me to get us a couple of drinks?"

"No, I probably shouldn't drink." She looked down at her lap. "Did you know that Billy…died?"

So that's what her reticence was all about? "Yes."

"I didn't know until…" Her voice broke. "A friend of mine asked me if I knew a Native America rodeo guy named Billy Rogers." She peered over toward the bar again. "I didn't think my brother would use his real name, so I showed him an old picture."

"And it was the man he knew?"

"Yes." She swallowed again. "One of the clippings

he had showed where he'd been hospitalized after getting into a bad car accident. Another one said he'd died."

Sadness radiated off her, and it took all his power not to pull her against his chest. "I know about his accident."

"We were never notified." Her eyes blurred with unshed tears. "No one knew to contact us."

No, that didn't make any sense. Billy had named his sister next of kin. Why would the hospital not contact her? They had called Dad, but not Cass. Why would they do that? Unless… William Rodgers was almost the same as William Rogers. Could that private investigator be right? Could Billy still be alive?

But, if that was true, where had he been the last three years?

"I still can't believe the hospital didn't call me or my parents."

His mind raced at the mystery. Dropping his foot to the floor, he studied her. Her tightly controlled emotions were really getting to him.

She wiped her unshed tears. "Did you get to the funeral?"

"I couldn't get there, but Dad made it to the gravesite." Jack pressed his nails hard into his hands. No good would come from him touching her now. His own painful feelings were too close to the surface. "Now I know why he didn't see you or your parents there. Billy told me he took off without your father's blessing, but that wouldn't have stopped the three of you from attending his funeral. Your dad was a gruff man, but he loved him."

"Yes." Cass twirled her fingers over the edge of the

table. "Even after I told Dad Billy was dead, he still refused to believe me. Like I would lie about something like that."

No, she wouldn't lie. The father and son argued, but they still loved each other. "And what about your mother?"

Shadows deepened under her eyes again. "I never told her."

"So that's why Mrs. Rogers hired Hank Wayne, the PI?

She sat tall, clamping her fingers tight to the edge. "How did you know about that?"

"He called me." Jack waved a hand toward the bar. Right now wasn't the time to speak about that PI. "Wonder when your friends will be back with the drinks."

Cass stole a quick look his way before focusing on the bar.

The band stopped playing, and people moved off the dance floor to the empty tables.

Only then did the clatter of male and female voices, the sound of laughter, and a few angry yells penetrate their conversation. For the last fifteen or so minutes, Jack had been so wrapped up in Cass he hadn't noticed the music or people milling around him.

Cass froze in her chair and glanced around, a little grin playing around the edges of her mouth. "The band stopped playing, and I didn't even notice."

He couldn't help it. Jack reached over and caressed his index finger down her flushed cheek. "Same here."

"Oh?" Her eyes brightened a deeper shade of green. "Really?"

The pleased look covered over the lingering

sadness and disbelief. He spread his fingers against her heated cheek and slid them down to the side of her neck, tightening them gently to pull her closer. An aching need to kiss her caught him completely off guard, blocking the sounds around him once again.

"Can't leave you alone for two minutes, can I?"

Thankfully, a mock-serious voice broke through the silence. He closed his eyes and dropped his hand. A punch against his upper arm sent him jerking sideways. He grabbed hold of the table edge and stopped his movement.

Maddie glared, hands clamped in fists at her waist.

A more subdued Angie stood directly behind her.

"What did you do to Cass?"

"Nothing."

"Nothing? Really?" Angie peered over her smaller friend's shoulder. "If you did nothing, then why does it look like she's been crying?"

"I haven't been—"

"You stay out of this." Maddie waved her clutched hands toward her, and then focused her studied look back on him. "She wasn't in the best of moods when she got here, but she certainly hadn't been crying." She leaned even closer. "What did you say?"

Cass did have some protective friends. "Nothing."

"He didn't do any—"

"Cass?"

"Oh, for crying out loud," she yelled. "Stop interrupting me."

Cass leaped from her seat and placed her arms around his neck from behind. His breath caught tight in his lungs, body going rigid with the shock of her sudden closeness. When she settled her chin on top of his head and brought her spread hands from his shoulder down his chest, he sighed in total contentment. He didn't have a clue why she was acting this way, but he was enjoying it.

"Angie?" Cass said.

The blonde woman glanced from his chest to her face. "What?"

"Remember what you told me at the diner?"

Angie's eyes narrowed. "We talk about a lot of stuff when you eat at the diner."

"About Johnny?"

The contentment he'd been feeling slid down a notch. Who in the world was this Johnny guy? And why was Cass bringing him up now?

"Or rather when you implied all men weren't like Johnny."

"I said that, yes," Angie said. "But it looks like I was wrong."

"No, I am a good guy."

Maddie settled into a chair beside him. "Oh, like decent guys make women cry?"

He jerked upward. "I didn't make—"

"Jack didn't do anything except remind me of my brother."

Cass straightened behind him, slipping her hands up his chest. He relaxed back into his seat. Her floral scent reached all around him, warming him completely. He could get used to this real fast if he wasn't careful.

"The tears were happy ones."

"Happy, how?" Maddie asked.

"Happy because I just learned someone Billy knew was at his funeral."

Both ladies looked toward him.

"He was?" Maddie asked.

"No, but his father was," Cass said lightly. "And that means someone who cared about him was there."

"Many people were there." He sat forward regretfully and glanced at her. "My dad didn't recognize any of them, yet…"

"You were like a brother to him."

Could Hank be onto something? Did that hospital get those two men mixed up? Rogers and Rodgers, except for one letter the names were basically the same. But, if that were the case, why hadn't Billy gotten in touch with his family? Three years have gone by since his accident. He should've gotten over his anger with his father by now.

"So," Maddie said, "You're fine?"

Cass pulled him back into the seat and pressed her chin against the top of his head again. "Yes, I'm okay."

The tone of her voice, her warmth, and her touch stopped the questions. He planned to talk with Hank again after the PI had time to check out some things. Time enough then to get these questions settled. Right now, Jack planned on enjoying this woman's closeness.

****

Pete dropped his cowboy hat onto the messy surface of his desk and sat hard onto the black leather chair. As the firm's silent partner, he only saw his office once a month. He could handle that. Daniel and Ed took care of the day-to-day business. Unfortunately, they still insisted he be at the annual board meeting.

Thank heavens he wouldn't need to meet with those pompous people for another twelve months. Man, he hated board meetings. He'd rather muck out horse stalls.

Daniel sat easily in his seat in front of the desk, crossed one leg over the other, and placed his hands in his lap.

He'd known some women less fussy than this man.

"I'm glad to tell you no one decided to sell their shares of Wholesome."

Even his partner's cultured voice got on his nerves today.

"Even though, you've ruffled a few feathers."

"Too bad." He raised his booted feet and set them on the desk, knocking the papers around the crowded space. One fluttered to the ground, landing next to the new leather sofa Daniel insisted he needed to freshen up the room's decor.

Leather? The only thing leather was good for was in saddles.

"I hate to admit it, Pete." He uncrossed his legs and leaned toward him. "I do look forward to you upsetting our board members once a year. They can be a bit boring."

"A bit?"

"You do have a way of taking them out of their comfort zones."

Did his partner just almost smile? Wow!

"Those seven people need to have that happen at least once every year," Daniel added. "They need to be brought down to earth."

"I'm here to serve," he said. "As long as it's on my terms." His leg slid a few inches to the side of the desk, sending a manila folder of unread letters to the floor. The folder opened halfway to the ground, spilling out a half-dozen or so documents around his desk. One landed face up near his chair, and he glanced down.

"Greenfield?"

Daniel stopped talking in mid-word and frowned "Greenfield?"

Kicking his legs from the desk, he snatched the paper. The address at the top left corner read *All Things Western Women's Clothing Store, Greenfield, Texas.* Indistinct memories skimmed through his mind, then faded. "Greenfield…"

"Are you remembering something?" Daniel sat forward in his seat, hands clasped on the edge of his desk. "What are you remembering?"

Pete set the letter down and glanced toward his older partner. Unexpected excitement rose hot at the implication of the unfamiliar feeling racing through his system. In a vague way, buried deep in his unconscious mind, the name rang as familiar. Was this where he'd lived before the abrupt ending of his bronco riding career? The memory faded, and he stifled the feeling of regret and drew in a deep breath.

"Are you remembering something?"

"For a moment, yes."

Daniel took the letter from his hand and read the return address. "Greenfield, Texas?"

"Seems…familiar."

Daniel focused on him before opening the envelope and pulling out the letter. "Have you read the letter?"

"No."

"This woman…Madeline Thomas…is confirming her interest in placing one of our lines of clothing into her store." Daniel glanced up again. "Does that name sound familiar?"

Pete closed his eyes and relaxed in his seat. Nothing more came. "So damn frustrating."

"Don't force it, Pete." The older man handed him the letter. "Maybe you should follow up on this. Go talk to this woman."

"Why?" Swallowing down the dryness, he leaned back into his seat and studied the envelope. Nothing. "Another waste of time."

"Read the letter," Daniel suggested. "It might remind you of something else."

He glowered at his partner and then skimmed over the short message. No flashes of buried memories broke through him. "Still nothing."

"Are you sure?"

"Wait a minute." Waking the computer, he opened a file and searched through it. "Here it is, Greenfield. I recognized the name because I just looked through this list before the board meeting."

Daniel leaned over the desk and glanced at the screen.

"That's why the name seemed familiar." Pete fell back into his seat. "I was hoping…"

The older man studied the screen. "There are at least ten other towns on that page alone."

"So?"

"Do you remember any of the other names?"

He shrugged. "Do you?"

Daniel waved his hand. "You reacted when you read the return address on the letter. I think that's a good sign. You should take a trip to Greenfield and talk to that shop owner. That'll give you a reason to check out the town and see if anyone knows you. What harm would it do?"

He reread the letter. Yes, what harm would it do? If nothing came of it, he'd at least have a chance to see another great town. Nebulous memories forced their way into his conscious mind so suddenly he sat forward. He focused hard on them, too hard because they slithered away just as swiftly as they'd come. "I loved the Main Street of that last little town Ed, you, and I went to a few months ago. I might like this one, too." He leaned into his seat, pushing the letter to the edge of the desk. It floated toward the floor, settling next to a dozen or so unread messages. "All the buildings there, according to that letter, are original to the Second World War period. Sounds like a unique and peaceful place."

A bewildering flash of a thousand memories barreled into him, followed by a single ghost-like image of a cute pre-teen girl. Clearer this time. Black hair flowed long and soft along her back, deep sienna skin glistening in the hot summer sun. Skin much the same color as his. "Who are you?" A name tried to form in his mind, and then disappeared along with the girl's image. "Damn!"

"Remembering that girl again?"

The light shade of his partner's eyes darkened.

"Did you catch a name?"

"No." He slammed his booted feet onto the floor. "I don't know what's worse, seeing that teenage face or not."

"It'll come," Daniel insisted. "You just need to give it time."

"Give it time?" He leaped from the chair, sending it crashing into the credenza behind him. "How much more time should I give it? A week? Month? Year? A decade? The rest of my life?"

"You need to calm down."

"Yeah, right, calm down." He twisted and stared out of the large side window. Traffic roared far below them, traveling to homes and families, to remembered towns and vacation areas. If all his memories could be laid side by side, it would barely reach the first streetlight. "Why bother finding out who I used to be, Daniel? Maybe it'll be better if I just gave up and lived the life I have now. Things are good. You and Ed are my family." He waved his hands around him. "My ranch is my home. Wholesome Natural Products is my life."

"I don't think that'll be such a good idea."

"Why not?" He twisted toward his partner. "It's hopeless."

Daniel stood and moved toward him, stopping a foot from his rigid form.

"Are you telling me you can give up looking for that teenager who looks so much like you? The one that could be a sister or cousin. Is that what you're saying?"

No, he couldn't do that. Not really. Silence lingered in the air for a few minutes.

"I would love to go with you when you visit Greenfield. I'm sure Ed would love it, too."

"Who said I was going?"

"You're going, Pete."

Sometimes this partner of his could be so maddening, especially when he's right.

"An old-fashioned town like that one would be a good choice for Wholesome," Daniel said. "I'm surprised Ed hasn't told the two of us about it."

"He's too busy with his new wife." Silence greeted his retort. He needed to get out of the stuffy office. He needed to feel the fresh early spring air of West Texas blowing against his skin. The day had barely begun, and he was already itching to get away. He stepped past the desk and headed toward the doorway.

"Pete?"

A soft, manicured hand stopped his escape. "I'm only going outside for some air."

"Ed has been alone for almost two years," he said. "And he's been grieving for Sarah far longer than that. He's lived with the specter of her cancer returning for almost a decade."

"I miss her." Heaviness weighed on his chest. "I still miss my angel."

"We all miss her, Pete," Daniel said. "Ed has the right to be happy."

"Yes, but…" Turning again from the half-open door, he looked toward the cluttered desk. "There's something about Whitney no man should trust."

Daniel studied him and then stood taller. "How about the three of us take a break from Wholesome and go see this unique town?"

Pete sighed. "Greenfield?"

He nodded. "Yes."

"That might be something to do." Pete dropped his misgivings surrounding Ed's new wife, and he pounded the wall beside him. "Yes, let's do that. Let's go now. Today."

"Today?" Daniel jerked straight. "I can't just leave now. Neither can Ed. We have a company to run."

Pete shook his head. "Isn't that why we have middle management and assistants?"

"Of course."

"And you would only be a text message or e-mail away." Pete gazed at him, leaning into the doorframe.

"What's so great about being the bosses if we can't take off once in a while?"

Daniel gazed at the cluttered desk. "What about this? We work through today and tomorrow afternoon. I have a few things I need to talk over with those middle managers and assistants." He glanced at him. "We can leave Friday afternoon and stay the entire weekend."

"Sure," he agreed. "I have a few things I have to take care of at the ranch anyway."

"Friday afternoon?"

Likely he would find out nothing about his past, but he'll see another wonderful small town. That'd be worth the trip. "Sure, Friday it is."

Chapter Eight

Bam-bam-bam.

Cass glanced into the front area of the bookstore. "What?"

Bam-bam-bam.

Sharp male voices invaded her space. She stood from her desk and wandered toward the office door. "What is going on over there?"

Something heavy slammed against the shared wall, followed by louder laughter. Heartbeat speeding, Cass straightened, her back muscles tensing. She moved into the main room.

More laughter rang out.

That was her building. Why was someone slamming and moving stuff around in *her* building? Mr. Martinson or his unresponsive lawyer never got back with her after she'd sent the requested rent payments, and now someone was inside her imagined new café.

She wasn't having it. Dragging in a long, cleansing breath, she raced toward the entranceway door and slammed it open. When she reached the building, she took another deep breath and crashed into the room.

"If I decide to buy this place," a way-too-familiar voice said. "You'll need to repair that damage."

"A tiny little scratch," a more cultured male answered. "You'll no doubt paint the wall, and no one would be the wiser."

"I would know."

Clamping her hands tight, she raced through the front store space and stopped at the open office door.

"Even if you cover it up, I'll still know."

Jack Fontaine. This was the person trying to steal her building out from under her. The hotshot ex-bullfighter, large-animal veterinarian who, with only one touch, caused her to rethink her values and hope to wipe away ten years. Not happening. "So, the rumors are true."

"Jack," the older man said, "It looks like you're in trouble."

"Hey."

She refused to let his pleased look and welcoming grin mess with her anger. She had the right to be upset...with both this man and the older one beside him. Until Mr. Martinson told her he'd decided to sell to another person, she had first dibs. And she didn't plan on giving that right up without a fight. No matter if the second choice had a grin that could melt a polar ice cap and a touch that could start her wildest imagining, she still had rights. "What are you doing in my building?"

"Sorry, honey," the other man said. "But I'm the owner's lawyer and have permission to show it to whomever I please."

So, this was the lawyer who'd been too busy the last couple of weeks to talk with her. "Mr. Brown?"

"At your service." He lowered his head in a slight bow. "Gary Brown, Attorney-at-Law."

"Shyster-at-Law, you mean." His conniving, totally untrustworthy smile sent her blood boiling. Jack's sputtering laughter was what jerked her forward.

"Something funny?"

"Yeah," he said. "If we had a full-length mirror around, you would see why I'm acting this way."

"What way?" Cass swallowed down a hard knot. "Acting like a fool? Or like a man trying to steal another person's building?"

"Stealing another person's building?" He peered at the other man. "It's your building?"

"Not yet," she said. "But it should be."

"Oh, you're the woman Gary told me about?"

"Like you didn't know that?" She glared at the lawyer. "Like Mr. Lawyer here, who can't be professional enough to call someone back, didn't tell you?"

"Yes, he told me someone else was interested." He moved his gaze from her to Gary then back to her. "But I had no idea it was you."

She placed her hands on her hips. "Oh, really?"

"Really."

Doubt stumbled over her temper for a brief second before she pushed it down. "Well, that doesn't matter, does it? He told you someone else was interested in the building."

The lawyer stepped forward. "There is no need for such a tone, young lady."

She jerked toward the older man so quickly her foot caught on a loose floorboard, twisting her ankle in the abrupt movement. Pain lanced up to her knee. She rested her weight on the other leg and lifted the sore foot an inch from the floor. "And you, Mr. Shyster Lawyer, need to stop being so condescending."

"Cass, are you okay?"

Figured he would notice her stupid, senseless

injury. "I'm fine."

"You don't look fine," he whispered. "You twisted your ankle, didn't you?"

"No."

"Stubborn woman."

Jack lifted her off the floor and carried her to a set of sturdy boxes near the joining wall. He hoisted her up and settled her on the nearest one, crouched, and tore off her left shoe. She yanked her leg away, drumming her heel into the front of the box. Pain raced through it, pulling a sharp yell from her mouth.

"Oh, yeah, you're fine."

"I'm not a cow or horse." Cass slapped his hand away. "I'm a woman."

"No kidding." He grabbed her leg and blocked her swinging hand.

His eyes showed her nothing. She couldn't read him. Yet something in the air softened her response. Then the pulse-pounding grin returned.

"Are you finished?"

And all her anger fled like the hot sun drying early morning dew. "I don't need your help, Jack."

He shook his head and probed his fingers gently around her ankle.

She bit her lip at a few sharp pangs, sighing when he stopped the painful movements.

"Doesn't look like anything is broken."

"I only twisted it."

"Gonna have to ice it down," he said. "And keep it elevated for a few days."

"I know what to do."

"You should get Maddie or Angie to help you out," he suggested. "I'm not sure about opening your bookstore tomorrow."

"That's no problem." She pulled her leg from his hand and glared at the lawyer. He hadn't moved from his spot near the office wall. "Seeing as I've been forced to put all my plans on hold until a certain lawyer could find the time in his busy day to return my calls, I don't have any reason to open my store tomorrow."

Gary raised his hand. "I was planning on calling you this afternoon."

"When?" Anger dissipating quickly, she closed her eyes and sighed. When she opened them, she dropped her gaze onto the still crouching vet. She couldn't find the strength to lift her look from the younger man. "When you got your answer from him?"

Jack shrugged.

"I want Jack to have the building," the lawyer said, "and Mr. Martinson wants you to have it."

"He's the owner, Gary," Jack said.

The lawyer pushed from the wall and glided toward them. "Yes, he's the owner."

"Then it's settled," Jack said. "Cass will get the building."

"And what about your mother's dream?"

What did Jack's mother have to do with owning this building? Cass remembered she used to come into the bookstore a lot with Jack in tow, but she never heard her speak about the Martinson building.

"You know how much she wanted this place." The lawyer waved his hand around him. "How she planned to open a thrift shop until the cancer returned?"

Jack shook his head. "That was only one of her many dreams."

"Maybe," he agreed, "but she still loved this

building."

Something in Jack's demeanor changed. Like so many years ago, after hearing of his mother's death, her heart softened. "Your mother wanted this building?"

"Yes." Jack stepped away. "But it was just a dream for her."

The lawyer moved in closer, glancing from Jack to her and back to Jack. "I think we have a stalemate here."

"Not if one of us withdraws our offer." Jack studied her for a long, quiet moment. "Seeing that she negotiated one with Mr. Martinson before me, I guess that will have to be me."

She jerked off the box, slamming her aching ankle into the floor. Discomfort knifed to her knee, but she pressed it away. "You made him an offer?" She twisted toward the lawyer, forcing in one deep breath after another. "An offer that you accepted?"

"You never signed a lease." Gary stepped closer. "The building is still available."

"So?" Lifting her burning ankle, she hobbled away from the two men. Looking foolish in front of this unethical lawyer was the last thing on her mind now. "A handshake and a promise used to be good enough until the legalese could be taken care of, until now."

"You need to calm down." Jack moved to stand beside the lawyer. "You're just making your ankle ache."

"Don't tell me to calm down." Jack didn't try to stop her limping movements toward the entrance. She'd been stupid to believe one comfortable, friendly conversation with this old crush would change anything. "I let my guard down."

"We'll talk to Mr. Martinson," the lawyer offered. "I'll set up a time with him. The two of you can sit down with us to discuss your plans for the building, and then let Mr. Martinson make the final decision."

"That seems fair," Jack agreed.

Cass nodded half-heartedly. "On one condition."

Mr. Brown leaned forward, close-set eyes widening. "Well, that would depend on what that condition is?"

Lawyers. "That you assign another lawyer to Jack."

"One of my partners will be taking over Jack's case." Gary studied her for an intense moment before glancing at Jack. "I hope you're okay with me transferring your case to one of our newer lawyers."

"Not really—"

"What?" She stood straight, clutching her hands against her hips. "Of course, it wouldn't be okay. Gary wants you to have the building to honor your mother, and Mr. Martinson will listen to him. Where does that leave me? You need to get another lawyer."

"Cass?" Jack lifted a hand. "You don't…"

"Guess I'll have to bring my own lawyer."

"Let me explain my reason."

She glared at Jack, and then focused a hard look on the unscrupulous attorney. "Mine will contact you today or tomorrow."

"That's not necessary."

She didn't bother looking at Jack now. Heat rose in her system, but it wasn't from the memory of his simple touch and warm grin. "I hope you will have the decency to call him back, Mr. Brown."

"Jack's new lawyer will do that."

"Good." As dignified as a person hobbling on a

twisted ankle could do it Cass exited the building, slamming the double entrance doors hard.

She couldn't believe him.

Ignoring the pain stabbing up her entire leg, she raced into her store and didn't stop until she reached her office in the back. She settled into the nearest chair, releasing a loud, drawn-out groan, then a sigh.

Stupid, stupid, stupid.

Cass didn't know what was worse, twisting her ankle in such a foolish way or believing Jack was a different sort of man.

It didn't really matter though because both caused her pain. Just in a different part of her body.

****

The ring of his cell startled Jack upward, pulling his gaze off the entranceway door. If he'd known Cass was the woman interested in this building, he would've never considered buying it. Just walking up and down the streets of Greenfield showed him three or four more available buildings. One store was as good as another, so why should he fight for the Martinson building?

Because his mother had wanted it, he answered his own question, and he wanted to honor her memory. He'd honored his father by starting a vet clinic here and buying the old farmhouse they'd once lived in. Now, he needed to honor his mother.

The phone buzzed again, pulling his mind off the dilemma.

"Are you answering that, Jack?"

He shook his head and grabbed the cell. "This is Dr. Fontaine."

"Falling Rain isn't doing well."

Falling Rain? Why was this woman talking about

the weather? Even though a storm did fit his mood, the sun burned bright in the sky. He stepped outside and glanced up. No rain in sight. His gaze dropped in the direction of the bookstore.

"Dr. Fontaine," the slightly anxious voice said, "Something is wrong with one of our mares."

Jack tore his gaze from the closed door. "Ma'am?"

"Oh, I'm sorry. This is Carol Williams," the caller said. "You came to our ranch to check out Thunder, one of our stallions, last week. He was down with the colic."

How could he forget that? He'd spent half the day and an entire night at their ranch. And he'd called back later the following day to see how he was doing. "Is he having more trouble?"

"No, Thunder is fine," she said. "But I'm worried about Falling Rain now. One of the ranch hands noticed she was favoring one foot this morning."

"Give me a half hour or so," he said. "I'm in Greenfield now."

"That'll be fine, Doctor."

Jack disconnected the call and slipped the phone back into its holder on his belt. "See you later, Gary. Got a lame horse I need to check out."

"Wait a minute.'"

The lawyer followed down the narrow building and out. "Are you still interested in this building?"

He walked to his truck, stopping at the driver's side door. "I'm not sure."

"Not sure?"

"Look, Gary, I like the building." He looked toward him. "And I want to do right by Mom's memory, but…" The older man studied him for so long

Jack wondered if he'd said something wrong. Or was he just waiting for him to finish his statement?

"You like Cass a bit more."

Is my interest in the woman that obvious? After all the women he'd been with over the years, he should be able to hide his emotions a bit better. Just because he'd compared every one of them with the memory of his best friend's sister didn't mean he hadn't learned how to hide his feelings.

"Tell me true now." Gary leaned in closer. "Part of the reason you set up your practice here in Greenfield and bought that old farm was because of that lady."

Yes, it was a part of the reason. But he had no intention of admitting it to his soon-to-be ex-lawyer. Bad enough her two friends sensed he was more than aware of her, but letting on to Gary about his feelings might not work to his advantage. He might have been his father's best friend, but even *he* didn't trust him completely. His dad had always been careful around the lawyer.

"Well, do you still want me to set up the meeting with Mr. Martinson and Cass?"

"You?"

"Yes," he said. "If it's good with Mr. Martinson, I'd like to stay your lawyer."

"I'm not sure that'll work." Jack stopped just inside the doorway. "I'm the newcomer here."

The lawyer raised his right arm. "Mr. Martinson knows all the attorneys in the firm. I'm sure it'll be okay with him, Jack. I'll let him decide."

"If it's okay with him, yes." Jack stepped to his truck. "You are familiar."

"Good." Gary moved past him and stopped near his

SUV. "No matter what happens, the firm will arrange the meeting with the old man and Cass."

Jack pointed his cell toward him. "And don't forget her lawyer."

"Of course," he said. "Before you give up the chance to get the building, you should talk to the owner. You need to think of your mother."

Gary was right. If his mother wasn't serious about the thrift shop, would she have collected and stored all those old knickknacks and period clothing in those lockers in Dallas? And all the old pieces of 1940s-style furniture? A treasure trove he'd never known existed until he searched through his father's things and found the key and contract for the lockers a few months after his death.

"As soon as you give the okay," Gary said. "My firm can make the arrangements."

Jack had no idea what was in any of those boxes, but he expected the stuff would be unique. No one ever accused his mother of being usual.

"Jack?"

Wiping his mother's image from his mind, he glanced over the truck's roof toward the man. "Yes, I'll talk with them."

"Good." He let out a long-held breath. "I'll set up the appointment as soon as I talk with Mr. Martinson. I'll update Michael, my junior attorney, and call Cass's lawyer."

"No hurry, Gary."

"The sooner the better." He snatched at the handle of his SUV and opened it. "Mr. Martinson is eager to lease out the building or sell it outright."

Then why didn't you allow him to accept Cass's offer?

Chapter Nine

"You need to keep your legs elevated." Angie gushed out a breath. "Sit back down, and I'll place this ice pack on your ankle."

"I'm okay." Cass sighed. "I'm fine."

She shook her head. "If that grimace is any indication, I doubt you feel as wonderful as you claim."

"I never said I felt wonderful," Cass muttered. "I said I'm okay."

A knock sounded on the front door. "Don't you dare get up, Cass. I'll get it."

Just thinking about putting pressure on her ankle hurt.

Maddie stepped through the door the second Angie opened it, not stopping until she stood at the side of the couch. "How's our patient doing?"

She loved that her friends cared, but this was ridiculous. "I'm fine."

"Irritable." Angie shook her head at Maddie. "Like you are a few days before…"

"Like me?" Maddie huffed. "You are in major denial if you think you act any differently when that time-of-the-month shows up."

"You're probably right." Angie grinned. "But are any of us at our best then?"

Cass sighed. She'd take cramps and bloating over being pregnant any day. Good news, maybe, is this morning she woke up irritable, like she usually did right before her period started, aching from the top of her head to the tips of her toes. Her head still ached, along with her ankle.

"I'll go and get our coffee." Angie stepped toward the little kitchen. "Why don't you reposition the ice pack, Maddie?"

Her legs lifted to the coffee table, followed by a chilled, wet ice pack settling roughly on her sore ankle. "Ouch."

Maddie patted the wet pack. "Is that better?"

Cass nodded, giving up the fight. Why bother asking them to leave her? Good people never left their friends to deal with things alone.

"Good." Maddie released the ice bag and grabbed for another towel to dry her hands. "Now don't move again."

"Or one of us will have to call your mother," Angie said.

"Oh please, not Mom." She lifted her hands in a pleading way, fighting a grin. That's all she needed now, Mom hovering like she was a helpless little child again. "I promise not to move."

Maddie dropped the towel on the coffee table. "Her attention is nice."

Yes, getting attention from her mom was a good thing. Unfortunately, hers wouldn't just hover now.

"Feeling any better?" Maddie sank onto the sofa and twisted toward her. "You look a bit more relaxed."

"My ankle is, yes."

Angie set three cups on the table, sliding them to the edge.

Cass reached for it gratefully, drawing a careful sip

before setting it on her raised thigh. The bitter liquid burnt the top of her mouth. "Perfect."

Maddie laughed. "Good and hot, right?"

Angie settled her bottom into the lounger kitty-corner to the couch and picked up one of the other cups. She blew into the hot liquid, studying her with intensity.

A hint of the spicy pumpkin creamer lingered in the air for a moment, then disappeared.

"Now tell us what happened when you talked with your mother," Maddie said.

Cass shrugged. "We settled the money issue. She's interested in decorating the café and has some good ideas for the lectures."

"That's good," Angie said. "But did you talk about Billy?"

"What about him?" If irritability was an Olympic sport, she would get the gold medal hands down. "We reminisce about both him and Dad all the time."

"Guess you haven't told her yet." Maddie sat forward. "If you wait too long, the harder it'll be. The PI will find out something sooner rather than later."

No kidding. She bit her lip instead of speaking the sarcasm out loud and took another sip of her coffee. A smaller one this time. "Good."

"You need to tell her the truth before he does." Angie leaned forward and reached over to rearrange the pack on her ankle.

Cold wetness eased her ache, and Cass relaxed on the sofa.

"It's not right to keep something like that from her." Sadness furrowed her well-shaped brows. "Your mother needs to know about Billy."

For the hundredth time, Cass wished Angie would open up about things. Even Maddie couldn't get any useful information about her divorce.

"It's always better to force things out in the open instead of letting them simmer unspoken inside," Angie whispered. "Better for you and the other people involved."

"I know, Angie." Her pensive mood brought heat over the situation back to the surface. "And, yes, I did try to ease my mom into the truth about Billy's death."

"No time for easing." Maddie sprang forward in her seat, splashing a bit of the liquid on the sofa between them. "You need to get your mother alone, take a deep breath, and just tell her. She'll be upset and might not believe you, but in the end, it'll be for the best."

"No, that's not the way to tell her at all." Angie sat at the edge of her recliner. "Cass needs to be gentle with her mother."

Maddie huffed. "Well, she had three years to do it the easy way."

"It's still not right."

"What's not right is her mother believing her eldest is still alive." Maddie sat tall, back straight. "That's what's not right. And with the addition of the private investigator who knows what will happen."

"I think he might have found out something." Cass glanced over at the chilly ice pack, feeling coldness dripping onto her foot. "Mom called me late last night and told me he wants to meet with us at his office in San Antonio this afternoon."

"Oh, no." Maddie relaxed her posture but didn't settle back into the sofa. "Are you going with her?"

"She can't. Not with her ankle the way it is now." Angie glowered at Maddie, then settled a softer gaze on her. "You need to tell her about your accident."

"She might not have any homemade chicken noodle soup ready to go."

Good-natured laughter broke through the uncomfortable silence, making her glad for friends like Maddie and Angie. Like her mom's chicken noodle soup and loving presence, their friendship meant the world to her. She would've been all alone if not for the two of them.

"Hey, why not spend the whole weekend in San Antonio?" Angie asked. "Until you find out something about that building, you can't do any work in your store. Especially with a sore ankle. It'll be good to get away for a few days. You'll have the chance to really talk."

The mention of that building forced her gaze to the ice pack. Her injury brought back the conversation she'd had with Jack and Gary. "You'll never guess who else is interested in it?" She didn't wait for a response. "Jack Fontaine."

"Mr. Hotty?"

"The new vet," Angie said. "How do you know that?"

"He seemed startled when I raced into the back part of the building to confront him." Cass took another sip of her pumpkin-scented coffee. "I had no clue it was Jack pounding on the connecting wall."

"Pounding?"

She ignored Angie's question. "Jack was right there, less than twenty feet from me, discussing my building with that lawyer. I'm meeting with them, Mr.

Martinson, and my lawyer's daughter, Lucy, on Monday."

"Jack wants your building?" Angie looked over at a fuming Maddie before once again looking at her. "Why would he buy it when he has the old farm on Old North Road? I heard he was setting up the barn as his vet clinic. He's no reason to buy the other building."

"Old Dr. Morgan's clinic is still sitting empty." Maddie jolted off the sofa. "That building was good enough for him, why isn't it good enough for Jack?"

Cass jerked her ankle a few inches from the table, landing down hard. Pain knifed through her, forcing out a groan.

"Oh, I'm sorry."

"I know you are." Her distraught friend settled the ice pack back on her sore ankle. The coldness swiftly numbed the pain. "The ice helps."

"Good." Maddie fiddled with the towel-wrapped pack before suddenly standing straight. "Hey, we can all go to San Antonio for the weekend. It's been a while since the three of us just took off somewhere together."

From mad to contrite to excited all in one second.

"How does that sound?" Maddie asked again. "And we could invite your mother?"

"Mom and I must be at that investigator's office at eleven thirty. Not all of us can close our businesses at the same time. Friday and Saturday are the busiest days of the week." Cass liked the idea of a women's weekend, plus one lovely mother. She just didn't see how it could be possible. "But you could meet us for lunch after. We should be finished with the PI in an hour or so."

"Then we can get a hotel room somewhere for the

weekend," Maddie said.

"No, I couldn't ask the two of you to do that," Cass said. "Mom might not want to spend time with me after finding out about Billy."

"I doubt that. Your mom will need to be with people she loves."

Angie nodded.

"My shop will open up tomorrow, whether or not I'm in town." Maddie glanced from her to Angie. "And Angie has an experienced cook and some fine older servers to take care of her parents' restaurant."

Angie frowned but didn't comment.

Another one of the strange, little mysteries surrounding her. This one was easier to understand, however. She didn't want to manage the café. Her parents just assumed she would.

"We need to go to San Antonio." Angie sat straighter. "We could spend the whole weekend there."

She studied Maddie again, seeing right through her reasons.

"Maddie's right," Angie agreed. "It'll be nice to get away from Greenfield for a few days."

"Even with my sprained ankle?"

"Yes," Angie said. "I'm looking forward to it."

Cass shrugged. The PI only talked to Mom on the phone five times. He had plenty of time to find out all he needed about her brother's car accident and death. Two whole weeks. Mom will need her support. "I guess I could go see the Alamo again."

"That's the spirit," Maddie said. "Maybe Angie and I can meet you and your mom at the Chinese Buffet and then find a nice room at a hotel in the city."

"Better yet," Angie said. "I can make reservations

now."

Cass settled into the sofa and stared at the wet ice pack. She wasn't sure she wanted to go anywhere now.

Maddie sat beside her, sipping her coffee.

"Let me check the computer." Angie wiggled her mouse and connected to the Internet. "I'll just type in the dates for this weekend, starting with today, and see what's available."

"We should register with one of the hotels along the Riverwalk." Maddie suggested. "Near enough to walk, so we can go and have a few drinks."

"Good idea." Angie typed the information into the search boxes. "Oh, good, there's one room left for this weekend at the Riverwalk Plaza. Two queen-size beds." She peeked over her shoulder. "How does that sound? Maddie and I will share one, and you and your mother will share the second."

"I've never stayed there before." She would love to go somewhere with Mom, but maybe not San Antonio. It was way too close to the PI. "I would rather visit some place farther away, though. Like the moon."

Both Angie and Maddie ignored her.

"Get my purse, Maddie, I'll pay with my debit card."

"No." Cass pulled the melting bag off her ankle and eased her leg to the ground. She stood slowly, pressing gingerly on her injured foot. Sharp pain raced up it. "Still hurts."

"Of course, it still hurts," Maddie said. "Sit back down, and Angie will bring you the laptop."

"That's okay. I don't need to see it. Angie knows how to pick a great hotel." She settled into the sofa, not fussing for them ordering her around. Lifting her foot gingerly onto the coffee table, she leaned back and sighed. "What I have a problem is with her paying now before we talk to my mother? Mom might have other plans for this weekend."

"Oh, I didn't think of that." Maddie grabbed the phone and threw it toward her. "Here, call her now."

Cass caught it with one hand and waved it. Normally, something thrown at her would bounce off and land a good distance away. Maybe this simple change would be the beginning of other, more meaningful ones. Like she'll start cramping up, or Jack will tell his new lawyer he didn't want the Martinson building.

Maddie only rolled her eyes.

Dialing the familiar number, she waited for the usual three rings. "Hey, Mom, this is Cass."

"Like she doesn't know who you are."

"Is that Maddie I hear complaining in the background?"

Even Mom heard her. "Yes, it's Maddie." Cass mock-glared at her. "I just called to see if you have anything planned for this weekend."

"No, just the appointment with that Mr. Wayne today," she said. "You haven't changed your mind about going with me, have you?"

"No, I'm still going." Even though every fiber in her being screamed to find a way out she couldn't allow her to face the truth alone. *Oh, why didn't I tell her the same time I told Dad and my friends here?* "Angie, Maddie, and I are thinking about taking off this weekend, and we'd like you to come. Interested?"

"Where are you going?"

"Not far," she said. "Just to San Antonio."

Quietness.

"I'm not sure."

"I mean, if you don't have any other plans."

"No, I don't."

Silence.

"If you're sure you three young ladies want an old lady hanging around, then I'd love to go."

"You're far from old, Mom."

"Forty-eight in two months," Mom said. "The three of you are only in your late twenties."

Maddie waved a hand, startling the phone from her ear. "I'm talking to my mother here."

"Is she joining us?"

Cass shrugged. "So, should Angie make those reservations? Looks like she entered all the information and is just waiting."

"Yes, I'll like to join you."

She lowered her cell and nodded. "Angie and Maddie will meet us at the Chinese Buffet around one. I figure you and I could check into the hotel room before we talk to that detective." Bile rose in her throat. "I just hope he doesn't have any bad news."

"It'll be good, honey."

She closed her eyes. *Oh, what have I done?* "I have a bad feeling, Mom. I hope you don't get your hopes up too high."

"Everything will go fine."

Cass heard the anticipation in her voice. She heard the hint of peace. She sank hard into the cushion. "Mom?"

"I've got to go," Mom said quickly. "A few of the ladies from my church are coming over for coffee, and I'm not even dressed yet."

"Okay."

"I'll see you around nine," she said. "Rumor has it you hurt your ankle, so I'll drive."

A dial tone erupted in her ear. She barely heard it. *Why didn't I tell her?*

"There." Angie powered down the laptop and closed the lid. "Done."

Yes, done is right.

When Mom finds out I've known about Billy's death for three years, she'll never talk to me again.

Chapter Ten

Jack stayed out of town all day on Friday, scrubbing and cleaning the downstairs of his new home from ceiling to floor. First, he swiped down the cobwebs in the corners, continuing to sweep along the lengths of the walls to the floor, and the floor itself, and then he mopped up the hardwood with lemony-scented cleanser. The scent whiffled up around him, reminding him of his mother. No matter what time of day, she'd always smelled like tangy fruit.

When his stomach growled for the fifth or sixth time in the space of five minutes, he glanced at his watch. "Wow, I totally lost track of time." And that probably wasn't the only thing he was losing, if the number of words he'd spoken out loud that morning was any indication.

"Oh, well." He pushed the mop bucket out the back door and tipped it over, splashing the cool, dirty water onto his jeans. He left the mop sitting inside it. "There, that's done." He patted his lower leg with the old towel hanging at his waist while looking around the clean kitchen. Sunlight found its way through the open window above the sink and the back door, bringing the cracked tile to sparkling life. A slight, refreshing breeze blew against his skin. He turned his face into it. His stomach growled out another loud protest. *Time to take a break.*

Jack walked over to the sink and scrubbed his hands, drying them with a fresh dish towel. He threw both towels onto the counter and opened the refrigerator, pulling out fixings for a quick sandwich, salad dressing, and a cold drink. Soon, wheat bread, turkey and ham slices, American and Pepper Jack cheese, shredded lettuce, and tomato slices sat on the table next to the small unopened jar of dressing and a chilled pitcher of iced tea. The appliance hummed, the motor running rough in the quiet. *Sounds like I've got another thing to place on my to-do list.* His list was slowly and surely getting longer and longer—and more expensive. Hopefully, he'll round up a few jobs soon. He poured the iced tea into a tall glass and swallowed it half down before refilling and setting it on the table beside the pile of food.

His phone rang. "Maybe that's one now." He shook his head and grabbed the phone. "This is Dr. Fontaine."

"Doc?"

"Yes." Jack stood. "How can I help you?"

"Are you taking over from old Doc Morgan?"

The man didn't give him the chance to say anything.

"I heard you were a vet, so I just assumed you were him."

He must have seen one of his business cards. "Yeah, it's me."

"Good." He sighed. "Good, because I'm a-needin' your help with one of my mares."

"What seems to be the problem?"

"Well, if I be knowin' that, why would I need a vet."

He bit his tongue to silence his response.

"Doc Morgan claimed it be asthma," the caller said. "I told him that was impossible."

"Why is it impossible?" He sat. "I'm Doctor Fontaine, and you are…"

"Oh, I guess I shoulda mentioned my name," he said. "It's Mitchell, Abe Mitchell."

"Nice to meet you, Mr. Mitchell."

"Abe'll be fine."

Jack relaxed against the chair's back. "So, why is it impossible for your horse to have asthma, Abe?"

"Simple," he said. "Asthma is a human disease, and horses can't get human diseases."

"Actually, asthma is pretty common in horses." He took a sip of his tea, swishing the liquid in his dry mouth. "Like humans, they can be allergic to different things, and that can lead to asthma."

"Yeah, right," Abe groused. "The same thing happened to Buttercup last year, and she got better."

Buttercup? At least, it was a mare rather than a stallion. He swallowed the tea and took another drink, setting the wet glass on the table.

"She starts coughing every time I have my boys herd the horses to the grasslands along the fence line touching my land with the Williamses'."

Jack glanced at his bread. That could mean a few things. "What did Dr. Morgan tell you to do?"

"Told me to keep a record of where she was when the symptoms happened," he said. "Thought old Buttercup might be allergic to something."

"Most likely that's the case." He nodded at the man's comment. "Did you do what he asked?"

"Started ta but she got better," Abe admitted.

"Figured didn't need to go through all that, if she wasn't feeling poorly anymore."

"Let me take a stab at this." Jack continued to speak before the other man could interfere again. "The mare starts coughing around May or June, right? And she only does it when she's at the fence line near the Williamses' land?" A loud huff was his only answer. Jack grinned. "Then her breathing comes easier when she gets back to the barn or to another grazing area."

"How ya know, Doc?"

He didn't answer Abe. "Is that the only place she has trouble?"

"Seems like it," he said.

"Okay." Jack slid from his chair and left the kitchen. "Let me see if Dr. Morgan left me a file on your horse."

"Buttercup has a file?"

What did the man think? That Dr. Morgan had a great memory. Jack shook his head and leaped from the porch, walking fast toward the barn. The overhanging doors swung open with a squeal, like a dull knife on a grinding stone. He wandered into his newly remodeled clinic office and stood just inside the doorway, admiring his handiwork. He'd spent the last week redoing the old barn. If you concentrated only on the building's outer appearance, it looked like it was about ready to fall to the ground. Yet, the interior told a different story.

"Doc?" Abe groused. "Ya there?"

"Yes." Refocusing on the man, he walked toward the bent, old filing cabinet behind his desk. And another thing he needed to add to his to-do list—hiring someone to modernize Dr. Morgan's paper files into the computer. "Let me just look under Mitchell."

"Wouldn't it be under Buttercup?"

He pulled out a thin file, ignoring the man's question. "Here it is." He searched through it and found the one for the mare. "Not much here."

"Now there wouldn't be, would there?" Abe asked. "Told ya, she got better."

"So, you didn't do as Doc asked?" Jack read through the few lines on the beginning pages, mostly just basic information about the mare like vital signs, age, weight, and height. On the next line, the older vet wrote *possible RAO*—recurrent airway obstruction. "So, how has the horse been since then?"

"Everything was okay until now."

So, that would suggest it was summer-pasture-associated heaves. He set the file onto the desk and settled down into his chair. Picking up a pen, he added this information to Buttercup's page and added the date, time, and his new instructions. "Why don't you take this week and do as Dr. Morgan asked? Keep a record of time of day, weather conditions, and the area when Buttercup starts acting up again." He pushed the paper out of his way, glanced down at the temporary, large calendar spread over the surface of his desk, and wrote Abe's name in an empty block under May twelve, nine a.m., a week from today. So far, three slots have been filled in May, a follow-up visit on the seventh, at two p.m., to check the Williamses' stallion, two days later at ten a.m. to check out the lame mare, and Mr. Mitchell's asthmatic Buttercup. "It's a start."

"Say something, Doc?"

He sighed. "Look, start keeping a record like I said. I'll come to your ranch next Friday, at nine a.m., to check out the animal."

"I can do that."

"Okay," he said. "I'll see you."

"Thanks."

"You're welcome." He spoke to a loud dial tone. "Goodbye." Before he could exit his office, the phone buzzed in his hand. "Dr. Fontaine."

"Are you the new vet?" a female asked. "Taking over for Dr. Morgan?"

Maybe business was finally picking up. "Yes."

"Do you take care of cats?"

He specialized in large animal medicine, and he wasn't all that fond of cats. Yet, how could he turn down a possible client? "Sure thing."

"Good."

Relief sounding clear. A hitch signaled in her voice, as if trying to stop her tears.

"My little Muffin won't stop throwing up. Can I bring her to see you now?"

Muffin? What's with these names anyway? His stomach growled out a warning. "Sure, I can see you at one today."

"I can't see you now?"

"One is the earliest I can see you." Did this lady not eat lunch?

"Well, okay, if that's the earliest."

Disappointment sounded clear in her tone. People really did love their pets.

"You're set up at the old Speyer farm, right? Off Old North Road?"

"Yes."

"Good," she said. "I'll be there, with Muffin, at one."

For some reason, Jack thought, if she's still alive. "I'll be here."

Three clients.

Yes.

****

Waves and waves of fresh green land filled Cass's gaze as soon as they left the town proper of Greenfield. She sat in silence, barely seeing the landscape until they reached the outskirts of San Antonio.

What will the investigator tell them?

"How are you feeling?"

"I'm fine, Mom." Cass angled sideways in the car seat, flexing her foot gently. "It helped I could keep my ankle iced and elevated most of the morning. I feel a lot better."

Mom peered down at her leg, swerving the vehicle slightly to the right.

Cass pressed against the door, releasing a low moan when her left foot rubbed against her sore right ankle. "Mom, you need to be careful."

"I'm sorry, honey."

She swallowed dryness. Mom wasn't one of the worst drivers she'd ever ridden with, but she was close. When she was preoccupied, like she was now, she joined the top ten candidates. Thankfully, they'd just turned onto Commerce Street only a few miles from their hotel to check in before meeting with the private investigator. Twenty minutes after setting up the girls' weekend, Mom had called back and told her the PI needed to change the meeting time from eleven thirty to three thirty. Instead of lunch, now Maddie and Angie would meet her mom and her at the Chinese Buffet for dinner, then all four would go to the hotel.

Mom turned into the hotel's parking lot, and she sighed. The car stopped directly in front of the entranceway door. "I'll let you out here and park the car." Mom helped her out and toward the door.

"Remind me to stomp Jack's foot the next time we see him."

"Jack? Did this Jack person cause you to twist your ankle?"

Oops, I really must stop speaking my thoughts out loud. "No, I did that all on my own."

"Oh?"

Her eyes widened, and then narrowed above a slight grin. A surprising look Cass hadn't seen in Mom for months. Maybe she should just stop talking completely. "It was nothing, Mom."

"Let me be the judge of that," she said. "You wouldn't have the need to hurt him if he hadn't caused your injury in the first place."

Cass did not want to talk about this now, for more than just the obvious reason. If she told her about Jack, she might remember he'd been Billy's friend all those years ago. Then that would remind her why and how her brother had left town, and that would bring up a lot of old hurts and questions Cass wasn't in the mood for now.

"Cass?"

In that one word, she heard the beginning of the old pain. "Mom, go and park the car, and I'll check us into our room."

"Yes, I'll do that." She pointed a finger. "But I want you to sit in the lobby and wait. I'll check us in and help you up to the room."

No argument there. Her ankle still ached a bit.

"Yes, I'll do that."

"I'll be right back."

Cass dragged in a deep breath and let it out slowly. Half walking and half limping along the wall, she hobbled on her good foot toward the double doors.

An older couple stepped out at the same moment. The man held it open for his wife to exit and waved her through. The simple gesture lifted her spirits, and Cass nodded her thanks.

"Do you need any help getting to a chair?"

Gingerly pressing her right foot to the floor, she put part of her weight on it. When only a twinge of pain moved up her leg, she shook her head and slowly wandered toward the nearest empty seat. She settled into the soft cushion.

"Miss?"

She smiled her gratitude. "Thank you."

"Are you sure?"

"Yes, I'm fine." A person helping her wasn't an uncommon thing. His friendly gesture touched her all the same. Her dad used to treat her this way when she was ill. During those sweet, precious times, she'd known her father had cared. Rarely had he shown her he cared, and even less than often had he said, 'I love you.' Amazing that she'd forgotten it. "Thank you."

The man nodded and beamed a bright grin, holding the door open for Mom.

A brilliant smile radiated from her.

Low laughter surprised Cass. She hadn't heard that rusty, gruff sound in over a year.

"Don't get up, honey."

"I don't plan on it." Both her parents had a hard time showing their feelings. That didn't mean they didn't have them. "This seat is way too comfortable."

Laughter rang out again, louder this time.

Cass sat straight in her seat and grinned.

A pink flush flowed across her chin to cheeks, eyes widening.

The blush looked good on Mom.

"I have no reason to laugh like that."

Maybe not, but it was good to hear it, tarnished and startled though it might be. Mom was too young, too warm and pretty, too vital, to act so old. Way too warm and beautiful if the look on the handsome older man's face standing by the door told the truth. "Mom, don't look now, but I think you've found yourself an admirer."

"What are you babbling about now?"

A slight flush rose in her features.

"No one is looking at me."

"Really?" She arched her head toward the tall, distinguished male walking toward them. "Oh, better put on your prettiest smile because that good-looking older guy is now walking this way."

Her flush deepened. "No, he's probably focusing on my beautiful daughter."

"Who happens to look just like her gorgeous mother." Cass fought back a grin. Her mom was really blushing. *Wow*. She glanced past her shoulder toward the man. "Hello."

"Hi."

The man never took his interested regard from Mom.

"I'm hoping you are the two women I'm looking for."

Oh, how hokey can you get? He had to be in his

late forties or early fifties. Shouldn't he have a better pickup line than that one? "Depends on what you were hoping for?"

"Cass?" Sharpness rang in Mom's disapproving tone.

"As in Cassandra?" the man asked. "Janessa and Cassandra Rogers?"

Her eyes widened, but Mom didn't react in any other way. A hint of fear replaced the shock a second later, followed by a totally unexpected look of shyness.

"Guess I was wrong," the man said.

"No, I'm Cass, and this is my mother, Janessa." Mom still refused to turn. *What is wrong with you, Mom?* She pinched her arm, causing her to jerk backward into the man.

"Oh, I'm so sorry." He stepped back. "Are you okay?"

"I'm fine," Mom said. "No problem."

The man recovered quickly, backing another step away while studying her mom with intense dark blue eyes. Cass wasn't sure she liked this man showing so much interest in Mom.

"My fault for standing so close behind you."

Oh, boy.

"No, it was mine."

A calmer, in control voice spoke now, the voice Mom used when she wanted to keep someone away.

"I stepped back too suddenly." She stood tall. "I'm sorry."

"I'm not complaining." He grinned.

Yeah, I just bet you aren't. Cass had about enough of this man hitting on Mom. She stood carefully from her seat. "Well, you know our names. We have no clue who you are.

"Cass, don't be rude."

The man's grin deepened, glee reaching all the way to his dark eyes. "Your daughter isn't being rude, Mrs. Rogers. I *was* checking you out."

Could the guy be even more unbelievable? He was like a train roaring unchecked down the tracks. Her recently widowed mother didn't stand a chance. Yet, when Cass glanced over toward her, a little grin played along her mouth. Dark brown eyes sparkled with a look that perplexed her completely. "Mom?"

Then she winked and turned toward the suddenly silent man.

What in the world is going on here?

"My daughter does have a point," she said evenly. "We don't know your name."

"It's Henry. Henry Wayne. I'm the private investigator you hired to find your son."

Oh, please, no. Cass couldn't win today. Just when she thought the entire situation couldn't get any worse, it got worse. Why couldn't the man be balding, with a paunch rolling over his middle? No, he had to be a hot older guy who showed way too much interest in her widowed mother.

"You're the private investigator?" Mom looked closely at the man.

And his interest seemed to be returned.

"Yes." He opened his wallet and showed his business card to Mom, then to her. "Proof."

Her mom stared for a long moment before nodding. "Henry Wayne. Wayne and Gray, Investigations."

"Someone called Mom early this morning and told us you needed to reschedule the appointment. We're supposed to meet at three thirty p.m."

"That was the plan," he said. "But another client cancelled so an earlier spot opened suddenly. I called both you and your mom but got no answer, so I called Jack."

"Jack?" Cass stood straighter, sending a rush of pain through her ankle. "Why would you call him?"

"His name came up a few times when I talked with some of your brother's old acquaintances," he said easily. "No one seemed to know Billy very well, but a couple of the guys told me your brother was close to the Fontaines."

"Yes." Cass peered at Mom. Would she remember Jack was the name of the guy who'd caused Billy to leave? "They were best friends."

"That's the impression I got," he said. "We talked a few times. Seems like a good guy."

"Yes, he is." Janessa shook her head. "Or rather he used to be. He and his father left town after his mother passed away years ago." She turned her attention to Cass. "Did you know he was back?"

She did remember him. "Yes."

"And you never bothered to tell me?" She caught the back of the chair. "Why didn't you tell me?"

"When I talked with Jack, he gave me the number for a bookstore and a diner in town."

The PI didn't give her time to answer, even if she had a good answer. Why would she tell her the man both her parents blamed for her brother leaving town was back? What good would it do? Like all small towns, his return wouldn't stay a secret forever. Tension sparked between her and Mom, yet the detective either didn't notice it or decided to ignore it.

Cass was fine with either scenario.

"No one answered at the bookstore—"

"Because I'm the owner." Cass looked toward the man. "And I was on my way here."

"Yes, I figured that out." He took a little notepad from his jacket pocket and flipped the cover. Searching through the pages, he read aloud. "A woman named Angie told me it was yours. She also said the two of you were in San Antonio at this hotel. That you were spending the weekend here, with her and another friend."

Cass took a deep breath. "She shouldn't have given you all that information."

"Why?" His eyes narrowed. "Hiding something?"

Oh no, what has this man found out? Has he discovered Billy died in that bad car accident three years ago? That he was rushed to a hospital and never awakened from his coma. That she'd hidden that information from the beautiful lady standing so quiet and intense between them now.

Oh, why did she have to listen to her father?

Chapter Eleven

The worried *cat lady* client had told him Cass and Janessa had gone to San Antonio around noon, but Jack still refused to go to town. Rumor had it Cass's two loyal friends planned on meeting them there a few hours later. Yet, he couldn't shake the ominous feeling. If he went into town today, something upsetting would happen.

Or maybe he was just being a coward, afraid he might meet with one of those ladies. The way Cass had raced out of the Martinson building yesterday didn't bode well. No doubt she'd told everyone some story about him causing her accident.

"Coward." He shook his head and shut off the vacuum at the clinic's door. "They're only women."

He wrapped the cord around the machine and set it in the corner of the reception area, unable to let go of the thought. A rattling sound echoed in the air, wood slamming against wood. *Fontaine Veterinarian Clinic.* Contentment pushed at his less-than-manly uneasiness. Long time in coming, but he'd finally made it. "Really need to go shopping, though."

Instead of going toward the house, he stepped to the other side of the barn and studied the broken fence surrounding the grassy corral. After he finished constructing the stalls at the back of the barn and fixed the fencing, the area would be used to hold any hurt animals in his care.

Dad would've been so proud. "Wish you could be here." His sight misted over. He wiped the tears away quickly and sped around the clinic to the house.

Dull, off-white bare walls and dark, hardwood flooring greeted him at the entrance, offset by his father's old black leather recliner in the corner with a stand beside it. He traced his hands over the coolness of the leather, remembering his father for a moment. He glanced around him, pleased by the changes to the place. All the windows gleamed with the warmth of setting sunlight, heating the interior. The small kitchen and half-bath in the back of the house also gleamed, as did the small dining room between them. "Tomorrow," he whispered, "the bedrooms."

Or at least the one he was using. And the upstairs bathroom needed scrubbing. "Should've done the upstairs first."

Maybe he should get a dog.

If he had a pet nearby, and someone came into his house or clinic unexpectedly, they would think he was talking to the animal. Didn't everyone who owned a pet talk to them occasionally?

A growl echoed in the quiet.

Other than a pound and a half of coffee, and containers of mustard, ketchup, and mayonnaise, both the refrigerator and pantry were bare. Was he truly that afraid of seeing Cass's blonde server friend from the diner? Or the other, even more loyal one Gary had told him owned the dress shop on Main?

Jack had never considered himself a coward, yet…

Wrangling bulls had been so much easier than facing an upset woman and her steadfast companions.

Or maybe he was afraid of facing the woman because she'd set his heart racing. The clean wildflower scent of her perfume had risen to trap him within its gentle fold that day she'd caught him and Gary in the Martinson building. The scent, the warmth, and the perceived softness of her skin kept him probing her ankle a few seconds longer than needed.

Then she'd gotten mad and limped out of the building.

Ring-Ring-Ring.

Startled out of his thoughts, he raced toward the phone. "Fontaine Vet—"

"You talked to that PI?"

He jerked backward. "Who is this?"

"Maddie," she said. "What did you say to that guy?"

How did Maddie find out about those conversations? "Nothing much."

A loud snort sounded in the line. "First, you break her ankle. Now you're acting all standoffish."

"Broke her..." Jack shot up tall. What an infuriating woman. "Is that what she told you?"

"How else would I know it?" Maddie said. "Do you have a habit of hurting women who disagree with you?"

"She tripped." He swallowed, staring down at his feet. "Twisted too quickly and tripped over her foot. I had nothing to do with it."

"Yeah." Maddie snorted once again. "Likely story."

Maybe he'd been right to stay out of town today after all. "Is she okay?"

"Why? Feel guilty about pushing her?"

"I didn't push her." He clutched the phone tight and counted to ten. "I know Cass is your friend. And I understand you care for her. But that doesn't give you the right to accuse me of hurting her. I would never hurt anyone."

She grumbled. "Yeah, you're probably right."

"Thank you for that."

"But I still need an answer to my question."

Question? The woman asked me a question?

"What did you say to that PI? What did you tell Mr. Wayne?"

"Mr. Wayne is what they called his grandfather." He climbed up the stairs slowly, stopping at his bedroom door. "They called his father, Henry. He's simply Hank."

"You do know him well?"

"Not really." He entered his bedroom, kicking off his left boot. "I only talked with him a few times on the phone."

"You know he likes to be called Hank, though."

He shrugged. "He told me."

Maddie snorted again.

Still at a loss, he kicked off his other boot. "Seems like a decent sort of guy."

"Cass doesn't think so," the woman said. "She told me he hit on Janessa, right before she invited him to dinner."

He had to give the guy credit. Foolish though his actions might be, Jack had to give him points for doing it. More power to him. "Well? She's a widow now, right? So, what's wrong with an available guy coming on to her?" He couldn't fight the grin forming. "If I'm remembering Janessa Rogers correctly, she's a beautiful woman."

"Yes," Maddie said. "She's gorgeous, but that's not the point."

He glared at the phone. "Then what is the point?"

Cass's friend went silent for a long moment. "Well, it doesn't matter if I understand Cass's reasoning or not. All I know is she called me to see if I could find out what you knew about this Hank guy."

Should he tell her what Hank suspects about the mix-up at the hospital?

Murmuring voices on the other line tore away his question.

"Who do you think I called?" Maddie whispered. "Of course, it's Jack." More low mumbling words. "Here, you talk to him."

"I don't want to."

"Then shut up," she said, harsh and abrupt, "so I can find out what he knows."

Only a sigh from Cass followed her comment.

"You still there, Jack?"

He shook away the cobwebs of his thoughts. "I'm still here."

"Like Chinese food?"

Both her question and Cass's loud protest in the background had him baffled. "Love it."

"Good," Maddie said. "The four of us—"

"Five," Cass said clearly. "Mom invited that detective to dinner, remember?"

Jack fought another emerging grin. The lady truly didn't like this PI showing interest in Janessa. "Are you asking me to join you?"

"Yes."

A louder negative comment followed Maddie's

laughing response. Just as obvious to Jack was Cass's perplexing reaction to Maddie's invitation. He might be tired and had no desire to drive the twenty or so miles into San Antonio, but he was starving. More importantly, he wanted to be there. He kicked his boots toward the bed and stepped into the bathroom. That room might not be as clean as he liked, but it'll do for one more shower.

"Interested?"

"Need to take a quick shower first."

"Of course."

He glanced at his watch. "It's quarter after four now." Unbuttoning and whipping his shirt off one arm, he flipped the phone into his other hand and finished the job. He let it drop to the floor before undoing his jeans and moving toward the relatively clean shower. "Should leave here in fifteen, twenty minutes."

"Okay."

He could almost see the grin on the vaguely remembered face.

"We'll be at the Chinese Buffet on Fredericksburg Road around six."

"That should give me plenty of time."

"Do you know where it is?"

"No," he said. "I'll find it."

Maddie did laugh then. "Can't wait to see you again."

"Same here, Maddie."

The last sound he heard before disconnecting the call was Cass's temper-filled sigh. Was that sigh because of Hank or him being invited to dinner? Or maybe it was a little of both. The phone rang again before he placed it on the sink. "Fontaine Veterinarian

Clinic."

"Hey, Jack, this is Hank."

Speaking of the devil. "I just found out you met Janessa."

"Yeah." He let loose a loud whistling sound. "Beautiful lady."

"That she is." He leaned against the bathroom wall. "So, what can I do for you? I was just getting into the shower."

"I need backup," he said. "I'm joining Janessa and her daughter for dinner. I could use some support."

"One of Cass's friends just invited me to the Chinese Buffet," he said. "I'll be there around six."

"Good," he said. "That's all I needed."

The PI ended the call.

Guess he's not all that tough.

Knowing Cass's friends, he understood completely.

Those two circled the wagons around both the mother and daughter, protecting them from whatever the PI had found out about Billy.

Chapter Twelve

"I can't believe you invited Jack." Cass moved away from the hotel's bed, placing her hands on her hips. "Bad enough we have one man busting into our ladies' only weekend, now we have two."

"Who said anything about ladies' only?" Maddie stared. "I don't remember hearing that."

"I did," Cass said. "I might not have said the words out loud because I just assumed you would know it."

Maddie snorted. "Well, you should've told your mother that."

Cass still couldn't believe her mom had asked that…meddlesome detective to eat with them. What had gotten into her? And Cass still didn't know what he'd found out about Billy. "First Hank, then Jack. Maybe I should ask someone to join us, so the two of you won't feel left out?" Two cowboys came to mind in a flash. "Give me your phone."

She sneaked a quick look at her. "Why?"

"I just thought of the two perfect guys." She reached out her hand, wiggling her fingers. "Give me the phone."

Maddie backed, hitting the end of a bed. She sank into the mattress and clambered up to the headboard. "I don't think so."

"Coward." The cowboy she had in mind would be perfect for Maddie, if she'd only get over the fact he used to go out with a lot of ladies. And Angie's ex-husband was still madly in love with her. "Ethan and Andrew are as hot as the two guys meeting us at the restaurant."

She let out a sigh. "Oh, so you're admitting Jack is hot?"

"Stop changing the subject."

"Who's changing the subject?"

"You are." Cass scowled, rubbing at the ache forming at the base of her skull. The headache overrode the slight pain in her ankle. "Whenever Ethan Bishop's name comes up, you change it. Denial is obviously not only a river in Egypt."

"Oh, very original." Maddie leaped from the bed. "You can do better than that."

Cass frowned.

The bathroom door opened, and Mom wandered out.

Warmth and fog flowed from the inner room, followed by the enticing scent of jasmine. "It's only the buffet, Mom." The sun could never be as bright as her beaming smile now.

"I know that."

Mom's unreasonable fascination with this detective overwhelmed her. Didn't she know he had the power to truly hurt her? Didn't she know he would find out Billy had died three years ago? "Since when have you gotten all dressed up to go to that place?"

"Maybe because…" Maddie offered. "She has a date."

The hotel room door opened, startling Cass's protesting words from her mind.

Angie breezed into the room and nodded *hello*

before tossing her overnight bag onto the nearest bed. "Sorry I'm so late."

"Where were you?" Maddie settled on the bed beside the new bag. "I went to the diner to get you, and they told me you weren't there."

Angie raised her brows but didn't make any comment.

"Okay, I get it," Maddie grumbled. "None of my business."

"No, that's not it." Angie glanced at Maddie quickly before turning toward Janessa. "So, tell me about this detective. Cass said he's nice."

Cass jerked around and glared at her blonde friend. She didn't say any such thing.

"He is," Mom agreed. "Did she also mention how good-looking he was?"

Angie nodded, settling on the bed beside her bag "That's what I meant when I said *nice*."

"Oh?" Mom glanced toward Cass. "She did?"

"Actually," Angie continued, "your daughter's exact words were—"

"Angie," Cass said. "Don't say it."

"Hot for an older guy." Angie grinned.

"Yes," Mom said. "I agree Hank is…hot."

Is Mom flushing?

"But I don't agree with the older part." Mom studied the carpet near her bare feet. "He's about the same age as me, and I don't see myself as old."

"No," Cass agreed. "But you are my mom."

"Yes, she is your mother." Angie widened her eyes. "But she is still a woman, Cass."

Cass focused on her. "I know that."

"Oh?" Maddie twisted toward her, "I don't think

116

you believe that."

"That doesn't mean it's easy to see her acting this way," Cass admitted. "Dad's only been gone a little over a year."

"Plenty of time." Maddie leaped off the bed and raced toward the bathroom. "My turn."

"Don't use up all the hot water," Angie said. "All of us need to shower."

Maddie waved a hand at Angie. "I don't have any reason to shower again today. I don't have a date like these two."

Angie studied Maddie for a second before turning her focus onto her. "*You* have a date?"

"Not by choice," Cass said. *And it's the last thing I want to do.* "Maddie called, and Jack accepted the offer. He's not *my* date."

"Sure, he isn't." Maddie stopped at the bathroom door. "You know, that's not true."

Cass shook her head. "I am *not* interested in that man."

"Keep saying it." Maddie's smirk widened. "Maybe someday you'll start believing it."

"Don't you need to use the bathroom?" Cass waved a hand in the direction of the small room. "Angie and I need to get ready also, you know."

Maddie raised her eyebrows and entered the room, closing the door with a bang and a loud laugh.

Totally unbelievable.

Sharp cramping roared deep in her belly so suddenly she encircled her arms around her stomach and groaned.

Oh, please, be what I hope you are.

"Honey?" Mom touched her upper back "Are you

okay?"

Please, please, please. Tomorrow, she'll complain about PMS symptoms, but not today. Today she would rejoice, cramps or not, and have a couple of glasses of wine with her two interfering friends, one lovely mother, and two hot guys determined to mess with her head. Another cramp knifed through her lower back and shot down her legs. She crossed her arms tighter around her waist and collapsed inward. "Please, please, please."

Mom moved in front of her. "Is it that time?"

"Oh, I hope so."

Cass raced into the bathroom the second Maddie exited, slammed the door behind her, and sighed out a lungful of air. An accident had never looked so good. Hopefully, all her other problems would resolve themselves as easily.

A knock sounded on the door before it opened slightly, and Angie peeked in, eyes widening. "Good news?"

"The best ever," she said. "Even though I do need to change my panties."

Angie sighed. "I'm glad."

"Never going through something like this again." Cass pointed toward her. "And you can just wipe that smile off your face."

"What smile?"

"You and Maddie were the ones who talked me into that Ladies' Night at The Corral."

"Yes, we did." Angie nodded. "But you were the one who decided to leave with Johnny."

"I wouldn't have done that if you hadn't forced me to go with you in the first place."

"And you were the one who called Maddie and me late the next day to tell us how great it was." Angie leaned into the doorframe. "So stop complaining."

Yes, that night was great. Just because the guy wasn't there when she woke up that afternoon, and she hadn't seen him in town since, didn't mean the whole night had been a bust. Now that no lasting effects existed, she could look back and enjoy it. But she was never doing it again.

"You could use this, I'm thinking."

She took the wrapped tampon and nodded. "Yes."

"Well, tonight you won't need to worry about leaving with some sexy cowboy." Angie grinned. "But next week…that's a completely different story."

A dark-haired man with mesmerizing blue eyes replaced Johnny's image so unexpectedly she dropped the tampon into the toilet.

"That won't do you any good there."

Thankfully, her friend was right.

"Here's another one." Angie handed her a paper-wrapped object. "Don't drop this one. You only have one more in your purse."

"You don't have any?"

She shook her head. "And I don't think Maddie does, either. Don't worry. We'll pick up some today."

"I'd appreciate that." She sighed. "Just take the money out of my purse."

Angie waved. "Don't worry about that, Cass."

"Well, okay, thanks." She glanced down at her panty. "Oh, before you leave, could you get me a clean pair?"

"Oops, guess I should've gotten those when I got the other stuff."

Angie and Maddie were gone when she exited the bathroom a few minutes later. She glanced over at Mom, catching a strange happy-sad look

Mom noticed her interest and covered it up, replacing it with her usual look of motherly care. "I have some ibuprofen."

"No, I just took something for the cramps."

She nodded. "Cass, I…"

"What's wrong Mom?"

"Nothing's…wrong." She looked over at the door, and then back. "You just seemed a bit…upset."

Does Mom expect I was worried about being pregnant? Or was this about that PI? "Me?"

"With me." Bafflement widened her eyes. "I'm a bit confused, too."

"About what?"

"Hank." Janessa shook her head. "No, it's not really Hank. Not really. It's my…reaction to him."

Cass let out a breath. She understood, even though she didn't want to. Mom's reaction to Hank was the same as hers to Jack. If Hank was anyone other than the private investigator she had hired, she'd be overjoyed. She'd love to see Mom involved with a good, decent man, the hotter and sexier the better. This PI seemed like all those things. Yet, he was a private investigator with the contacts and abilities to find out about Billy.

"You know, honey, I loved your father." Her soft voice roared loud in the quiet room. "He was my life."

"I know, Mom."

"I thought we would have so many more years together. Get to retire and play with our grandchildren one day." A sweet smile graced her gentle mouth. "I never expected him to have a major heart attack and die soon after having a second one. I never thought I'd be alone in my late forties."

Cass didn't know how to respond. Rarely did Mom speak of her father's death.

"And I never thought…"

The skin of her lower face flushed, clearly showing her uneasiness with the discussion.

"I never thought I would miss…" She shook her head. "Well, I'm not sure what I want to say."

"I think I understand Mom."

She glanced up before lowering her guilt-filled gaze toward the floor again. "No doubt I'm getting ahead of myself, but…" She sighed. "Your father stopped looking at me the way Hank did today…years ago." She dragged in a deep breath, shook her head hard, and forced her look upward. "Many things happened after Billy left."

Shock pulled her up straight. "You and Dad stopped…?"

"No, we didn't stop…that," Mom said carefully. "At least, not right away."

"Mom?" Tears formed in the corners of her eyes, and she wiped them away. "I didn't know any of this."

"A woman gets used to things," she said. "We didn't stop loving each other." Sadness sounded low in her voice. "But we did start being careful how we…shared it."

"Oh, Mom." She lifted her arms and gathered her slight figure into them. "Why didn't you tell me this before? Dad was grieving." The half-lie hurt to say. "So were you. Billy was gone."

"But you were still here," she said. "You are still here."

Swallowing the old memories, she tightened her hold around her mom's waist. Time for her to let the pain of the last few years go. The pain, the guilt, and the bitterness needed to be buried deep if she ever wanted to find her peace.

"Can you ever forgive me?"

Can I ever forgive her? The real question is, will she forgive me when she finds out what's been hidden all these years?

"Honey?"

No answer came to her question. "Mom, you haven't done anything to deserve my forgiveness."

"That's not true." She stood back, shaking her head. "After Billy left, I withheld myself from you." She looked past her shoulder again. "And so did your father." She dragged in long, deep breaths and forced her gaze on her. "Both of us were scared you would leave us like him, and we couldn't allow that. Your father tried to hold on too tight, but I didn't try at all."

"Mom." She touched her wet cheek with a tender finger. "I can truthfully say I never wanted to leave Greenfield. I love that town. I love the bookstore. I've never thought of going anywhere else."

She studied her. "You're happy?"

"Yes, Mom, I'm happy." And she was, if only the nagging little voices inside would shut up. One voice screamed to tell her the truth before the PI could do it. But that other weaker, frightened one whispering *your mother will never forgive you* silenced her confession.

The cell phone on the stand vibrated under the force of its ring, silencing both voices in her head. She grabbed it. "Hello."

"Cass?"

Her heart skipped at the sound of the man's voice. How in the world could she recognize it? "Jack?"

"Just wanted to let you know, I'm on my way."

Mom glanced at the phone. "Jack?"

She nodded. "We'll meet you at the restaurant in an hour." She gazed at the digital clock on the stand. "Say around six."

"Sounds good."

Squeals of a door opening blocked out his next words. The door slammed shut, and an ignition roared.

"You wouldn't happen to have the address to the restaurant handy, would you?"

"Yes, Mom wrote it down. It's around here somewhere." She searched around the objects on one bed and then the other before moving toward the stand in between them. She gave up and glanced at her mom. "Do you know the address to the restaurant?"

"I have it." She reached into the side pocket of her purse and pulled out a colorful sheet of the hotel's paper. "Here."

Cass read off the address.

"Okay, I think I know that area."

"We'll meet you there."

"Yes, around six."

Cass glanced at her mother at the window and lowered her tone. "I'll meet you outside the building. We need to talk."

"Can't wait to see me alone?"

The teasing laughter in his voice caused her heart to flutter against her ribcage. "No."

"Ah, I'm wounded."

Even if she'd wanted to, Cass doubted she could've stopped her grin. "Somehow, I doubt that."

"You don't think a man can be wounded," he whispered. "I'm crushed."

Like a feather tracing low over her back, the deep whisper sent shivers over her spine.

"Oh, well," he said. "At least, you want to talk."

Boy, the man was impossible.

"See you at six."

The echo of his pleasant laughter still lingered when he disconnected the call. "Unbelievable."

"Nice, isn't it?"

Mom's gentle, pleased tone twisted her toward the window. She set the phone on the bed.

"Not to mention, a bit strange."

"Strange?" Cass stepped closer. "What's so strange?"

The beaming grin Cass had noticed since the PI walked out of the lobby a few hours earlier warmed her face again.

Cass loved seeing that warm, alive look.

"It's strange you and I are going through the same thing."

"You mean, Jack and Hank?"

"Exactly."

Yes, it was odd to be in the same predicament as Mom over a new man, but it was also good. Cass only wished her mom's new guy wasn't a PI looking for her brother, and hers wasn't the man who ultimately caused him to leave Greenfield in the first place.

Other than that, all would be well.

Chapter Thirteen

GPS sucked.

Jack slammed his hand against his dashboard. Was he even on the right road? Slowing at the next intersection, he ignored the honking horns behind him and read the sign. Yes, he was on the right one. So, where was that restaurant?

A car zoomed past him, the driver waving that universal sign of displeasure. Jack shrugged and continued to creep his way a few miles below the speed limit. Three more cars passed him before he finally spotted the Chinese Buffet and turned on his signal.

Another driver squealed his brakes, slamming his hands on the horn for a long few seconds before letting it go and roaring past.

"Well, that's what you get for riding my bumper." He sighed out a loud, relieved lungful of air when he spied a shapely shadow moving away from the building. Air caught tight in his lungs once again, and his heart sped up. The memory of the perceived softness of the skin of her ankle played through him, as tingling warmth flowed.

Wow, this woman had a way of getting to him.

He pulled into the lot and parked his truck in the middle row.

She twisted around and gazed out at the evening traffic, leaning forward slightly, before turning a full circle and moving under the nearest light.

He stepped out of his vehicle.

"There you are."

Did her voice really sound breathless? Or was it just wishful thinking? "Cass."

"I thought you changed your mind."

"No." He moved past a row of cars and stopped near her. "Stupid GPS wasn't working properly."

"That's been known to happen."

A welcoming grin softened the skin around her lips. Man, those lips needed to be kissed. Shaking the thought away, he crossed his ankles and leaned into the building.

"I was about ready to give up and go inside."

"So, you needed to talk."

The grin faltered, a quick unexpected look of embarrassment flushing her cheeks. "Ah, yes."

"Does this have something to do with Hank?"

Relief covered her uneasiness. "In a way, yes."

"In a way?"

"Yes." She glanced at him quickly before looking over his shoulder toward the traffic. "He cancelled his meeting when Mom asked him if he wanted to join us for dinner. I'm afraid of what he'll tell her."

I wonder what the man has found out. "I think it might surprise you."

She shook her head. "I know Billy's dead, Jack."

"Maybe." He bit his tongue. He had promised Hank when he called back after he'd gotten out of the shower, he wouldn't say anything to anyone until he could completely check his theory out. "I mean, things might not be as we both were led to believe."

"He's gone, Jack." She glanced at the car behind

him. "I can see why my father didn't want to believe me, but your father was there at his funeral."

Oh, why did I promise Hank not to say anything? "At the burial," he said. "My dad didn't get word in time to attend the service. He told me there was no viewing. The funeral procession had already reached the burial site when he arrived. The casket was being lowered into the ground."

"Your dad didn't make it to the funeral?" Tears welled up in her eyes. "I thought you told me he was there. That my brother had at least one person who cared in attendance."

He'd said too much. "Many people were there, Cass. Dad recognized a few of the guys near him."

"But no family members." Her face reddened, eyes glistening with unshed tears. "Mom and I are still waiting to be notified of his death. I even called the hospital he'd been taken to, according to that newspaper article I read, and they never called me back."

"Maybe the hospital—"

"No."

"Maybe—"

She lifted her right hand and placed it lightly on his chest. Her fingers flexed into his shirt, relaxing him slowly. She dropped her hand. "He's gone, Jack."

Sadness lingered when she turned and raced into the restaurant. "Cass, wait."

Her trembling figure stood at the check-in counter. He spied the familiar blonde from the diner standing at a back table.

Angie grinned and waved their way.

"There's your friend."

"Angie," she said. "Everyone is here."

"Waiting on me." He waved back at Angie and nodded at the young Chinese server. "We're with that group at the back booth."

"What would you like to drink?"

"Coffee," he said. "Cass?"

"Oh, I have mine."

He followed her and the server to the table.

Angie sat on the same side as an older man and a familiar woman.

"Mrs. Rogers?"

"Hello, Jack."

"Good to see you again." He helped Cass into a seat beside her shorter, dark-haired friend and then settled in front of the only other man in the group. "So, you're the detective, Hank Wayne?"

"That's me. And you must be the new vet in town, Jack Fontaine." The PI reached across the table, a broad grin breaking across his face.

Jack accepted his firm handshake.

"Good to put a face with the name." Hank dropped his hand and glanced around the table. "Been hearing a lot of good things about Greenfield. Sounds like a great place to live."

"It is," he agreed. "That's partly why I decided to set up my practice there. When I found out the long-time vet wanted to retire, I grabbed at the opportunity."

"Yeah, when opportunities of any kind come your way"—he peered at the older lady—"you've got to go for it."

He had a feeling he would like this guy. Looking down at the flustered woman's daughter sitting quietly beside him, he nodded. "I couldn't agree more."

"Oh, brother, anyone got any boots I can borrow?" Maddie pushed at Cass. "Stuff is getting deep here."

Both men laughed.

She winked across the table at Angie. "But it is fun seeing both Cass and her mother getting rattled at the same time, isn't it?"

"Nice for a change," Angie said. "It's usually one of us acting goofy around men."

The older lady sat straight. "My daughter and I are not acting goofy, young lady."

"Sure, you're not." Maddie didn't give anyone time to respond. "Now let's eat. I'm starving."

"I told you to start eating." Cass glanced at Maddie. "You didn't need to wait."

Jack stood and stepped back, waiting for the ladies to step past him and Hank toward the steaming metal buffet. He traveled his gaze over her curvy figure accented by the loose, swinging skirt.

"Are all the women from Greenfield as fine as these four?" Hank asked.

"I don't know." He grinned. "I haven't met every one of them yet."

"Think I need to seriously consider moving."

Jack looked over at Hank and shook his head. The PI seemed as taken with the mother as he was with the daughter. Twelve years ago, Cass had been a pretty but awkward teenager, just coming into her own beauty and charm. Dark hair waved easy down her back then as now, brushing its smooth straight ends along the top of that tempting bottom. Deep sienna skin, like her Comanche ancestor's side of the family and the dark green eyes of her father, gave her more than just beauty. It made her exotic and striking, unusual in a good way.

Gorgeous.

"You're from this area?"

Hank's question pulled him back into reality. No use imagining what couldn't be now, if ever. Once Cass found out he hadn't been there to stop her brother from driving while under the influence, he'd never get any closer to her. Jack might have never promised he'd look out for Billy with outright words, but that's what he'd meant all the same. The day her cocky brother had shown up at his and his father's doorway all those years ago, claiming he could never go home again, he became more than just his friend. The two had become a substitute family for Billy.

He would never have climbed into that car if Jack had been there to stop him. No matter how stubborn Cass's brother got, Jack could talk him out of reckless acts. Until that day he'd caught him sneaking out of the house of a woman he thought he'd loved. He'd punched him to the ground and left the area. Less than a week later, his father had mentioned seeing more than a few cowboys leaving that same home, but Jack had still stayed away. More because he'd felt like an idiot for believing the woman's lies rather than because of his argument with Billy.

"I need to ask you a quick couple of questions while the ladies are away from the table."

Jack turned to Hank gratefully. "Ask away."

"It's about Billy." The PI leaned forward onto the table. "Doesn't anyone in town know he's dead?"

The question jerked him tall in his seat. "Ah, I assume so. He died three years ago." He peered at the women quickly before looking back at the detective. "I think they might all know but none of them believe it.

Except Cass." He shook his head. "If they believed he'd died three years ago, why would Mrs. Rogers hire you?"

"Good question." He leaned into the table. "Seems like everyone I talked with was shocked when I told them Billy was dead. Everyone thought he was alive, bronco riding in the rodeo still. That he'll probably come back home after he found out his father had died."

"Really?" How could that possibly be? "Have you found out any more about that other guy? William Rodgers with a *d*?"

"Still working on that," he said. "Ah, looks like our ladies are returning."

"Keep me in the loop, okay?"

"Sure will." He leaped out of his chair so Angie and Janessa could slip into the booth. "Leave any food for us?"

Maddie snorted at his comment.

Cass set her plate down and followed in after looking toward her flushing mother. Her mouth angled downward into a slight frown.

Jack understood why in a way. Hank was a little rough around the edges, but he seemed like a decent guy. Or was that the reason for Cass's frown now? Did she want no man to be interested in Janessa, or just this one? This detective?

A hard slap slammed against his shoulder, rocking him off his feet a bit. He grabbed the back of the booth and twisted toward the smirking man. "Let's go and get something to eat. I'm starving."

Rough or not, Jack liked the guy. For the next two hours, Jack stuffed his stomach with way too much

Chinese food and listened to the four women gossip about both the male and female residents of Greenfield. He tried to make a comment once or twice but gave up and just sat back and enjoyed the view. By the time he placed his last plate at the edge of the table, he knew more than he wanted about the townsfolk. At one time, in his younger years, he probably cared more about which women slept around, which unmarried lady was pregnant, and by which married man. Or who was getting a divorce. Now that information barely held his attention.

What did intrigue him, however, was the quick look passing between the three younger ladies when the conversation had first turned to babies. Maddie had winked at Angie, who sighed as if in relief. Cass had frowned toward her two friends. Jack would love to find out what the reason was behind those guarded looks.

"Wow, how many people live in that town?" Hank set his plate on top of the unbalanced pile.

The server came by and picked them up, a sweet smile warming her face.

He grinned at her before turning toward Janessa. "Lots of stuff going on for such a small town."

"Two thousand people live around the town."

A hint of wickedness widened the older woman's dark brown eyes. Jack could see why the PI was so taken with her.

"And men and women are the same no matter where they live," Janessa added. "Small towns are no exception."

"There is no way you can hide a secret here." Maddie winked at Cass. "Especially if it's good news."

"Maddie?" She nodded toward her mom. "You promised."

Janessa reached across the table. "So, is it really *good* news, Cass?"

"How did you know I might be—?" Cass glared at Maddie and Angie. "One of you told her."

Janessa shook her head. "No, neither of your friends gave away your secret."

Jack sat straight in his seat. *What in the world are the two talking about?*

"Then how?"

Janessa glanced down at her clutched hands. "I saw your…scheduled doctor's appointment on the same day Susan at the pharmacy mentioned you…asking for something, and I put two and two together." She looked up and touched her arm. "I guessed."

Cass straightened for only a second before relaxing into her seat. "I had a feeling talking with Susan would come back to haunt me."

Maddie snorted so loudly the others at the table jumped in their seats. "That's what you get for not doing what I told you."

"I didn't feel like driving to another town." Cass raised both hands in the air and let them drop. "Susan should've kept her mouth shut."

"Since when has anyone done that?" Maddie handed Jack her empty plate. "Everyone always has to know everyone else's business in Greenfield."

"If that's the case," Hank said, "why doesn't anyone know that Bill—"

Jack kicked his foot a bit too hard, sending the other man out of his seat.

Hank glared. "What was that for?"

133

He slanted his eyes toward Janessa and shrugged. "Wait until you find out more."

"More about what?"

Hank sighed. "It's nothing."

"Does this have something to do with Billy?"

"Well, I… Ah…"

"I'm not a weak woman." Janessa stood to her full height. "Neither is my daughter. We can handle anything you've found out. I want to believe he's still alive because we've never been notified of his death, but…"

Sadness lowered her voice. Oh, if only what Hank suspected was true.

"It's time I accept my son is gone, and he's never coming back."

Jack shook his head at the pleading look in the detective's eyes.

"I have…" Hank looked his way again, and then closed his eyes. A heated glare burned out of them when they reopened. "Jack and I are looking into a few things."

Two sets of look-alike eyes stared him down now. Not in color, but in shape and intensity. *Well, I guess I deserve that.*

"You know something about my brother?"

Unlike the older man, Jack refused to back down from this lady.

"Jack?" Cass studied him for a long moment before she turned to include Hank in her stare. "If the two of you know something about Billy, then Mom and I have the right to know what it is."

"I'm checking on a few leads now," Hank said. "I don't want to say anything until we're certain."

"What leads?" Janessa never took her gaze off the detective. "Why didn't you mention this when we met earlier at the hotel?"

"Ah." Hank sent another despairing look his way. "Didn't think about it?"

Shouldn't detectives be a little less tongue-tied when talking to a client? Or is it just this client? Jack wasn't stepping up to help him out, was he? But, then again, he wasn't a detective. He was just a lowly, small-town vet.

"Hey, when the poor guy has something to tell you two…" Maddie interrupted the quiet impasse. "He'll tell you."

"Maddie's right," Angie said.

Jack breathed in deeply at the blonde's friendly grin and wink.

"Now," Angie said. "Maddie and I will get some wine."

"We will?" She blinked rapidly. "Why?"

She raised her eyebrows at Maddie before swiping her look over the other occupants at the table. "Yes, we will."

"Well, I guess I could go for wine. It's been a while since the three of us have had a night out." She looked over at Janessa. "And Cass's mom has never been a part of one. It'll be nice to get together and gossip."

"Like you haven't been doing that," Jack spoke under his breath. "What else is there to talk about?"

"Or rather who else." The relief in Hank's voice rang out through the restaurant. "Good thing I need to get back to my office."

"And I need to get back to Greenfield to finish

adding things to my computer database." He would've burst out laughing at the quick look passing from Angie to Maddie at his words. Instead, he swallowed it down and winked at the older man.

Hank winked back.

A slight snort brought Jack's look back to Maddie.

Looks like even she has finally caught onto Angie's blotched plan.

Maddie opened her mouth, then slammed it shut.

The server arrived at the table with the check.

Jack reached for it at the same time as Hank, and they stared at each other.

A soft hand pushed both of theirs away and swiped the piece of paper from the table. Janessa's hand. "It was my idea to eat out tonight, so I'll pay."

"No, you won't." Hank yanked the ticket from her and stood. "Call me old-fashioned, but I still think men should pay for their date's dinner, not the other way around."

Dates? Yes, Jack liked the sound of that. "And I'll pay the other half."

"Let's see." Maddie tapped the tips of her fingers. "Two men. Four women." A wide grin softened her mouth. "A little bit one-sided, don't you think?"

Cass's eyes brightened in a wicked way.

Jack liked that look.

"It wouldn't be this way if you'd allowed me to call Andrew and Ethan," Cass said.

"You need to let that go, Cassandra Rogers." Angie placed her hands hard onto the table. "He lost his chance when he believed his mother's lies about me."

Maddie only snorted her disapproval.

Warm laughter rang out from the woman beside

him, accelerating his heart. Even under his clothing, his skin tingled at her warm closeness.

"I would rather pay for my own dinner for the rest of my life," Maddie finally said. "Rather than have that cowboy pay for it, thank you very much."

"Honey, you know that's not true." Janessa's comment stopped the dark-haired woman's next words.

"Jack and I will pay the bill for all of you," Hank offered. "Half and half?"

He nodded. "Sounds good."

Jack stood from the booth and followed Hank and the ladies toward the front of the restaurant. He paid half of the bill and then stepped out of the building. Laughter flowed toward him.

"I hope we're right about Janessa's boy," Hank said. "I really like that smile of hers."

Jack started to speak, but then his cell rang. He pointed his finger at the phone. "This is Dr. Fontaine."

"This is Mr. Williams," the gruff voice said. "Could you come to my ranch? One of my milking cows is having a problem?"

"I'm in San Antonio now." He didn't give the man time to speak. "But I'm on my way home. I can be at your ranch in thirty or so minutes."

"I'll be waiting, Dr. Fontaine."

Hank was still standing beside him, looking toward the mother and daughter when he disconnected the call.

He pulled his look off the ladies and walked into the parking lot.

Jack followed him. He opened his truck door. "Hey, Hank, let me know what that lady tells you tonight."

"It'll be late," he said. "After eleven."

"That'll be fine." Jack slid into the seat. "No matter what she has to say."

Hank just nodded.

He sat in silence as the man got into his vehicle and drove away. Yes, he wanted to find out what that woman knew, but, more importantly, he wanted to find out what that cryptic conversation between the women meant.

He really wanted to know why all the ladies seemed so relieved.

Chapter Fourteen

Taillights disappeared in the traffic a few minutes after Jack left, and Cass finally allowed her held-in sigh to escape. A soft night breeze blew over her, pulling her gaze from the disappearing truck to the harsh lights encircling the parking lot. Over a decade ago, she'd had a major crush on him. Yet, those feelings were nothing compared to what she'd been experiencing sitting so close in that booth. Every time he moved, every look, and every word he spoke stole her breath and sent her heart rushing rough under her breasts. No man had ever had her so out of control without even one intentional touch, and she wasn't sure she liked the feeling.

And was it really an appropriate reaction? They barely knew each other. If she wanted to get technical, they'd only just met a few weeks ago.

The loud ring of her cell phone jerked her upward.

Mom pressed her hands against her breast, and then she laughed.

Cass glanced at the display, mouthing *Maddie* before pressing the connect button. "Why are you calling? I can see Angie's car about ready to pull out of the parking lot."

"Do you still want wine?" she asked.

Cass looked over the car roof. "Still want to do an all-girls' night, Mom?"

"I'm too old for something like that."

"We already went through this, Mom." She shook her head. "You're not."

Mom looked out toward the large vehicle idling near the exit. "Well, if you want to add an old lady to your group, I'll like to join you."

"You're not old, Mom."

"Cass?"

"Mom still thinks she's too old to join us," Cass said.

Maddie only snorted.

"But she's willing to." She lowered her voice a degree. "But you need to remember she is my mother."

"No teasing about Hank?"

"None at all."

A sigh escaped the line then. "Okay."

"We'll meet you back at the hotel." Cass glanced over at her quiet mother. "I'm looking forward to having a drink or two with Mom."

"Same here, honey."

More like two friends now, rather than mother and daughter, Cass liked the direction their relationship was heading.

"Tell you what," Maddie said. "We won't mention Hank's name if we can talk about that hot new vet."

Did she really want to talk about Jack in front of Mom? "No."

"And you and your mom can bring up that cowboy's name," Maddie conceded. "And Andrew's."

A protest sounded on the line. "It sounds like Angie doesn't want to talk about her ex-husband."

"And I don't want to talk about Ethan." Maddie groused. "And I don't think you want to discuss Jack, either, but everything's good."

Good? Suddenly, Cass didn't think drinking wine with her two best friends was a good idea. The last time she'd gotten call-a-cab drunk was at The Corral for Ladies' Night, and she'd left with a man who didn't have the decency to stay around until she woke up the next morning. Yes, her missed period was just a late one, but she'd fretted for weeks before things got back on track.

"Angie and I will get the wine," Maddie said quickly. "We'll meet you two back at the hotel."

Cass ended the call and placed the phone into her purse.

A few seconds later, Mom pulled out into traffic behind the luxury car and headed in the opposite direction. Traffic crowded around them. Janessa stopped at a red light behind a dozen or so vehicles and glanced over at her.

The dull, empty stare meant she was thinking about Billy again. She always displayed this type of restlessness before she bought up his name. Any repetitive motions like pacing or combing her fingers through her hair spoke the same thing; now she was sliding her clamped hand around the steering wheel. Cass hated seeing her this way.

A horn blared, and she straightened. She drove through the early evening traffic without saying a word until they reached their turnoff. The downtown area was even more congested than the outer roadways, forcing her to slow down and concentrate. Both gave out a sigh when the lights of the hotel appeared and they pulled into the parking lot, stopping near the middle of the building.

Silence entered the car a moment later. And that

was fine. Mom wasn't the only one thinking about Billy. Something was going on between Jack and Hank, and she couldn't help but think it had to do with her brother. She sensed it in their careful conversation during the meal. A few times, the younger man had silenced the older one by changing the subject or by some other means. Once he'd even kicked him, causing Hank to jump from the table. They were hiding something. Maybe it was something regarding her brother. Maybe, just maybe, it'd all been a mistake. Maybe, Billy hadn't been killed in that accident.

Could he still be alive? Her heart sped up at the thought. Wouldn't they have been notified? Cass wondered why no one had told them of his accident and death in the first place. Wouldn't the PBR have the cowboys fill out emergency and next-of-kin forms? He might have been upset at the way Dad had been acting, but he wouldn't have disowned him completely. Billy would've put their parents' address and phone number on the form. Or at least hers. "He's hiding something."

"Honey?"

"Nothing," Cass said quickly. "I was just talking out loud."

"Oh?" Mom studied the building in front of the car. "I like Jack."

Cass didn't know how to respond.

"I've always liked him," she whispered in the silence. "He had a…calming effect on Billy."

"Yes, I remember that." Mom didn't add to her comment. "Billy was so full of himself, thinking he was better than he really was." That restlessness sang around them again. Not as strong as before but *there* all the same.

"That's why your father and I didn't want him to leave."

"I know that."

"Yet, Jack…" She shook her head. "Jack and his father lived the kind of life Billy wanted to live."

"Yes."

Mom stayed quiet for another long second. Her fingers once again caressed over the steering wheel. "I will admit I was angry at Jack and his father for a long time. I needed someone to blame, so I blamed them."

All Cass could do was nod.

"Your brother would've never been happy here," she said. "If it wasn't Jack filling his head with wanderlust ideas, it would've been someone else." She gazed at her clutched hands. "You belong here, Cass, taking over the store for your father, but your brother needed to find his own place."

A hint of the usual bitterness rushed into her. Cass pressed it away. No use thinking about that now. "It's all I've ever wanted to do, Mom. I had ideas on how to change things about the bookstore. But Dad never seemed to think much of them."

"Oh, he liked them."

"You told me that before."

"But you didn't believe me." Janessa peeked at her. "You still don't?"

"Not really."

Mom nodded, a soft smile lifting the dullness a bit from her eyes. "I know he never told you this, but he was especially interested in your expansion plans. He wasn't sure about leasing the Martinson building, though, but he liked the idea of finding more room for the lectures."

"Really?" She jerked her head back, touching her throat. "I can't believe that. Every time I mentioned the lecture series or the café, he changed the subject. He never wanted to discuss it."

"No, he liked the lectures series," Mom admitted. "But he wanted to expand it like me. He wanted to hear about other things and subjects."

"Oh?" She sat even straighter. A part deep down inside wanted to believe what she said, but something stopped her. Dad had never said anything positive about the lectures at all. "That's what I'd planned on doing. In fact, I've already approached a history and psychology professor from Texas A&M and a well-known area writer. I've got feelers out to a few other people, too."

"That'll be nice." Janessa glanced at her. "The ladies at my church had a few topic ideas, and I've been researching them. And some of my friends on the reservation have interesting stories to tell. Would it be okay if I invited a few people to speak at the café also?"

Excited that Mom wanted to get involved, Cass nodded. Then yesterday came to mind, when she'd caught Jack and that lawyer in her building, and her ankle suddenly started to ache. "Oh, maybe we shouldn't get ahead of ourselves, Mom. I don't have the building yet."

"You'll get it, honey."

She opened the car door and exited. "I'm not so sure of that."

"Why?" Janessa followed her out and around to the passenger side door. "I thought you told me Mr. Martinson wants you to lease it."

"Yes, he does." Cass sighed, stepping to the front. She lifted her sore foot and leaned into the vehicle.

Being near Jack had taken her mind completely off her pain. Now small twitches were returning. No doubt it was mostly in her head because they were discussing that building and not about the old injury. "Mr. Martinson's no-account lawyer wants someone else to have it."

"So, what if Gary wants that?" She stood tall, placing her hands on her hips. "Mr. Martinson wants you to have the building."

A firmness rose in her voice. Cass focused on her mom's face.

"Mr. Martinson owns the property, doesn't he?" She dropped her hands to her side. "I've known Mr. Martinson for ages, you'll get that building. We'll get the building, Cass."

Mom could be sure of things because she didn't know the total truth. "And Gary Brown has been his lawyer for just as long, Mom."

"Honey, look at me."

Cass glanced back. Mom's brown eyes brightened, highlighting the deep sienna of her skin. Dark hair, with a few strands of gray, curling around her ears and down to her shoulders, bounced lightly against her upper back. No one could deny that they were mother and daughter. Her hair was darker and longer than Mom's, eyes rounder and a completely different shade, but their features were so much alike they had to be family. Mom was gorgeous.

"Now do you remember what Gary looked like the last time you saw him?" Mom grinned. "Think about it?"

Yes, short, and bald, with a slight paunch over his belt and closed-set eyes, like a used car salesman. A totally untrustworthy looking character. "I remember."

"Now, which person do you think Mr. Martinson will favor?" Her grin widened. "You or that lawyer?"

"Okay, Mr. Martinson would pick me," she said. "But Mrs. Martinson has a say in who will own the property, too, won't she?"

Janessa rolled her eyes. "We're talking Gary Brown here, honey."

"Yes," Cass said uneasily, "But we're also talking about the other person interested in the building."

"Oh, and who is that?"

"Trouble." She swallowed dryness. "Big trouble."

She raised her right hand toward her. "Does *big* trouble have a first name?"

"Jack."

"Jack?" Her eyes narrowed, then widened again. "Your Jack?"

"He's not my Jack, Mom." That smile was back, that wicked grin she'd only now noticed on her mom's face.

"But you want him to be, don't you? Didn't you have a crush on him when you were younger?"

"So?"

Her grin widened into a full-fledged smile. "Now, don't lie. I remember how you used to act around him."

"That was then, Mom."

She looked toward the road. "And, by the way he was acting at the buffet, I got the feeling he liked you before he left with his father years ago, and I still get that impression."

Oh, really, Mom. Well, guess what? Two people can play this game. She'd told Maddie and Angie not to tease her about the detective, but that was before her rarely seen playful attitude popped up to mess with her head. Mom hadn't acted this way since Dad's death. Cass hadn't heard her laughter in a long time or seen her truly smile. She missed her mischievousness.

The reason why she was acting like a freer woman now seemed obvious. Cass might be leery of what the man would find out, but she couldn't fault the way his attention had brought her mom to life. "And what about Hank?"

Janessa's skin flushed. "We're not talking about the private investigator."

She shrugged. "I considered letting it go until you teased me about Jack."

"Cass?"

She ignored her warning. "At first, I was upset by how you were acting around him, but now I like it."

"You do?"

A horn blared. Cass jumped, knocking Mom into the side of the car. Her ankle ached slightly. "Oh, I'm sorry."

She rubbed her upper arm and nodded.

A giggling Maddie leaped out of the SUV, waving a large bag around in front of her. Soft clinking sounds echoed in the quietness of the parking lot. "What are you two doing out here still?"

"We were talking." Cass grinned at Maddie. "How many bottles did you get?"

"Probably a few more than we need." She glanced over the car's roof at the blonde. "Angie went crazy."

"Only because I wasn't sure what Cass's mother liked to drink." Angie glared back over the roof at her giggling friend. "Maddie was supposed to ask you."

"Cass and I like the same thing," Janessa said.

147

"Let's get into our room so we can start drinking it."

"Mom?"

She encircled her arm around her mom's waist, glancing behind her at her two frozen friends. "Well, come on. I can't wait to hear everything about Jack, Ethan, and Andrew."

A loud snort followed her laughing comment, and then by a low, whispering sigh.

"Oh." Cass looked at Maddie. "Remember who I mentioned we weren't allowed to talk about?"

Maddie nodded.

"Well, forget I mentioned it."

"Cass?" Mom narrowed her eyes. "I wish you wouldn't bring him up. I just met him."

She winked. "Well, I haven't seen Jack in years."

"Please, honey?"

The guilt at her action rose until it was wiped clean by the razzing look in Mom's eyes. Oh, yes, she liked seeing her widowed mother this way.

Chapter Fifteen

Traffic had been heavy all the way through the 1604 loop of San Antonio and a few miles beyond. Jack didn't think he'd ever get back on the open road home. He'd forgotten how much he hated driving in thick traffic. The denser the traffic, the stupider the drivers. He'd had to slam on his brakes more than once because someone was paying more attention to his cell than to the road.

Cell phones? Some smart people should invent a device that would automatically shut them off as soon as a person stepped into their car. Would save a lot of heartache. He turned onto the secondary road leading to the Williams ranch.

A smiling older man stood near a smaller barn.

"You have a hurting cow?"

"Nope," he said. "I have a young grandson who worries way too much about his prized cow, is all."

Jack let out his breath. He should have been upset, but he wasn't. He acted the same way with the first horse he'd ever owned. "I'm here, so I might as well check out the cow."

"If you want," the older man said. "But he's fine."

The man was right, but unfortunately his grandson didn't believe either of them. The boy insisted Jack check out the animal from head to heel, and after that, Mrs. Williams offered him pie. No one could ever refuse her pie, even if he'd just eaten.

When he finally exited the ranch property almost three hours later, a light rain had begun to fall. The rain turned into an unexpected downpour less than two miles from his home. He slowed his vehicle to a crawl. Even the wipers going at the quickest speed didn't give him much visibility. Thankfully, the rain lessened ten minutes later. The phone buzzed then, and he ignored it. If it was important, the caller would leave a message. If not, it didn't matter if he answered.

The rainfall changed into a soft sprinkle, then stopped completely.

He turned onto the secondary road leading to his new home and clinic, huffing out a few breaths. The second he parked in front of his house, the phone buzzed again. He glanced down at it. He let the unknown number stop ringing and waited for a message. When no indicating sound rang in the air, he opened the car door and slid out. Sweet, rain-clean air breezed over his skin. He breathed it in and let it out slowly, enjoying the invigorating aroma.

The phone rang a third time.

"Oh, for crying out loud." He pressed the proper button. "This better be important." Jack could care less if he offended the caller. "You called me three times in the last minute. Do you have any idea how late it is?"

A gruff voice laughed. "Ah, sorry."

He didn't recognize the voice. "You've got me now, so who is this?"

"Hank," he said quickly. "Sorry, guess I should've left you a message."

"Yeah, would've been nice."

"Sorry."

Relaxing a bit at hearing the familiar name, he slammed his truck door and moved into the house. A second later, light brightened up the late evening darkness.

"Sometimes when I get excited by something, I tend not to think straight," Hank said. "Sorry about that."

"Yeah, yeah, you don't need to repeat yourself." He kicked off his boots and wandered into the kitchen. "To be truthful, I never talk on the cell when I'm driving."

"I try not to," Hank agreed. "But in my line of work, sometimes I have to."

Jack reached for a cup from the drainer, poured the last of the coffee into it, and placed it in the microwave. "Why did you need to call me?"

"Are you still in San Antonio? Can you come to my office?"

"No, I left there hours ago." Jack pressed the half-a-minute button on the machine three quick times. "I was at the Williams ranch, checking out some of their animals. The grandson insisted his prized cow was sick, but she was fine. I stayed around to check out a few other animals." He grinned. "Mrs. Williams brought me a piece of apple pie, and I couldn't say no. She makes the best pies."

"Pie?"

"The best."

"Yeah, I bet," he said. "I was hoping to tell you this in person."

His heart pounded against his rib cage. "Is it about Billy?"

"Possibly," Hank said "I didn't get much

information from the hospital, but the person I talked with did tell me a man died in the operating room that day. She refused to release his name but did admit it was close to Billy Rogers."

He tensed. "Really?"

"Yes, looks like they might be covering something up."

Jack jerked at his tone. "You found out more?"

"A bit," Hank said. "I'm getting the impression the higher-ups are leery of releasing any more information, though."

"Why?"

"Probably afraid your lady or Janessa might sue them," he said.

"Cass isn't my—"

"Give me your email address," he continued. "I'll send you all the information I have so far."

He nodded, reading it off to him. "My laptop is in my clinic. Give me a few seconds, Hank."

"Sure," the detective answered. "I'm sending the stuff now."

He raced out of the house to the barn, flipping on the overhead lights. A minute later, he powered up his laptop. "Okay, I'm online."

"I don't have much now," he said. "But I emailed you everything."

Jack logged into his email and clicked on the most recent one. "I'm opening the attachments now."

"Okay, let me know when you check it all," Hank said. "I sent you what I found out about Mr. *Rod*gers, with a *d*, also. I have a lead on his daughter. She promised to call me tonight around midnight. She works second shift. She's going to be out of town for the next week or so, and she'd rather take care of things tonight. Hopefully, I'll have some answers for your lady and Janessa by tomorrow."

He didn't try to correct Hank this time. And what was wrong with having someone think that fine sexy woman was his lady? He could think of way worse things for people to believe.

Stupid for him to think he had a chance with her anyway. First was his part in her brother's horrible accident, and second was the Martinson building. Maybe before she'd found out he was interested in that structure, but not now. She'd gotten so upset at him and Gary, she'd twisted her ankle. She couldn't get away quick enough.

He needed to study that list of things Mom and Dad stored away. He'd found it in his father's paperwork but hadn't really looked it over yet. Once he figured out what was in those lockers, he could make his final decision. Maybe he could co-lease the place with Cass.

"Jack?"

What are you thinking, Fontaine?

"Are you there?"

Taking in a deep breath, he blew it out and glanced through the rest of the attachments. "Not much here." He saved the documents before settling back in his chair. "But then I guess there is a privacy issue involved. Hospitals probably can't release information beyond the basics."

"You're right about that." A hint of annoyance darkened his voice. "HIPAA laws."

Jack fought a grin. "Would you want some stranger looking through your medical history?"

"Who wants to look at any medical records?"

His irritation sounded even thicker.

"All I want to find out is who actually died on the operating table that day—William *Rodgers* or William *Rogers*?"

Jack agreed. The answer would change everything. "Good question."

"Is that really too much to ask?"

Another good question. "Maybe you'll find out something from the daughter."

"That's what I'm hoping," he said. "I really like your lady's mother. I would hate to be the deliverer of bad news."

Jack stood from his chair and wandered to the office door. "Yeah, must be tough."

"Telling people upsetting news is never easy," he added. "Normally, it doesn't bother me all that much, though, but it's different this time."

"I understand." Cass hadn't been happy when she found out he'd made an offer on that building. She would be even more upset when she found out he wasn't forfeiting his bid like he'd tentatively promised her.

His parents might be gone, but their dreams were still alive. Returning to Greenfield and opening his practice was his father's, and now it was time to fulfill his mother's. And part of his mother's dream involved that corner building.

Maybe co-owning or leasing wouldn't be such a bad idea.

****

"We should've eaten breakfast before we left Dallas." Daniel released his seat belt and glanced at

Pete. "Greenfield is so small. I doubt they have a decent restaurant."

Pete shook his head at his older friend and partner while slipping out of the driver's seat of his truck. A brand-new, high-end vehicle pulled to the curb and stopped at the same time his partner stumbled from the side door. He glanced up and down the main street, taking in the charming, old-fashioned storefronts and clean sidewalks. An empty park sat on the opposite side of the road with a slow river flowing past. Pete grinned at the peaceful setting.

Ed raced around the luxury car and pulled the passenger door open. He stood aside and waited for his wife to exit the vehicle before shutting the door.

"So, this is Greenfield?" Whitney asked. "Not much to it."

Oh, why did Ed have to bring his wife? Couldn't he manage to spend one night without her? Just looking at the woman gave Pete a bad feeling. He'd broken it off with Whitney over two years ago, and yet, he got the feeling she wasn't over him. Just like that woman he'd fought over with Jack. A worthless woman who—

"Jack?" The vague memory faded quickly, the elusive image of an unclear face.

"Pete?"

He shook his head and stepped back, looking over at Ed and his new wife.

"Not much to look at, is there?" Whitney pushed bright fingernails through the bouncy curls of dyed-blonde hair "I doubt the town even has a decent coffee shop."

"Coffee's coffee." Anger surfaced, more at Pete's inability to recall his past than the woman's condescending words. Vague images and memories—mostly of that Native American girl and now a less clear male—teased in his mind. "I prefer regular black coffee anyway."

She frowned at him, then glanced toward the buildings. "Oh, there must be a coffee shop in this town." She flipped her hair behind her back and linked her arm with Ed's. "Hopefully, they'll have something decent to drink."

"And something to eat," Ed said. "I could use some eggs and bacon."

Whitney sighed. "You know you're not allowed to have bacon."

"Oh, honey." Ed groveled. "Even my doctor said bacon once in a while won't hurt me."

Pete shook his head. "I'm with you, Ed."

"Peter?"

He ignored Whitney's whine. "Let's go get something to eat before we talk with… What was her name again, Daniel?"

"Ah, let me see." Reaching into the still-open door of the truck, he clicked the latches of his briefcase and reached for a sheaf of papers. He glanced quickly at the top one before setting it down and closing the case. He shut the truck door and turned toward him. "Maddie Thomas."

"Maddie?" Whitney huffed. "So, country."

Pete had about enough of this woman. "I like the name."

"You would now, wouldn't you?"

Something in her voice burned through his easy-going nature, setting his teeth on edge. "What do you mean by that?"

"Pete?" Daniel set a hand on his tensed shoulder. "Whitney? We're in the middle of the street. No need for the entire population of Greenfield to know our business."

"Doesn't look like anyone is around to hear them argue, my friend." Ed slipped an arm around his wife's small waist. "But just to be on the safe side, I agree with Daniel." He looked at Whitney and then focused on Pete. "Lead the way, my friend."

Pete stood still for a moment longer, then shrugged and turned left. "Let's go this way."

"Why that way?" Daniel asked.

"Seems...right." Before Pete could second-guess his belief, he rushed down the main street until he stopped in front of an entrance door. A sign waved gently in the early morning wind, slapping against the wood above it, *Main Street Café*.

"How quaint!"

Main Street Café? On the edge of his mind, where memories from his past sat in a gray, foggy darkness, another sign slammed into the front of a building. "This is not right."

Ed and Whitney moved past him, not hearing his whispered words.

Yet Daniel did. "Pete? What's wrong?"

"I...know this place." That male image broke through the mist, vague and unclear—more indistinct than the young girl. "Something about this..."

The entrance door opened, and a tall, lean cowboy stepped out, almost bumping into Daniel. The cowboy waved without looking up. "Sorry."

"You have no need to worry." Daniel stepped backward. "I'm fine."

The man set his cowboy hat lower over his forehead and raised his cell phone from his mouth. "Got an emergency."

Pete's recollection faded once again, disappearing into the hazy place at the back of his mind where his past lived. He let it go as another memory moved to the forefront of his mind. Not of the young girl who looked so much like him she had to be a relative of some kind, but one of a more mature nature. One with the smell of assorted flowers, mixed with gentle smiles and words. Then that tentative thread faded.

"Pete, are you remembering something?"

The image of another business sign broke through him so abruptly he jerked straighter. "I…think…"

Daniel touched his arm. "You are, aren't you?"

Without answering Daniel, he stepped away from the diner's entrance and looked down the street. He raced away from the restaurant, glancing briefly at the back of the cowboy still talking on his cell phone.

The man finished his call and slipped into a truck, bringing the diesel engine to life.

Pete caught the name on the side of it—*Fontaine Veterinarian Clinic*. Something about that name rang familiar. But why?

"I thought you were hungry, Pete."

Daniel's slightly out-of-breath voice slowed his pace. Something about that name—Fontaine—spoke to him. He'd heard the name before.

"Pete," Daniel said. "Will you please stop running?"

He stopped and glanced at the dark truck. "Daniel, do we know anyone named Fontaine?"

The older man leaned forward and gasped in a loud

breath. Taking in another, he let it out slowly and faced him. "Fontaine? Why…are you asking?"

Once again, the ambiguous memories plummeted from its insecure footing. "Never mind."

"No need to start running again."

A dozen slow steps later, Pete stopped at the double doors of the second-to-the-last business on the west side of Main Street and stared into the dimly lit front store area. Small tables and chairs sat haphazardly around the empty shelves, with boxes of books and other containers surrounding them.

"Doesn't look like it's open for business yet."

"The Horse and Bridle." A familiar place but, like the diner, different. Wrong, somehow. "Or, at least, I knew a place like this one."

"Knock and see if anyone is inside." He waved both hands toward the building. "Someone might recognize you."

"That would be nice."

A thin, bald man stepped out of the building to the right. He locked the door and wandered toward them. "The bookstore isn't open this weekend."

"We can see that." Daniel said. "From the looks of the front area, it hasn't been open for a few weeks."

"More like a couple of months," the man said. "Cass decided to remodel a few things after the fire."

"Fire?" Pete turned toward the park-like area on the other side of the street. "Yeah, I think I remember reading about that."

"It happened about a year ago." The bald man studied him, eyes narrowed. Shaking his head, he turned toward the park. "It spread quickly along that side of the street, damaging most of the businesses."

"No one wanted to rebuild?" Daniel asked.

The man shrugged. "Most of the buildings were empty anyway, and the owners of the businesses still operating relocated to this side of the street. The town council decided to clear the area for safety reasons."

Daniel glanced at the park. "So, you all voted to open a park?"

"Yes."

The unknown man answered Daniel's question without taking his focus from him. Pete tensed at the unwanted attention.

"It's a popular place during the holidays."

"I like it," Daniel said.

Pete gazed at his partner. "Yes, it looks...peaceful." Pete ignored Daniel's questioning look and stepped into the road, wandering into the park. He stopped at one of the dozen or so benches and settled his lean body onto it. "I like this area."

"Greenfield is a nice place," the man said. "Great place to raise children or to retire.'

"Yes." Peace filled him. Only when he was alone at his ranch had he ever felt truly at ease with his past. Somehow, that building and this small town were a part of it. Deep down, he knew it to be true. "This is what I've been missing."

"Pete?" Daniel sat next to him. "Are you remembering something?"

"No." Pete looked at his friend, enjoying the warmth settling into his body. Then he turned toward the other man. "You wouldn't happen to know if anyone is looking to sell a ranch or something outside of Greenfield."

"You want to move here?" Daniel jerked tall.

"Why would you do that?"

The other man stood straighter and pulled out his wallet. He handed him a card. "Here's my card. I'm a lawyer, but I can help you find a realtor."

Pete studied the card. "Gary Brown."

A cat-like grin rose on the lawyer's face. "At your service."

"You can't be serious, Pete."

Even his friend couldn't bury his hope. "Oh, I've never been more serious."

"But Greenfield is only one of many small towns in Texas." Daniel leaned forward, clamping his hands. "All you know for sure is you might be from a small town in Texas."

"Actually," Pete said easily. "All I know for sure *is* I'm from a small town."

The lawyer looked from him to Daniel, then back. "You don't know where you're from?"

"No," Pete said. "Or my real name, or my family, or my age."

"Oh?" He sat forward in his seat. "You lost your memory?"

He nodded. "The first thing I remember is waking up from a coma, in a hospital bed, three years ago. The nurse, Sarah, told me I'd been in a car accident."

His eyes widened. "And you don't remember anything before that?"

"Not a thing."

"Really?" The lawyer settled on a bench directly in front of him, chin jutting over raised eyebrows. "You look like you have some Native American blood."

"Maybe." That pre-teen image flashed clear in his mind. Dark, almost-black hair, hanging down to her waist and a warm, deep tan sang in his mind. "Maybe."

"Cass's mother is Comanche." Gary raised a hand and then dropped it to the bench. "And she had an older brother."

"Cass?" Daniel asked.

The lawyer pointed behind his back. "She owns the bookstore, The Horse and Bridle."

The Horse and Bridle?

"That's what you called it, Pete." Daniel stood and moved toward the edge of the road, glancing at the building. "But how could you have known that?"

"I saw the sign," he said simply.

"What sign?" His voice rose in the soft morning air. "There isn't one."

Pete froze for a moment at his words, then leaped from the bench and moved toward him. He glanced up and down the building, seeing no wording at all. Shaking his head, he stepped into the empty street. Still no wording showed on the windows or the door, and no faded sign flipped in the soft breeze around him. Yet, two large hooks sat in the wood directly above the entrance door. *Strange.*

He still didn't remember anything.

The answers would come in time.

He'd found his past.

Chapter Sixteen

"Cass, this is Lucy Cobert," the voice on her shop's answering machine said. "Call me back as soon as you get this. The number is—"

Cass stopped that message, listened to the rest, then hung up the phone.

She really needed to get this business with the Martinson building settled before she lost any more time and money, though. She couldn't afford to keep the store closed for much longer. Her teen workers were kept busy filling out and sending all the online orders that could barely keep up with the monthly bills. Glancing outside of her open office door, she sighed.

Jack Fontaine might look good in a pair of jeans with a cowboy hat bent low over his forehead. He might talk sweet and have a good Southern way about him, but that didn't mean she was giving up her building.

She dialed Lucy's number. A young female voice answered her call.

"Hometown Realty, how may I help you?"

"Could I speak to Lucy, please?"

"Who may I say is calling?"

"Cassandra Rogers."

"Just one moment," the polite voice spoke. "I'll transfer you."

Cass's head still ached from all the wine she'd

drunk Saturday afternoon into the wee hours of Sunday morning. On Friday, they had decided to forgo the wine and go float down the San Antonio River, and on Sunday, before starting home, Mom wanted to go to the Alamo.

Her mom?

Cass shook her head at her antics during the weekend. She'd acted so silly, blushing like a teenager with her first crush when Angie and Maddie teased her about Hank.

She'd never seen her act that way before. Was a mother even supposed to act so free and out of control?

"Hello, Cass," a hurried voice said. "Can I help you with something?"

"Hey, Lucy." Cass shook the sweet image away and focused on her phone call. "I just got your message."

"Oh, right."

Clicking from a computer keyboard sounded soft on the line.

"This is about the Martinson building, right?"

"Yes."

"One of my dad's associates sent over the information about the place. Give me a minute."

More clicking sounded as Cass settled into her seat, then a rustling of papers.

"Here it is."

Should the best realtor in the county be so disorganized? "Still writing everything down and forgetting to put it into your computer calendar?"

"Hey, that's my dad. Not me." Lucy laughed.

Cass had to grin at her comment. The elder Cobert and her own father were built from the same type of cloth, stuck in their old ways of doing things. When she started working full-time at the bookstore, her first new improvement was a software program to keep track of new stock and another one for accounting. Yet, her father still wrote everything down longhand, in his small, squiggly writing. All she'd managed to get him to do was print his notes. It wasn't much of a concession, but his printing was easier to read.

"Dad has set up an appointment with you, Mr. Martinson, and Jack Fontaine for one this afternoon," Lucy said. "Mr. Martinson and the new vet have already called me back saying they'll be at the meeting. I'll be representing my father." She stopped and dragged in a long breath. "Oh, and I believe one of Gary's team is the old man's new lawyer."

She'd heard about that change and didn't like it. "I can't believe Mr. Martinson decided to change guys."

"No, Dad said he's okay with it," Lucy said. "Jack knows Gary so that's why he's decided to stay his lawyer."

"And your father doesn't see anything wrong with Gary being his lawyer still."

"Like I said, he doesn't see any problem."

"Good." Cass let out a long sigh of relief. If Lucy's lawyer father was fine with the situation, she couldn't complain. "So, where are we meeting? I hope it's at your dad's office. Or at Hometown Realty."

"That's what I was hoping," she said. "But Gary thinks a more neutral place would be better. Dad will contact me when they agree on where."

"I guess that will be okay." Cass didn't like the shyster lawyer having the final say, however. "I hope it truly is a neutral area."

"Don't worry. Dad and I will make sure it is."

Silence filtered through the phone line, broken up only by the soft clicking of the keyboard.

"Oh, I just noticed one other person is interested in the building."

"What?" Cass didn't believe this. For almost seven years, that building had stood vacant, with not one person making an offer. Now, two other people wanted it. "Do you have a name?"

"Daniel White."

"Daniel White?" She cocked her head to the side. "I don't know anyone by that name. Is he from the area?"

"No."

Rustling sounds echoed low in the air.

"I have the information here, somewhere," Lucy said. "Oh, here it is. Dad must have been in a hurry when he wrote this. I can barely read his handwriting."

Impatience had her leaping from her seat. Someone else wanted her building. Cass couldn't believe it. "Lucy?"

"Hold on."

Soft country music replaced the silence. "Lucy?"

Less than a minute later, the music stopped.

"Dad told me Daniel White is the business manager of Wholesome Natural Products. Have you ever heard of them?"

"Yes, that's the company Maddie is working with now. She's thinking of adding a line of naturally made products and sleepwear for married couples to her shop. The Intimate Marriage Collection, I think she called it. A representative from Wholesome called my shop a few times in the last month." Cass paced around her desk, stopping at the doorway. "Why would that company want my building?"

"It's not technically your building until Mr. Martinson gives the okay," Lucy said calmly. "Until you sign the lease, it's still up for grabs."

"But we shook on it." She tightened her right fingers around the door handle, headache returning like a freak storm, quick and fast and overwhelmingly powerful. "And I sent him rent payments for the next twelve months."

"I doubt if he's used the money yet, Cass."

Placing her left hand over her aching forehead, she stepped back to her desk and sank to her seat. It squealed under her weight. "I can't believe this."

"Don't worry," Lucy said again. "The Martinson family has known you since you were first born. Mrs. Martinson and your grandmother used to be best friends when they were younger. Dad thinks that should bode well."

She hoped so.

"Don't worry so much." Her voice lowered to a soft whisper. "It'll give you wrinkles. I'll see you later," Lucy said. "Goodbye."

Cass stared at the phone in her hand for a long moment, and then set it gently into its base. The jingle of the bell over her entrance door startled her out of her frozen stance. She shook her head to clear it, resting her forehead in her hands before rising slowly from the chair.

"Hello," A male voice echoed in the half-empty storefront. "Is anyone here?"

While her world was crumbling around her, life for others still went on. The slightly cultured voice sounded vaguely familiar. "I'm in the back."

"Do you have time to talk with us?"

Us? "Depends."

Hard and determined footsteps strolled through the cluttered aisle of the main area of the shop. Light laughter rang out around the room, followed by a smart comment about her needing an interior decorator, sent her heart into her throat.

Jack.

This sweet, sexy voice she recognized. His deep bass laughter got stronger and louder as he moved closer to her back office. How dare that traitor show his face in her shop! That building stealer. And that only meant the other voice must belong to that lawyer. "Lucy just called me about the appointment. You can't wait five more hours before you start harassing me about *my* building?"

The bald man froze, backing up two steps. He covered up his emotions and moved through the doorway, settling into one of the two visitor chairs. "It's not *yours* yet, Cass."

Jack wandered into the room, stopping behind the lawyer. No laughter rang from his firm mouth now. No hint of pleasure warmed those mesmerizing eyes. No emotion whatsoever showed in his features, or in the way he stood so strong and tall.

"Your attorney and I talked this morning," Gary continued. "I'm just here to see what you know about the third person interested in the Martinson building."

"Daniel White from Wholesome Natural Products." She focused on the ex-bullfighter vet. "You're here, Jack, so you might as well sit."

The left side of his mouth lifted slightly in a quick

grin a second before he nodded and settled into the empty chair. Breath caught in her lungs, heart beating rough in her chest at his simple gesture. She hated feeling so out-of-control. That grin could so easily turn into a full-fledged smile, one with the power to fog up her mind completely. And she could live without that now.

"Did Lucy tell you anything else?" the lawyer asked.

She pulled her look off Jack and settled into her seat, forcing it tight to the front of her desk. "No, only his name and company. I guess her father didn't have any more details."

"Have you ever heard of this company before?" Gary glanced at Jack and then focused on her. "Or the man?"

Cass dragged her gaze off Jack's relaxed body and looked at the lawyer. This man didn't seem to notice the energy racing throughout the room. It crackled from one corner to the other, electrifying every inch of the area. "The company, yes, but not the man."

"How did you hear of them?" Gary leaned forward. "I've never heard of the company."

Cass tore her gaze from Jack and studied the lawyer. "Maddie's thinking of selling some of their line of products in her shop." Way safer to look at him than Jack. Especially since that sexy guy was studying her just as hard back, with a look that told her he knew exactly what she'd been thinking.

Gary nodded. "Guess I'll have my legal assistant do some research."

"Maddie did." She took in a couple of deep, slow breaths, and still her irritation over the situation didn't completely fade. Bad enough having only one other person interested in buying the Martinson building; two were too many. She couldn't believe this was happening. "Wholesome Natural Products sent her some stuff, but she also did a computer search. It's a legitimate company. Young and growing, and it's gaining a good reputation."

"Did she tell you anything about the owners?" Gary asked.

"No." She placed her arms on the desk, rolling the chair back a bit. "I'm sure she'll be willing to share her information though."

"I'll talk to her." Gary stood. "But I think I'll have my girl look into it first."

"If Maddie thought the company wasn't legit, she wouldn't be interested in the Intimate Marriage Collection." She swallowed another dry breath. "Maddie's the most distrusting person I know."

"Don't I know it." Gary smirked before turning to face the vet. "Have you had the pleasure of meeting Cass's friends yet?"

Jack nodded. "Maddie and Angie, yes. We had dinner together in San Antonio Friday."

His brow arched. "Really?"

"Yes." Jack set his left ankle on his right knee and hooked his cowboy hat over his boot. "Went to a Chinese buffet with Cass and her friends, as well as Janessa and Hank."

Gary straightened. "Hank?"

"The private investigator Janessa hired." Jack softened his tone, eyes wrinkling around the edges. "Janessa hired him to search for Billy."

"Billy? Are you talking about your brother, Cass?"

The older man glanced quickly at her, then at Jack. "Rumor has it, he's…" Gary looked back at her before lowering his gaze to the cluttered desk.

An uneasiness filtered through Cass.

"Ah, will never return home."

Her heart burned. "So, people in town have been talking about my brother?"

"Yes, a few years ago," the lawyer said. "But I haven't heard anything recently."

Oh, amazing. Cass hadn't heard anything about her brother taking off a few days after he'd turned eighteen. When she'd graduated and moved back to Greenfield, she'd been too busy modernizing the bookstore to pay any attention to the townsfolk. Getting to the shop an hour early and leaving an hour after closing time was the only way she could implement some of the newer software programs necessary to run the business more effectively. The only way her father would allow the changes was if he didn't see her installing them.

"Cass?"

She shoved her thoughts aside and glanced toward the desk front. She'd been so caught up in her past she hadn't noticed the older man had exited the office. "Where's Gary?"

"He left like a minute ago."

The smirk warmed his eyes again. She liked it. She liked him. If only he wasn't after her building. "And he didn't drag you out behind him?"

His grin widened. "No."

"Isn't he afraid we might come to some type of agreement?"

"Could we come to an agreement?" The corner of his lip lowered. "I don't particularly like lawyers."

"I guess we do agree on something then." Cass stood from her chair and moved around the desk. "I don't like lawyers, either. Especially ones like Gary Brown." Minty warmth breezed over her cheekbone. Her mouth dried at his nearness, heart skipping a beat. She raised her hands and backed away. "That's close enough, Jack Fontaine."

His eyebrow arched upward. "Oh, I think I'd like to get closer."

"Jack?"

"Okay." A wicked glint burned in his eyes, then he winked and settled back in his chair. "Just checking to see if you still react the way you did when you were younger."

She backed hard into the edge of her desk. "When I was younger?"

"You were fifteen or sixteen when I left Greenfield." He sat forward, hands pressed onto his knees. "You haven't changed much."

"You remember me?" Taking a wide path behind his chair, she fell onto the other one and crossed her legs. "That's surprising. I don't remember you ever talking to me."

"Billy never let me near you."

She sat straight and stiff in her seat. "You're kidding! My brother did that? Why would he act that way?"

Jack shrugged. "I was a different type of man back then."

"Oh?"

"I'm not proud of the way I acted when I was younger."

Something unreadable flashed across his face. Why

should this man feel bad for liking someone? She'd a major crush on him back then. A lesser man would've taken advantage of her innocence, with or without a brother to protect her.

"But at the time I was doing so well on the rodeo circuit, I was way too cocky. Nothing could possibly hurt me."

"Billy had been that way." She tightened her hand around the arm of the chair. "My brother had always been interested in bronco riding. He'd never admitted that until you and your father showed up in town."

He didn't comment.

"Dad and Billy used to fight about it." Cass glanced at her clamped hands. "They fought all the time."

"I remember," he said softly. "My dad had to calm yours down a few times.

She gazed at him. "He did?"

A hint of a grin formed over his harsh mouth, softening it.

Whatever negative emotion he'd been feeling faded as he relaxed into his seat and faced her, long legs stretched out toward her desk. Nice firm legs that went so well with his toned arms and flat chest. *Why the heck am I thinking about his body?*

"Billy and your dad didn't seem to agree on anything," he said.

That oh-so wicked grin once again warmed his features. The more she saw it, the more she liked it.

"He showed up at the ranch so many times late at night Mr. Speyer set up a cot in the living room."

"Really?" Sweet memories rose inside her, mixed with the not-so-good ones. "I know my dad and Billy fought, but I didn't realize it'd been that bad."

"Oh, it was." He twisted in his seat, leaning in closer. "At least once a week."

"Wow."

"Yeah, wow."

His voice lowered, softened, and changed so quickly a rush of shivers soared into her. She glanced at him and sighed. That wicked look still shone in his eyes, but something else vied within it. Something warm, and real, and unexpected pressed her into her seat now. She recognized the look. Her entire being responded.

"Cass."

He traced a finger down the length of her cheek, over her jaw to her chin.

His touch paralyzed her.

Whispering her name again, he lifted her head gently while leaning closer.

Heated breath breezed over her trembling mouth a second before his lips dropped to hers. A gentle touch, a sweet kiss, one that had her heart pumping fast and loud inside her chest. Her hands floated from the arms of her chair, creeping over his biceps to his firm neck.

What is wrong with me?

His fingers played over her face toward the back of her head, pulling her closer. Groaning out her name, he snatched her and stood from his seat. His entire body tightened against hers, fingers plunging deep into her hair as he delved his tongue inside her slightly open mouth.

Oh, she needed to stop this now.

He released her and inched away.

Part of her was glad, but another part screamed

inside to pull him back. Her sensible side won out.

"Shouldn't have done that."

"No." She swallowed hard. "You shouldn't have."

He glanced at her, then moved toward the office door. "I should leave before things get out of hand again."

"No, don't go."

He froze a few feet inside the front area but didn't turn.

"I'm not sixteen anymore, Jack." She moved into the main room, stopping an arm's length away. "I'm not that innocent girl anymore."

"Like I haven't noticed," he said. "That's exactly why I need to leave."

Pleasure dashed through her heart at his admission. "Are you telling me the hotshot veterinarian who used to wrangle bulls for a living is afraid of the little bookstore owner?"

"No, I'm not saying that at all."

"Yes, I think you are." She touched his face lightly. "I know you are."

Chapter Seventeen

Could Cass understand him that well? Could she really see his fear? Not of her, but of the situation. He *was* afraid of the little bookstore owner. He took another step into the half-empty room. "A bit."

"Oh, so you're acknowledging it."

Jack shouldn't have kissed her, but not for the reason she thought. Never had a simple little kiss affected him. Not even a deep tongue-to-tongue battle had ever left him feeling so hot and needy.

"Are you okay?"

No, he wasn't okay. He was confused by his reaction to her nearness. Guilt from the part he'd played in her brother's accident fought inside him with this new feeling, leaving him unsure of what to do. When she found out he left her brother to fend on his own because of a woman—a questionable woman who wasn't worth losing a friendship over—would she still want him near her? Or would she push him away? "I've made my share of mistakes with women."

Her eyes widened. "I'm a mistake? That kiss…"

Why was it so hard to find the right words sometimes? "No, that's not what I meant, Cass."

"Then you like kissing me?"

Was this sexy lady teasing him, or was she that uncertain? He turned and studied her for so long she placed her arms around her waist and glanced down at her feet. "You're still a bit innocent."

Cass glanced at him.

He placed his right hand on one of the boxes of books. "Yet, you do know how to kiss."

A grin angled over her sweet mouth.

"You've kissed a few guys before."

"Of course." She jerked her head upward. "I'm not that virginal girl anymore."

Unexplainable jealousy raced through him. The disbelief in her eyes now ate at him. That look was neither innocent nor unsure. She was gorgeous. She was hot. Of course, she wasn't a virgin. He doubted any female in this day would still be one. How many twenty-eight-year-olds still were, statistically speaking?

He'd lost his virginity with the older sister of his best friend when he was fifteen. Two months before he settled in Greenfield with his mother and father.

"Could I ask you a question?"

Her soft voice pulled him out of his past. "Of course."

"It's about…Billy."

Billy? He swallowed and nodded. If he didn't find a way to tell her about his part in her brother's car accident, the guilt might tear him completely apart. He stepped through the large room, hoping the boxes and boxes of books mixed with the café tables and chairs would shield him. "Sure."

"Okay." She followed him into the room and stopped near the end of a long row of empty bookshelves. "Was he happy before…he died?"

He blew out a sigh, relaxing against one of the heavy boxes. "Yes, he was."

"I'm glad." She choked out the last word. "Did he

talk about me or our parents?"

"Yes, he missed the three of you."

Her eyes widened. "I can't believe Billy talked about Dad."

"Yes, even your father. Billy hated the way he left things. A couple of times, he picked up the phone to call him."

Tears shone in her eyes.

Jack lifted his right hand to wipe them away but dropped it.

"Why didn't he?" Cass lowered her head. "Was he afraid Mom and Dad wouldn't want to talk with him? Or me?"

"He knew you and your mother wouldn't hang up," Jack said. *I can't tell her much, but I can tell her this part.* Until Hank found out more about Billy, he needed to be careful. "But he wasn't as sure about your father."

"I don't know why he would think that way."

Hardness lined her mouth. Not as strong and noticeable as before, but the emotion showed all the same. Whatever was attacking her mind now didn't sound like her.

"He was always Dad's favorite." She clamped her hands together. "Even after he left town the way he did, he was still Dad's favorite."

Her intense words cut into him, causing him to raise his arms up a few inches from his side. He pressed the need down and lowered his arms. Yet, the need arose once again when he spied the tears rolling over her flushed cheeks.

She swiped them away quickly.

A yearning entered his heart. His arms ached to hold her. Yet, he kept still in his place near the boxes.

"I hate feeling this way toward my father and brother," she spoke softly, wiping at her shedding tears again. "I know my dad loved me. Even after I told Dad about Billy's death, he refused to believe me. He made me promise not to tell Mom or mention it to anyone else in town."

Why would he do that? "So, that's why Gary didn't seem to know about it?"

"Dad figured if it was really him, someone would've notified us."

Hank's conviction that something odd happened at that hospital and his own knowledge about Billy's next-of-kin form left him hoping her dad had been right. But if he had, where had Billy been? No one had heard from him or seen him in years. If he was still alive, by some miracle, shouldn't someone know about it? Shouldn't his family?

"Dad wanted Billy to run the bookstore and not me."

Firmness sounded in her voice, with just a hint of bitter sadness. "I know, Billy told me. That was one of the reasons he left Greenfield. Your brother didn't want to be a part of the family business."

"Dad didn't care about that," Cass said. "Neither did he care I was way more capable than Billy. No matter what I did he still wanted my brother to be a part of it. Every improvement and idea I produced, my dad shot down." She glanced at the connecting wall to the contested building. "At least until I mentioned an expansion. He acted like he was against it, but Mom told me recently he started to warm to some of my improvements. She told me he'd mentioned a few of my ideas. That surprised me."

He grabbed onto the hint of a safer subject. "Is that why you want the Martinson shop? To expand?"

"Yes." She pointed to the back. "We were using the backend of the bookstore for the lectures, and the area was getting too crowded. People were walking out of the building without paying for their merchandise."

"Oh, really?"

She nodded. "The stealing got so bad we needed to hire a few new people. One person roamed around the store area, and the other stayed by the door and check the receipts."

Jack shook his head. "Bet that didn't go so well?"

She nodded. "Some of our regular customers were upset."

He stepped toward the nearest unopened package and placed his hand on it. "So, that explains all the tables and chairs. You plan on using the front area of the Martinson building for the lectures alone."

Cass looked at the box where his hand rested, and then moved her gaze around the room. "I should've probably waited to order all this new stuff until after I'd signed the lease. But I was so sure I would get it."

"Maybe."

"I figured it was safe to do." She scowled. "Seeing that the building had stood empty for years. Mr. Martinson told me I was the first person to show any serious interest."

Did he still want that building? "My mother loved that building, Cass."

She opened her mouth, then pressed her lips tight together. Taking a deep breath, she studied him for a long, quiet few seconds. "You told me your mother had a lot of different dreams."

"She did."

She stood tall. "You want to honor your mother's memory by opening a thrift shop?"

"You remembered me telling you that?"

"Yes." She raised her right hand and nodded toward the doorway. "Do you have a few minutes? Or do you need to get back to your clinic?"

What was she up to now? Actually, except for an appointment at one, his whole day was free. His vet practice wasn't booming with business. Hopefully, in a month or so, things would pick up. Thankfully, he had enough money put aside to pay for his expenses for the next six months. And then, if needed, he had all those collectibles his parents had stored away. He could always sell them online.

"I'd like to show you what I plan to do." She moved toward the entranceway door and stopped. "My lawyer—or rather Lucy, my realtor—will probably be upset, but I don't really care."

"Me neither," he said. "Gary is more interested in this whole thing than I am. I still like it. My mother liked it."

She focused her intent look on him. "Your mother liked it, and you want to do right by your mother's wishes. I can understand that."

Jack didn't know how to respond, so he only nodded.

"But what I'm wondering..." Cass added. "Is if you've planned anything beyond leasing the building? Other than turning it into some kind of thrift shop? Running a shop is a bit different than an animal clinic."

His heart leaped in his chest at the change in her demeanor. A strict, totally in control businesswoman looked at him now. Jack liked this side of her. "Well, I haven't thought about it much."

"I didn't think so."

No bitterness, no anger or confusion deepened her tone. Her back stiffened a bit as she pushed on the entranceway door.

"That's the difference between you and me." She turned and held the door open. "I do have plans. I've had tentative plans for that building a year before I even talked to Mr. Martinson."

He had no idea what he wanted to do with the building. "Oh?"

A grin played over her mouth. "I've only mentioned all my plans to Angie and Maddie."

"And now you're telling me?" Her smile warmed her entire face, brightening up the emerald color of her eyes. *Sweet.*

"Even my mother doesn't know their full extent. I told her about the coffee shop and expanding the lecture series program, but not about what I plan for the back section of the building."

"Wow." He placed his left hand over his chest in a mocking way and bowed low to the floor. "I would be honored to hear about your plans."

Her grin faltered a bit at his unexpected gesture before she rolled her eyes and stepped through the door. "Ready?"

"Ready."

Maybe her plans wouldn't be as thought-out as he expected.

Because beyond selling Mom's stuff, he had no goals at all.

****

Man, her heart was beating like crazy. Cass needed to get it back under control. *How in the world does he do this? How does Jack manage to throw her off all the time?*

"Lead the way, Cass."

Her heart skipped inside her chest once again. Where did that professional woman go? Where did that woman who'd just held all the control fly away to? A hand touched her back, and she leaped a few inches away. Without looking at his reaction, she rushed to the entrance door of the Martinson building and grabbed hold of the knob.

Nothing happened.

"You might need a key."

Sure, like she hadn't noticed that. "This door is usually unlocked. Guess one of the Martinsons locked it or Lucy."

"Or Gary."

Cass heard the grin. "Or him."

Low laughter boomed close behind her.

"Stay here." She needed to get away from the confusing man for a few minutes. "I'll go get the key."

"I'll be waiting."

His tempting laughter followed her all the way through her shop to the back office. She grabbed her purse and unzipped it so quickly the teeth caught on an edge of the material, ripping it slightly. "Great." Reversing the zipper, she freed the trapped leather and opened it all the way. She was acting like a little pre-teen schoolgirl overwhelmed by her first crush.

Cass slipped her hand into the bed of her purse, quickly finding and retrieving the large, horse-shaped key ring Mr. Martinson had given her months ago. She threw her purse onto the desk and raced out of the office. The man stood where she'd left him, with that same wicked grin. Cass wished she didn't like that smile so much. But she did.

"Ah, I was about to come searching."

At least, he wasn't laughing now.

"Have a hard time finding the key?"

Cass fought a smile.

A moment later, blaring overhead lights pushed away the gloomy dimness of the large room. "Thank you for turning on the lights."

"Easier to see you with," he said. "You're gorgeous when you're mad, you know that?"

Okay, about now she could use a dose of that professional woman persona she'd worked so hard to develop over the last few years. Instead of this breathless girl she'd given up the first time she'd kissed a boy in the ninth grade. Shoot, she shouldn't have let *Jack* kiss her.

"I'm surprised how good a shape the building is still in."

Thankfully, Jack let go of his teasing attitude. Cass sighed.

"Gary told me it sat empty for a couple of years."

"More like a decade." The more professional side of her took over once again. "I think the last person who'd leased the building was an accountant. He stayed for about a year before he moved his business to San Antonio."

"Oh?"

Cass moved to the center of the main room. "He was a nice man."

"Not much business coming his way?"

"No."

Jack wandered through the door of the back room and stopped at the crates and stacked-up old wood near the side wall. He placed his right hand on the same box he'd set her on the other day. Her body warmed at the memory of his hands moving over her sprained ankle in a delicious, soothing way.

"Guess a town this small wouldn't have much need for a CPA, would they?"

"No." She swallowed past a lump in her throat. "Except at tax time."

His grin widened.

Her younger self pressed against her control, and she pushed it back.

"I'm wondering," he said. "Did this building ever house a thrift shop?"

His question brought her professionalism back to the forefront of her brain. Cass stood tall and straight. "Why are you asking?"

"Just wondering."

"Mr. Martinson would know," she said. "Or Lucy."

"I'll have to ask Gary."

She huffed. "Yes, I'm sure that shyster lawyer of yours will know the answer."

"Tell me something, Cass." His eyes narrowed. "Why is my lawyer a shyster and yours isn't? Or should I say your realtor?"

"Simple." Completely under control again. Maybe this time she would stay that way. "Lucy and her father want the right person to lease this building."

"Meaning you?"

"No, the right person."

He shook his head. "So does Gary."

"No, he wants *you* to win." She raised her finger to her lips. "At least according to my mom, I mean. She told me this weekend Gary will do anything to win a case."

His lips tightened. "Isn't that what all good lawyers do, win the case for their clients?"

"Not like him," she said. "And that's why I decided to tell you my plans for the building."

He stood frozen at the box before reaching toward her and touching her arm. "I wouldn't allow him to do that."

"No, maybe not." His attitude pushed at her control. Closing her eyes, she pulled away. "But we're talking about your mother's dreams here, aren't we? You want to do right by bringing one of her dreams to reality, and all I want to do is expand my business." Jack stayed quiet for so long, she expected him to turn and walk out.

Yet, instead, he moved in front of her and relaxed his entire body into the middle wall.

"Even to me, honoring a deceased family member is a better reason to get the building than expanding an existing, thriving bookstore."

He groaned. "Tell me about your expansion."

"You still want to hear about it."

"Yes." A gentle grin lined his mouth. "Then I'll tell you what I'm thinking about doing with the building."

She glanced at him. "I didn't think you had any ideas."

"Nothing concrete."

Truth sounded clear in his tone.

"I do remember a few things my mother wanted to do." Suddenly, he stood tall and waved her way. "You

186

go first, Cass."

Oh, great!

"Well?"

And, just like that, she'd lost all control over the situation once again.

Chapter Eighteen

"I'm leaving to meet with Mr. Martinson's lawyer now." Daniel moved a step into the hotel room.

Pete stood at the large window, staring out onto the half-filled parking lot.

"Are you sure you don't want to come with me? Either you or Ed is always a part of the discussion when it involves the business."

Pete twisted from the window and moved a step toward his friend. "No, I trust you."

"Yes, I know you do." Daniel froze with his hand on the doorknob. "I wish you would talk about what happened the other day. I know you remembered something."

"Yes, but it was just more about that girl." Pete wasn't sure what had happened at that bookstore. A confusing mixture of feelings and faces had flooded his system, overwhelming him. He still had a hard time separating the old memories from the newer ones. "And a few other things."

"A few other things?" He stood taller. "Well, why didn't you tell me or Ed? Why are you hiding what you sensed from us?"

"I'm not...sure."

"Maybe you'll find out more if you go with me today." Daniel opened the door halfway, still not looking away.

A hint of pine breezed into the room. Pete just wanted his friend to leave. He needed to be alone.

"If you didn't want to see the town again, you would've gone back to Dallas with Ed and Whitney."

"Not now." *Just go, Daniel, please.* He trusted this man, but he still didn't want to talk to this man about Greenfield. At least not now.

"If you went back into town, then someone might recognize you."

He twisted back to the window. "I don't think I'm ready for that."

"You can't mean that."

Just go, Daniel.

"I'll meet with the other interested buyers at one while you go and wander around Greenfield," Daniel said. "You might remember something more."

That's what he was afraid of. He couldn't articulate why he sensed real pain was waiting when he finally remembered his past. Why he was afraid to find out who he had once been? "I just don't feel like going there now."

Daniel focused an intense look before shaking his head and stepping into the freshly cleaned hallway. "All right, Pete."

"Thanks."

He smiled. "I'll keep you posted on what's happening."

"Sure."

Penetrating quiet followed his disappearing footsteps. He stepped back to the window and watched his friend get into his car and drive away.

Greenfield belonged in his past somehow. He couldn't explain his strange knowing. He sensed it to be true, though. One moment he'd been excited about finding out more about the town, and the next he was afraid of what he might discover. Something in the area spoke to him, on a deep, subconscious level. When he'd investigated that closed, under-renovation shop, he'd known it was a bookstore. The name just came to him. Just like he'd known the diner had been named something other than Main Street Café at one time, and that the burned-out, one-story building near it used to be a veterinarian clinic.

And that girl, with the long dark hair and deep sienna skin, was a real person. Someone he used to love and care for. Somehow, that girl was connected to the bookstore.

He was connected to that store, to this town, and he wanted to find out how. Fear stopped him from moving forward, however.

Pete liked the person he was now. He wasn't so sure of the one he used to be.

****

"Now let me tell you what I plan to do with the other half of the building."

If it was as sensible as the coffee shop for the bright, breezy front area and the expanded lecture series, Jack didn't think he wanted to hear about it. The more Cass told of her ideas, the more he wanted to let go of his offer on the building. Mother's dream or not, this lady's hard, thought-out planning deserved to be finished.

Yet, he could think of no way to get rid of the collectibles, clothing, and furniture taking up space in those storage lockers. Just a simple, quick walk up and down Greenfield's streets showed more than a few empty buildings. Why not focus on one of those less-visible storefronts?

Or why not go completely online with the business? He really didn't know much about doing it that way, but he could surely learn. But what about honoring his mother's dream? She had wanted the Martinson building.

"Follow me, Jack."

He gathered his courage and stepped through the backroom toward the side entrance of the building. He waved at a cobweb in the farthest corner and leaned into the back wall. His eyes watered and nose itched at the dust flowing around his head. "This part of the building hasn't been cleaned in a bit, has it?"

"Mom and I only cleared the front room." She glanced at him. "My plans for this room aren't as clear yet."

"Oh?"

"Maybe set up a few smaller offices for home business owners to use." She looked around her, wandering to the center of the room. "Two computer desks with a thick privacy wall between them."

"You plan on setting up businesses here?"

"Yes, a few office spaces." A proud grin beamed across her deeply tanned face. "I'm still figuring things out, but I can see the finished area in my mind."

"Greenfield has enough people for that?"

She nodded. "I'm thinking *yes*. Our library has a few computers for personal use, but not space and privacy. I know a few people who would like to find a cheap place to run their home businesses. This will be perfect."

Even though he could clearly envision the coffee

shop-lecture area, he couldn't see a bunch of businesspeople working in this dark, dingy backroom. His imagination wasn't that powerful. Three unpainted walls and rough, uneven flooring didn't put to mind a great place for a business, along with no windows to bring in natural light. "A lot of work will need to be done here first, I'm thinking."

"Now," she said. "But when I'm finished, you'll see sunlight and cleanliness."

"That'll be nice."

"I'm also thinking about offering other business services." She glanced at him. "I'm still working everything out."

"Are you?" Jack still couldn't see it. "Really?"

"I am." She stepped a few more feet into the dim room. "I can see it clearly in my mind."

All he could see was a big empty space.

"What an amazing project it will be." She wandered to the opened interior door and stopped. "I haven't talked to my mom yet or a contractor to see if the changes are possible, but I'm excited."

"Needs to be lighter." That was all he could think to say. "It's dark."

"That's one of the problems."

"Major one." Still not seeing her vision. "You could always put in overhead lights, but natural light would be better."

"Right, that's what I was thinking." Her grin widened. "If it's possible, I would like to build two windows on the side wall near the entrance door and maybe a long, narrow one in the upper part of the interior wall." She pointed toward the wall. "I think this room was always used for simple storage. That's why it's so dark and rough."

Her excitement must be rubbing off, because he was starting to see the dark room in a brighter light. Yet, Jack thought it should be kept as a simple storage area. Or maybe a separate place for Mom's collection.

"So, what do you want to do with this room?" she asked. "Your plans?"

His plans? All he'd planned so far was to store all the stuff his parents had packed away in those large storage lockers. This room would be perfect.

"You can walk around, if you want."

"No, I'm fine."

Cass stepped close, touching his arm.

His heart picked up its beat. Her clean, sweet scent rose, enveloping him in a delicate trap. He liked it.

"So, what do you think?" She pinched his shirt sleeve. "I'll like to know."

He sighed. "It sounds like a lot of work."

"Maybe," she whispered. "But all that work will be worth it in the end."

"Perhaps." Someone needed to be the voice of reason here. "But would it be feasible or profitable? What if no one comes to use the spaces?"

"They'll come," she said. "And they'll pay, because it'll be secure and safe."

"Libraries don't charge." He lifted his hands. "Why not just keep this room for storage?"

She sighed, then looked around the basement area. "Maybe."

"My mom left me a bunch of stuff." He touched her arm and led her back to the coffee shop area. "I need a new place nearby to store everything."

"Your mom?" She studied him closely, eyes

narrowing slightly. "Is this the stuff she collected for her imaginary business?"

"Yes."

"That's why you want my building?" Her voice lowered. "To use it to store your mother's things?"

Store his mother's stuff? Well, his things now. He needed a place to sell those things. Why not do it in this back room? "We could do it all."

"All?" She jerked back. "We?"

"Yes." He ignored her reaction. "You could have the front room for your lectures, and I could set up a shop in the back to sell Mom's collection. It'll be perfect."

She twisted around before shaking her head and moving halfway into the cleaner, brighter front room of the building. "Jack?" Cass crossed her arms around her waist. "Are you saying you want *us* to lease the building?"

He backed away and raised his hands in front of him. Oh, what was he thinking? Jack couldn't believe he just voiced his plans out loud. "Forget I mentioned it."

"I'm not sure if…I can…share my building."

When will he ever learn? No matter what he said from now on, he figured would be the wrong thing. Several emotions surged over her features. At least, she didn't appear angry. Hopefully, that was a good thing. If her temper wasn't up, she might be willing to consider his misspoken suggestions.

"Jack?" She bumped into the door on her way out to the sidewalk. "We shouldn't be talking about this without our lawyers."

"No, don't go yet," he said. "We need to talk about

my suggestion."

She stopped at the door.

For some reason, his idea seemed to be bothering her, but something in her eyes said she wasn't too surprised. Did that mean she'd thought of it herself? That she'd come up with the same solution to their problem. "You'll think about it?"

"Yes." A slight grin lifted the edge of her mouth. "Lucy won't be happy, though." A handful of black hair lifted in a slight afternoon breeze. She snatched it in her hand and turned toward the bookstore. A few strands escaped her hand.

He brushed the stray hairs behind her ear, lingering his fingers for a second near her soft earlobe.

She stopped and twisted slowly toward him.

"Neither will my lawyer." Jack dropped his hand and backed away. "Yet who cares what they think, right?"

Her grin erupted into a kissable smile.

Before he could stop his action, he traveled his fingers over the smoothness of her cheek down to her chin.

She froze under his touch but stood near him. A deep breath, followed by a low sigh.

Jack wasn't sure if the sound came from her or him. He moved closer, tracing his fingertips over her chin to the back of her neck.

Another sigh.

A breeze blew gently over his face, warming the surface of his skin. Her clean, flowery scent invaded him, blocking out the afternoon smell of the town.

"You're not fighting fair, Jack," she whispered. "And there's no need. I said I'd think about your plans."

"Oh, well."

She grinned again and moved her fingers to his shoulders, one clutched tight into it as the other opened and combed easily through his way-too-long hair.

A soft laugh heated his chin and neck, sending his heart to beat rough and fast.

"You need a haircut, you know that?"

A safe subject. "I haven't found the time to get one yet."

She moved her fingers through his dark hair, tracing her fingertips over the top of his scalp in light, circular motions.

A tingling sensation rushed through his head, down his body, relaxing him into the rough wall behind him.

"It used to be short."

Fingers from her other hand moved into his hair, smoothing it down the back of his head.

"It's nice, though."

"Hey, now who's not playing fair?"

Sweet tenderness rose in her eyes. "You like this?"

"Oh, yeah." How could a woman touching the top of his head be so right, so soothing, and so nerve-racking at the same time? "If you don't want me kissing you again, then I would stop doing that."

She froze in place. "You want to kiss me again?"

Her hands tightened around the bottom end of his hair, pulling it lightly. The professional businesswoman who'd been telling him of her plans dissolved as a more insecure one took her place. Fear, uncertainty, and indecisiveness rose and fell in her look. "I'm sorry, Cass."

"No."

He traveled his fingertips over her face before pushing her away. "I shouldn't have kissed you the way I did earlier."

"You don't need to apologize, Jack." Her mouth quivered. She dragged in a deep breath, clutching her hands at her side. "It's just been…a long time."

"Since someone kissed you?"

"No," she said. "It's been a long time since…I wanted someone to kiss me."

Ah, this woman is so good for me.

Chapter Nineteen

Three hours later, when Cass logged off her work computer, she still wondered why she'd reacted to Jack's nearness the way she had. Why had his actions scared her? Was it because he'd kissed her earlier or almost kissed her again? Or was it because of his suggestions about sharing the building? Or could it be that her instantaneous answer to the compromise was *yes*? "Let it go."

She gathered in a breath and glanced at the clock above the office door. Fifteen minutes to one. She'd stalled long enough. Time to find that professional businesswoman attitude and face him. The phone rang the second she stepped around her desk. She reached down and grabbed it. "The Horse and Bridle Bookstore," she said. "How may I help you?"

"Cass, this is Lucy."

"Lucy?" Why was she calling? Hopefully, Mr. Martinson needed to reschedule the meeting for next week or month. Or, better yet, he'd decided the building should be hers without meeting the other interested parties. "I was just on my way to the Martinson home."

"I'm glad I caught you then." A hint of laughter sounded in Lucy's voice. "That would save you some time."

Please tell me he canceled. "What's going on, Lucy?"

"We're meeting at the Main Street Café instead. Gary just notified my dad about the change in the meeting site. Mr. Martinson suggested it."

"I wished you would've called me an hour ago," she said. "I ate lunch already."

"Sorry about that, Cass."

"It'll be fine." She glanced into the front of her shop. Still as empty as this morning. "I guess I could always get a cup of coffee."

"That's the spirit." Full laughter rang out on the line. "Jack knows about the change, but no one can get ahold of the other man interested."

"He probably left for the meeting." *Maybe they'll have to postpone it. Hopefully.* "What if he doesn't make it? We can't talk about the building, if all the interested parties aren't there."

"No problem," she said. "Gary's assistant will direct Mr. White to the diner."

Another thought followed that one. "And what about your dad?"

"I'll be sitting in for him," Lucy said. "It'll only be an informal meeting, anyway."

Her relief was short-lived.

"I'm leaving now."

A loud squealing and soft footsteps echoed in the phone, pulling Cass back to their conversation. "I'll meet you there."

"Yes, you'll probably beat me to the café." A door slammed hard. "Gary and Jack should be waiting."

Figures.

"Nothing will be decided today, but Dad reminded me to tell you not to discuss anything important until I get there." A car horn honked in the distance. "Give me about ten minutes, okay?"

Great! Cass started to tell her about her conversation with Jack earlier, but she let it go. She wasn't sure if leasing the building together was a good thing or not, even if she did automatically think it the perfect solution. It would be best to keep that information to herself for now. At least, she should talk with Mom before anyone else. "I won't say anything."

Another door slammed, then the sound of a well-tuned engine. "To be on the safe side, keep the conversation focused on other things."

"I'll do that."

"I trust Mr. Martinson, but not that lawyer," Lucy added. "And I've never met the new vet, so I'm not sure about him."

"I agree about the lawyer."

And with everything else she said, except for the part about Jack. The more time she spent with the man and talked with him, the more she trusted him. The more she understood his reasoning for wanting the property. A thrift store wasn't a bad idea.

Would his mother's things be small enough to sell in her coffee shop? She'll have to— "No."

"Cass, are you okay?"

What was she thinking? First, she liked his idea about using the back area as simple storage, instead of her tentative plan of setting up two office spaces. Now, she was finding a way to incorporate his parents' stuff into her plans for the front portion of the building.

Hard for her to admit, but merging his parents' stuff with hers did seem like a better way to go. Just like using her father's money was better than taking out a loan. Dad's money? She could use his money to fix up the building, no matter what she decided to do.

"Cass?"

She shook her head. "I'm here, Lucy."

"Oh, okay." Silence lingered on the line. "I thought I lost you."

Cass sighed. "I was only thinking."

"Unsettling thoughts?"

Were they unsettling? "Yes and no."

"Well, ah, I guess I'll be seeing you at the diner in a few minutes." Lucy grumbled out a swear word. "Stupid drivers."

"Be careful, Lucy."

The realtor mumbled out another set of choice words before saying a quick goodbye and disconnecting the call. Cass placed her phone in its base and grabbed her purse. Five minutes later, she stopped at the large window on the left side of the diner's entrance. Inside the large room, to the right of the long, front counter, sat her rival for the property and the lawyer. Sitting between them was an unfamiliar older man.

Guess the third party interested in the building made it on time.

"Going inside, hon?"

She pressed her right hand against her chest before twisting around. "Oh, you startled me, Ethan."

"Sorry."

A lazy grin eased up his lips. How in the world did Maddie stay away from this man? He exuded charm to spare.

"Didn't mean to do that."

Cass nodded. "You're forgiven."

The cowboy winked and leaned past her shoulder to look through the window. "Tell me you're meeting with that sexy friend of yours."

"Which one?" She grinned. "Angie or Maddie?"

"Well, either will do." He arched his brows, then groaned loudly. "But I'm partial to dark-haired ladies with a sharp tongue."

"Maddie?"

"Yeah," he said. "I'm a glutton for punishment."

His smirk told her he was strong enough to take it. "No, I'm not meeting her today."

"Too bad."

A rush of peace raced through her at his comical look. "You're unbelievable."

"You don't know the half of it, honey."

She stifled a laugh and rolled her eyes. "My friend doesn't stand a chance."

"That's the plan." Slapping his cowboy hat against his thigh, he arched his brows. "She's a stubborn woman, though."

"Yes, she is that."

Loud scraping interrupted their silly conversation, followed by a firm hand falling on her back. She jerked forward into Ethan, strangled breath rushing into her lungs. The hand on her back glided over her upper arm and tightened, pulling her away from the stunned cowboy.

Ethan's look changed into recognition a second before he backed away. "Hey, Jack."

"Ethan."

She relaxed into Jack. "You two know each other?"

Ethan nodded, grin widening his mouth. "You need to try that when I'm talking to Maddie."

"I'll remember next time," Jack said. "Right now, Cass has a meeting with my lawyer."

Earlier, Jack was friendly and warm. Now, tension stiffened his body. "And mine."

"Technically, Lucy's dad is your lawyer," he said lightly. "And he's not coming in today."

"Same difference, Jack."

Ethan laughed. "Oh, no, seems my lady is rubbing off on yours."

Both men were unbelievable. If Ethan knew what Maddie really thought of him, he'd be singing another tune. And she wasn't anyone's lady, especially this building-stealing ex-rodeo star. What was wrong with her? Had she seriously been considering sharing that building? Using Dad's money for the renovations he wanted?

Jack moved toward the cowboy. "Looks like it."

"See you around," Ethan said.

"Yeah."

Jack stood quietly for a moment after Ethan departed. Then, he took in a loud, deep breath and turned toward her. "Gary and I have been here for fifteen minutes."

"Oh?" Pulling her arm away, she wandered past him toward the other two men. She didn't need these uneasy feelings now. She didn't want them. "Don't yell at me. Lucy just told me five minutes ago."

The two older men stood from their seats.

An old-fashioned gesture men rarely did anymore. It was sweet, even if it was done by the shyster lawyer.

"Hello, Cass."

She nodded at Gary, then twisted toward the newest rival for her building. Shivers raced down her spine at his intense stare. She shook the feeling away and settled in the chair next to Jack.

Gary sat in the chair between Jack and the still-staring newcomer.

Wanda placed a cup on the table in front of her and poured coffee. She refilled the other cups and wandered away.

"Is your attorney on the way?" Gary asked.

"No, but Lucy is. She said it was just an informal meeting." She glided her look over the lawyer before focusing back on the unfamiliar man. Middle-aged and lean, clad in a suit and tie, he was a bit overdressed for the town. She picked up her cup, wrapping her suddenly chilled hands around it. "You must be Mr. White?"

His dark eyes colored over before he nodded. "Yes, Daniel White. I'm with Wholesome Natural Products." His eyes narrowed. "You're Cassandra Rogers?"

"Cass, yes."

"Cass?"

Shivers at his concentrated look erupted on her skin, pushing away all thoughts of her previous conversation with Jack. "Do I know you?"

"No." He glanced from Gary to Jack and then back. "You just…remind me of…someone."

"She does?"

Something like optimism sounded in Gary's short question.

"She reminds you of someone?"

"Yes," Mr. White said. "Yes, someone close."

"What's going on?" Lucy spoke. "I told you not to talk until I got here."

Lucy's harsh words stopped the strange conversation cold. "No, you told me not to discuss the Martinson building, and I'm not."

"Oh, okay. Good." Lucy looked from her to each man, focusing her widened gaze on her once again. "Things looked a bit…intense when I stepped into the diner."

Gary stood and pulled out a chair, waving his right hand toward the new arrival.

The other two men rose also, sitting as one after Lucy settled into the offered seat.

Gallant of the man to pull out a seat for her. However, Cass still didn't trust this lawyer.

"We were just introducing her to Daniel," Gary said. "No matter what you might think of me, I would never start discussing official matters until you arrived. Especially when only one of the interested buyers has his lawyer present."

The server returned, placed another cup on the table, and filled it with coffee. "Would anyone like anything else?"

"No, we're fine, Wanda." Jack grinned "Maybe later."

"Okay." The server disappeared into the kitchen.

Cass glanced around the table, and then looked toward the door. "I guess Mr. Martinson is running a bit late."

"Oh, didn't Lucy tell you?" Gary said. "He won't be able to make this meeting."

Cass looked up at Gary's words.

Jack raised his left hand to silence her. "The old man just called Gary ten or fifteen minutes ago. When he found out about Daniel, he decided to cancel the meeting. It was Gary's idea to still meet informally."

"What?" Quick heat burned into her. She pressed it down and looked over at Lucy. "Why didn't you mention this when you called?"

"I didn't know then." Lucy sat forward in her seat. "I found out on the way over here, after I'd called you."

Cass swallowed. "Why are we still having this meeting if Mr. Martinson can't attend?"

"It's what he wanted." Gary glanced at Lucy before refocusing his attention on her. "Good news is Mr. White has decided not to pursue his interest in the building."

"Oh?" Lucy said. "Why have you changed your mind, Mr. White?"

"I was never really interested." He slid his gaze quickly over Cass. "When my other partner showed an interest in the bookstore—"

Cass dragged in a deep breath, then let it out slowly. "I'll never sell my bookstore."

"He doesn't want your business," Gary said easily. "And with Maddie selling Wholesome products in her dress shop, they have no reason to bid on the building."

"Then why did he show an interest?" Lucy placed her arms on the table. "For that matter, why did Jack?" Toughness sounded in her voice now, riddled in her words. "Being Mr. Martinson's lawyer, you knew Cass had made a tentative deal for the building. She paid him the rent you insisted on for the privilege of using it."

"Yes."

Gary sounded just as strong and forceful as her realtor. By the look on Lucy's features now, Cass sensed she could handle him.

"But he still hasn't used any of those funds." Gary placed his hands flat on the table. "So you bringing up the rent payment is moot."

"Because you told him not to, Gary." Lucy stood

and leaned toward him. "You had no right to give him that type of advice."

"I was his lawyer then, Lucy. I had every right."

"Yes, you were also Jack's attorney at the same time. Didn't you see that as a conflict of interest?"

Fury deepened her words, flashing hot in her look. Cass was so glad she was out of the line of fire.

Gary opened his mouth and then shut it. A few quiet breaths later, he nodded. "You're right. I let my memories of Jack's parents get in the way of my professionalism. I should've never agreed to represent their son."

"Right," Lucy agreed. "You finally fixed that problem, even though Dad thought you'd hand Jack over to one of your associates instead of Mr. Martinson. So, what do you propose we do now?"

Jack lifted both hands. "I know what to do. Cass and I—"

"Stay out of this." Gary waved his hands toward the vet. "Lucy and I will figure something out."

Cass glanced at Jack, then at the quiet newcomer.

He dropped his gaze to his clamped hands.

Apprehension intensified within her. Something about the man bothered her, and she wasn't sure why. A small man—almost feminine in his ways, with a quiet, controlled manner—shouldn't make her feel so uncomfortable. A gentle hand landed on her leg and squeezed tight, forcing her gaze away from the older man.

Jack leaned in and whispered a breath of warm air around her ear lobe.

She shivered at his closeness.

"Let's talk."

She swallowed and moved his hand from her.

He pulled her from the seat. "While the two of you argue about lawyerly stuff, Cass and I will go to another table and come up with a way to fix the problem."

Cass pulled her arm away. "No, you and I won't be doing any such thing."

Circling his arm around her waist, he half-carried her to an empty table in the back corner of the suddenly quiet diner and set her into the booth. "Move on over."

"No way." She jumped from her seat. "I'm not saying anything without Lucy present."

"Yes, you are." Forcing her gently back into the seat, he slid in beside her. "I know it's only been a few hours, but have you thought about leasing the building together?"

Her anger subsided a bit at his words. Yes, she had been thinking about it. The more she considered his compromise, the better it sounded. If they both owned the building, or only leased it, then her limited supply of funds would open for other things.

But did she really want to get more involved with this man? Just this morning, she'd run from him because of a simple almost-kiss. Should she seriously be considering his plan? This would force them closer together, not further apart.

"Remember me telling you about all that stuff my parents collected?"

Sweeping her concerns away, she nodded.

"They left me two large storage units," he said. "Boxes and boxes of stuff, packed to the ceiling, along with larger things like stands, dressers, and bedframes, and some sofas and chairs. I believe there's also an old

1940s-style radio and telephone in the lockers." He grinned and winked. "Kind of looks like your bookstore right now."

"I don't have boxes stored up to the ceiling, Jack."

"To be honest, I have no clue what's inside those boxes. I do have a list of what's in storage, but I haven't looked it over yet. It could be junk for all I know or treasure."

"Junk to one person is another person's treasure." Almost against her will, she relaxed in the booth. He had her trapped, so she might as well listen to what he had to say. Her mind was telling her it'd be good, but her body was screaming *no way*. "But what does all this have to do with the building?"

"You want to expand your bookstore with a coffee shop." He placed his left arm on the back of the booth, rubbing the tips of his fingers over the side of her head. "I want a thrift shop to honor my mother's dream. I was thinking maybe we could have both. The coffee shop in the front and the thrift store in the back.

"Both?" She moved her head from his sweet touch. "You *were* serious this morning when you mentioned leasing the building together?"

"Not at first, but now I'm thinking it might work." He settled both of his hands on her shoulders. "We could lease it together. Or we could even buy it."

Could that work? Would Mom be okay with this solution? "I don't know."

He sat back. "Why?"

"You said you didn't have any clue what was in the boxes," she said. "How do I know the stuff is right for my image of the building? I want everyone to feel comfortable coming into the place with their children."

He jerked back. "Are you saying my mother had bad taste?"

"No," she said quickly. His answering grin relaxed her back into her seat. "I remember your mother. She used to come into the bookstore all the time."

"I hated going with her," he said. "Until that day I saw you." He placed his fingers gently against her cheekbone. "She never had to beg me to go again."

She jerked from his touch. "What?"

"No one could keep me from going," he whispered. "After I'd finally met my best friend's little sister."

She froze at his words, then relaxed. He couldn't be telling her the truth, could he? "Really?"

Chapter Twenty

"Yes, really."

The diner customers sitting around her faded as Cass focused on Jack's face. Her heart slammed in her chest. Was it true? Was she the real reason he'd showed up at the bookstore almost every day back then?"

"I really did forget how to breathe," Jack whispered. "The first time I saw you."

Placing her right hand on her chest, she dragged in a deep breath. Was this true? If he'd been so taken with her back then, then why hadn't he spoken to her? Why hadn't he let her know how he felt? Maybe because you were only a kid, a loud sarcastic voice inside said, and he was a decent guy.

And Billy had been her overly protective brother.

Billy. She missed him even more now.

Warm tingles spread down her cheeks, in line with his tracing fingertips. No matter how many men touched her, none of them made her feel so alive. She sighed and glanced up when he moved his hand around her neck and pulled her gently toward him.

"I'm forgetting how to breathe again."

He wasn't the only one. "Nice, isn't it?"

Eyes widening, he grinned and kissed her on the forehead before releasing her. "Wrong time, wrong place."

"I agree."

Disappointment heated in the brown of his eyes. "Next time." His expression changed then, and he lowered his hand from her neck.

Cass couldn't tell what he was thinking now.

"Tell you what?" He grinned. "I figured a change of subject was in order here."

She arched her brows.

"Don't worry." He winked. "Next time I get close enough to kiss you, it won't be on your forehead."

Boy, this man is something else. "Thanks for the warning."

"You're welcome." He choked out through his deep laughter. "Now, stop interrupting me."

"Me? Interrupting you?"

"Let's get back to our conversation."

"You might be charming, Jack Fontaine, but I'm still not agreeing to your scheme without discussing it with Lucy and my mother first." She backed away. "Mom will need to agree. She's in control of the lectures."

"Of course, Janessa will have the final say." He wiggled his eyebrows. "That's what I want to talk about."

"Jack, stop stalling."

His grin was back. "You need to see the stuff, right?"

She nodded. "Mom and I both, yes."

"And I need to move it out of those storage rooms in Dallas to my ranch."

She backed into the side wall. "You want me to go to Dallas?"

"No," he said. "I was thinking you could check out the stuff once I got it stored away at the ranch."

Warmth rose within her at her misspoken words. "Oh, I could do that."

"But if you want to go to Dallas." He arched his eyebrows upward, tracing his touch along the skin of her lower arm, "I'm good with that."

I'm sure you are, Jack Fontaine.

"But I can tell by the look on your face, you would rather not do that."

Shouldn't it bother her he could read her so well? "That would be better, yes."

"I think so, too."

A hot ache rumbled through her now at his intense look. Tingles raced along her skin, like demanding fingers over a naked body. His fingers traced over her body. Johnny had looked at her in the same way. Yet, she'd never lost control of her heartbeat or fought to keep her lungs filled with life-giving air.

"So, it's a date then?"

Date? What was he talking about?

"I'll take you to my ranch sometime later this week, so you can check out my stuff."

Said the bee to the flower. Thankfully, she'd managed to hide her reaction this time, or maybe he decided not to comment on it. Either way, she was glad. The laughter in his eyes told her the truth, though.

"Some of my friends promised to help me move it the day after tomorrow, Wednesday. You're welcome any time after that."

"Saturday or Sunday would be better."

"Saturday it is then," he agreed. "Maybe I'll even make you dinner."

With everything in her, she wanted to say *no.* Yet, she only nodded.

"Good." He slid out of the booth and grabbed her hand. "Let's go and tell the others what we're thinking about doing."

The image of him gathering her into his arms and placing his lips against hers in a hot, demanding kiss flashed in her mind. She wiped it away before the kiss turned into something a bit more R-rated.

"No, I'm not talking about that." His gaze lowered to her lips. "No one needs to know about *that* particular part of our plan."

Oh, wow, she really had to learn how to hide her thoughts a bit better. She shook her head and led him toward the other table.

"So, have the two of you ironed out your differences?" Lucy asked.

Gary and Daniel rose from their chairs, settling back after Cass sat.

"It would solve everything if you could come up with some plan to work together," Gary added.

"Maybe not everything." Daniel focused his attention on her. "But things have a way of working out."

Cass picked up her warm coffee cup and looked from the newcomer to Gary. Something between the two men had changed since she'd left the table. When she peeked over at the other woman, her belief deepened. While she'd talked with Jack, she realized the lawyer, realtor, and business owner had their own conversation.

"Seems like Cass and I weren't the only people discussing things."

If she was hoping the trepidation was only her imagination, then Jack's words proved her wrong.

"Yes," Gary said quickly. "But it has nothing to do with the Martinson building."

"Then what does it have to do with?" Cass asked. "Didn't we all meet today to discuss who would ultimately gain that property?"

"Yes, the meeting was about that." Lucy placed a hand on her arm. Her mouth fought against a smile, losing the battle. "But Mr. White"—she glanced at the older man—"Daniel provided us with some interesting information about things."

Jack settled into his seat. "What things?"

He asked what she'd been thinking. Cass sat beside him and glanced around the table.

"Neither of us can say right now." Gary gave away nothing. "Time will tell."

"Gary?"

"Lucy?"

"So," the quiet newcomer said. "What have the two of you decided about that building?"

Something was going on here. The quick responses and guarded looks meant something was not right.

Cass just hoped it had nothing to do with the building.

She couldn't handle another setback.

****

That night, Cass invited Maddie and Angie to her apartment above the store to talk over her misgivings. Unfortunately, the only words the two heard were the stuff about Dallas.

"I would go in a second." Maddie settled on her sofa. "That'll be fun."

Oh, why did I have to mention that? When will I ever learn? "Then go." Cass clamped her fingers around her wine glass. "Just go."

"Jack didn't ask me." Maddie twisted her little body, splashing her wine onto the cushion. "He asked you."

"So?" She sipped her wine, not taking her gaze off her more unpredictable friend. "If I'm remembering correctly, Ethan asked you to check out his horse training school and you didn't go."

"That's different."

Angie laughed, dripping a few drops of wine onto the coffee table. "Oh, and why is that?"

"It just is." Maddie glared at Angie. "Stop laughing. You're spilling wine all over the floor."

"Not to worry, Angie. Gives my old floor character." Cass sipped the sweet liquid again. "Good wine."

Angie raised her glass. "One of my ex-mother-in-law's favorites."

"She does like her wine, doesn't she?" Maddie said quickly. "Guess she isn't all bad."

"So, what have you decided?" Angie sat forward in her seat. "About sharing the Martinson building, I mean?"

"I'm not sure yet," Cass said. "The front will be perfect for the lecture series, and there's plenty of room in the back for…whatever Mom and I decide. A contractor is checking tomorrow to see if the windows I want will be worth it. I haven't talked to my mom about Jack's mom's stuff yet."

"I think you should work with Jack," Angie said. "That way all the responsibility for maintaining the building won't fall onto you and your mother. It would also open your father's cash for all the tasks your mother mentioned last weekend."

"I still can't believe she's been thinking about the bookstore all these years." Cass glanced at her glass. "That surprised me."

"And that she told her ideas to your father," Angie added. "Not everything she mentioned would be feasible, but still, your father never even considered them."

"You don't know how much that upsets me." She tightened her fingers hard around her glass again. If she wasn't careful, she would bust it next time. "Dad always led me to believe she didn't want anything to do with the business."

"I always thought your mom was a smart lady." Maddie relaxed, twisting her legs under her and turning again. She took a sip of her wine. "But I never realized she knew so much about running a business."

"Me, either." Cass studied the dark wine in Maddie's glass. "I'm her daughter. I should've known."

"Why?" Angie sighed. "You've no need to feel guilty."

"Maybe, but that doesn't change how I feel." She shrugged and relaxed her hold on her glass. "Mom and Dad hid many things." She glanced at Angie, and then focused on Maddie. "That's what parents do, right? Keep bad stuff from their children."

"Good ones, yes," Maddie agreed. "But I wouldn't know because mine were crazy."

"No, not crazy, just different." Cass leaned back and took a sip of her wine. The fruity, sweetness flowed easily down her throat. "At least, you know where you stand with them. Nothing was hidden from you, or by you."

"As far as I know," she added, under her breath. "My brother, Jeff, looks nothing like Dad."

Angie glanced at Maddie before frowning and twisting toward her. "You're thinking of Billy again, aren't you?"

Cass just nodded.

"And now with the addition of this private investigator—"

"Oh, please don't mention his name." She tightened her fingers around the wine glass. This time, she swore she heard a cracking sound. She stared at the glass, forcing her hand to soften a bit. "Having him searching around wouldn't be so bad if he wasn't so interested in Mom and if it wasn't a mutual attraction."

The empathy in Angie's eyes changed to sympathy. "Has he found out anything yet?"

"No," Cass said. "At least, he hasn't contacted Mom or me."

Maddie slammed her right hand against her shoulder. "You need to tell her before he does."

Drops of the chilled liquid splashed against her bare legs, traveling down toward the sofa cushion. Cass wiped at the dampness with her bare hand. "Be careful."

"In fact, you need to call her now." Maddie flipped her the phone. "While Angie and I are here, you need to talk to her."

The device settled upside-down on the sofa beside her. She gazed at it but didn't pick it up. "I'm not telling my mother about Billy's death over the phone."

"Well, then, the three of us will go to her house." Maddie leaped up from the sofa and grabbed her hand. "Come on, let's go."

She yanked her arm down. "Not now."

"Why?" Angie leaned forward. "You need to tell her."

"No more stalling, Cass," Maddie added. "Call her now."

"I can't." Looking around the room for any way out of her predicament, she focused on a row of photos and knickknacks lining the top of her bookshelf. "I wonder what Jack's parents have stored away in Dallas."

"Changing the subject, are you?" Maddie asked.

She ignored her. "If they're small and old enough to fit my forties theme, I might be willing to use that backroom for them. It'll be up to Mom." Silence roared around her.

Angie sat back and sighed low.

Maddie fell back, splashing her wine once again on her sofa.

"At least, Jack is the only other person interested in the building." Cass closed her eyes. "The other guy decided he didn't want it."

Maddie snorted.

Angie just sighed low again.

Typical reactions, grudging acceptance of her need to let the subject go. Just like she'd known they would act this way now, next time would be a completely different story. Next time, Maddie wouldn't allow her to get out of telling Mom.

"Mr. White came to the dress shop today," Maddie said. "He brought samples of The Intimate Marriage Collection. One of everything Sarah from Wholesome Natural has designed for the collection. Nice, sexy stuff."

"Oh, really?" Cass took a sip of wine and set it on the table. "I thought he went back to Dallas. Why would he return to town so soon?"

Maddie shrugged. "He talked with his other partners about my interest in the collection. I guess the three of them decided to visit the town this weekend again. The other two should be here later tonight."

"I hope they aren't reconsidering the Martinson building." Bile bubbled up into her throat. "Negotiating with Jack is bad enough."

"Not to worry," Maddie said. "Mr. White asked me if I wanted to add the whole collection to my store, and I've decided to do it." She picked up her glass and took a sip. "Some of the stuff is a bit...risqué, but I like it. It'll no doubt shock the church folks, though."

"Risqué?" Angie leaned forward, a wicked grin lifting the edges of her mouth. "I would love to check out the collection, if that's all right with the owner."

"Sure, he gave me samples for that purpose." Maddie nodded.

The sparkle lighting her eyes heated Cass's skin. *What are you up to now?*

"And maybe you can borrow some of the things for your date when you meet Jack at his house tomorrow. That should be a real test of the products." Maddie added. "Or I'll just give it to you."

"But what if Angie and I don't want the stuff?"

"Wholesome Natural supplied samples of almost every design. The company expects me to give it away." Maddie shrugged. "So, you have no excuse not to get a nice garment to wear on your date with Jack."

Oh, boy, she'd mentioned meeting with Jack only once, five minutes after Angie had opened the wine bottle. Could Maddie ever leave anything alone? "It's not a date."

"Oh, really." Twinkling laughter sounded, then she winked. "You are such a bad liar."

Cass didn't need this now. "Maddie?"

"But it could be, with the right enticement." She gazed at Angie. "Right?"

Angie just nodded.

Cass sighed. "The last thing I want is to entice Jack."

"Oh, come on." Maddie swallowed the last of her wine. "Want to see the collection now?"

"I do." Angie stood. "Let's go do that. We can take the wine."

"Sounds good." Maddie grinned at Angie before she refocused her attention. "You with us, Cass?"

Her brain told her not to go, but her body cried, *why not*?

"Come on."

"All right." She slipped off the sofa and stood between her two friends. "But both of you will be trying on some things, too."

"Why are you assuming I haven't done that?" Maddie winked. "Trying on some of those nightgowns almost made me wish I had a man to model it for."

"Ah," Angie whispered. "Ethan Bishop."

A loud snort was her only answer.

"Good thing we only need to go a few blocks." Angie moved gracefully out of the door. "The three of us are pretty drunk."

"Speak for yourself." Maddie snorted again and lowered her right hand. "Let's go."

Cass sighed. "I'm coming." Even if she'd wanted

to change her mind, the speed and quickness of her exit down the stairs and through the front door next to her bookstore entrance gave her no time.

Maddie stumbled off the curb of the first side street, giggling like a schoolgirl. She emptied the last of the cool liquid down her front.

"No more wine, Maddie." Cass snatched her left arm. "You can barely walk as it is."

A totally unladylike splutter was her only answer.

"Stand straight," Angie said suddenly. "The last thing I want is to have my ex-mother-in-law find out I've been drinking. She thinks I'm a bad mother already."

"Maddie and I will act right, Angie." Cass wanted to question Angie about her comment but decided to let it go. "I promise."

"Me, too. At least until we reach the safety of the dress shop," Maddie yelled. "Then all bets are off."

A diesel truck roared down the lane, slowing near the café at the end of the street before speeding toward them.

Cass glanced up at the same time the vehicle passed her. "Oh, that's Mr. White."

The older man's eyes widened, and then he looked quickly toward the tall, lean driver. Something familiar rang through her for a breath as the truck slowed near the bookstore almost to a stop before speeding again and roaring out of sight.

"Hey, we're not letting you get out of trying on some of that sexy lingerie." Maddie pulled at her arm. "Need to find something for your big date."

Okay, she had about enough. Freezing a foot from the entrance door of the dress shop, she jerked from

Maddie's grasp. "For the last time, it's not…a…date."

Both turned toward her.

"We are discussing the possibility of co-leasing the Martinson building, that's it."

Angie shook her head and glanced away.

Maddie only continued to stare with that smirking look. "Well, it'll be more if you wanted it to be."

Cass couldn't win.

"Angie and I will pick out a sexy nightgown."

She shook her head. "I give up."

"Good." Maddie grasped her arm and pulled her toward the entranceway. "Jack won't stand a chance."

"Let's go inside." Angie tilted her glass upside down, wobbling a bit. "Ex-mother-in-law be damned, I need to refill my glass."

"Then why not refill it?" Maddie giggled. "You have the bottle in a bag in your hand."

"Yes, I'll just do that." She laughed softly and wiggled the bag. "I forgot I had the wine."

"None of us needs to be seen drinking in the middle of the street." Cass swallowed the last of her wine before tipping her glass upside down. "My glass is empty, too."

"I guess I'll have to unlock the door."

"That'll be good." Angie grinned. "The two of us have to pick out something sexy for Cass."

Should've realized changing the subject wouldn't be that easy this time around.

Chapter Twenty-One

In the soft glow of the streetlights, Pete walked down the main street in Greenfield. Warm feminine laughter flowed from the locked entrance door of a women's clothing shop, the sweet sound warming over his troubling thoughts. That younger female image lifted to the surface of his mind. "Who are you?"

The answers were here, in Greenfield. He sensed it clearly as he walked out of range of the laughter toward the dark building filled with unopened boxes.

If Daniel was right, the owner of this shop could be his sister. His sister?

Fear of the unknown battled through him, causing him to freeze near the entrance door of the dark bookstore. Something had kept him from approaching when he'd first arrived in town hours ago. He'd planned on walking right into the building. Yet, he couldn't force his feet out of the truck. He barely even slowed before speeding and racing back to the motel with Daniel. A sense of anxiety he couldn't explain tightened his throat then. It burned in his heart now.

His hard-won control was slipping, the same as it had after Sarah's death. Familiar slow footsteps echoed in the night silence, stopping a few feet from him. Pete recognized those steps. "I didn't mean to wake you, Daniel."

"You didn't," he said. "I wasn't asleep yet. I

figured you would be here, so I got dressed and followed you."

Pete nodded, not taking his gaze off the dark front area of the store.

"How can I help?"

He shrugged. "I don't think you can."

Daniel stayed quiet.

Pete appreciated his friend's consideration. "I'm afraid to see her. I'm afraid of what I might find out about...my family. About Billy."

"Everything I've heard about...Billy Rogers...has been positive, Pete."

Daniel's words sounded loud in the quiet night air, echoing all around him.

"If this Cass Rogers is your sister..."

"If Cass is my sister that means my...father might be gone." His throat tightened around his words. "And she and my mother might have been alone for the last year." He swallowed away his tears. "It feels as if we..." He swallowed again. "That my father and I have unfinished business. A disagreement that might never be settled between us if he's...gone."

"Your father's death is only a rumor," his friend said. "If you don't make contact with that woman, you never know for sure, Pete."

He knew that.

"What did you hope to find here so late at night?"

"I wish I knew." Silence answered his unspoken questions, a loud silence roaring with one memory after another. Bombarding him with sudden, quick flashes of familiar faces and images. He stepped backward at the emotional impact. Remembered warm smiles and laughter, learning and failure, joyousness and sadness sprinted across his mind. The young girl mixed and merged into an older woman with the same black hair and warm eyes. Bright laughter and the remembrance of small arms wrapping around him in a motherly hug broke through his uneasiness. He tightened at the overwhelming memories bombarding him. "I remember my mother. And Cass…Drea."

Two other faces drifted into his vision, one dark and one light. Those two girls used to follow him all over town, making him feel as if he could do no wrong. Just like his sister had a crush on Jack— "Jack Fontaine." He jerked and twisted toward his friend. "The vet… That man who almost knocked you down the day we first arrived in town."

Daniel rubbed his chin. "Oh, yes. He's interested in the Martinson building and your sister."

"He always was." The rest of his hidden memories rushed him, so quickly he couldn't catch all of them. Memories of a friend, Jack, teasing his sister mercilessly, just to see her blush. Laughter bubbled in his dry throat. "Man, he had a major thing for her. So bad I had to put my foot down more than once." He shook his head. "She was only sixteen at the time."

"You're remembering everything?"

His grin must have said it all because his friend beamed.

"That's wonderful."

Then the argument between him and his father came back in full force, and he slouched. "Dad wanted me to take over running the bookstore. He was against me leaving to follow the rodeo." He gazed into the building. The streetlight reflected his dull, empty expression in the glass. "I left town a week after my eighteenth birthday. Jack and his dad took me in a few days later, and I haven't been home since. I called home only once, and my father refused to talk. I never contacted them again. Not even my sister."

"And then you drank a little too much and got into a car accident." Daniel set his left hand on his shoulder. "I don't understand why that hospital never got in touch with your family. I know you left without the doctor's permission and without letting anyone know where you would be, still…"

Another painful memory invaded. "I deleted their names from the notification form. Jack's father was my emergency contact, but I left the other part blank."

Daniel narrowed his eyes. "So, that's why no one told them you were hurt?"

Jack wouldn't have told them, either, because he'd been with him when he took care of all that business. His friend had insisted he put his parents' names down, but it hadn't sat well with him. Pete went back an hour after that phone call with his father and deleted the information.

"What a fool." Fingers clamped deep into his shoulder blade. Pete gazed at his friend. "I'm such a fool."

"Stop thinking that way, Pete. We've all done things we wish we could change."

"I need to see Jack." He pulled from the man and headed toward his truck. "I need to see him now."

Daniel sputtered. "It's late, Pete, and we don't even know where he lives."

"I know where he might be." He slid into the vehicle. "He used to live at a farm on Old North Road with his parents. They had to move into town after his mom got sick, but he'd always told me how much he missed that ranch."

"How can you be sure he's there?"

"I spent many a night at the old Speyer farm after my dad and I had one of our many arguments." The engine boomed in the quiet air. "Are you coming or not?"

He opened the truck door. "What if he's not there?"

Jack shrugged. "If there was any way Jack could buy that farm, he would've."

"But you don't know if it was for sale."

"Only one way to find out." He raced the engine. "Are you coming?"

Daniel shook his head, then slipped into the truck. "I'm awake, so I might as well join you."

"That's the spirit."

****

Cass really needed to slow down with the wine. The more she drank, the more willing she was to model the way-too-sexy Intimate Marriage Collection. The more comfortable she got showing off her body to her two best friends, the more talkative she became. And the more talkative, the more she wanted to admit her meeting with Jack was a date. As soon as she said that, she told Maddie and Angie she wouldn't mind Jack seeing her in one of the revealing nightgowns. The crush she'd had on him when she was younger hadn't faded like most first loves. The crush had only gotten stronger.

And she was okay with that. His actions told her he was just as interested.

"Oh, wow."

Shoving her thoughts away, she looked in the direction of the fitting room.

Angie stepped around the area with an easy glide, clad in a tight, neck-to-bare-feet, black leather bodysuit.

Her model-thin body, long legs, and smooth skin, blonde hair swishing over the curve of her shoulder and a mock come-hither look, showed why she'd been such a well-paid model. If she hadn't known her forever, the blonde could easily make her feel less than beautiful.

"No way could I ever pull off something like that." Maddie whistled. "I'm too short, with the waist-less body of a pre-teen girl."

Angie twisted toward her, flipping her hair into her face. "But I bet Ethan would love it."

"No way."

"Yeah, way." Angie stopped in front of Maddie. "You've already admitted you would like to be with him. You can't take it back now."

"Sure, all right. I think he's hot." She crossed her arms at her waist. "But that still doesn't mean I want to wear something like that."

Cass giggled, swallowing the last of her wine. "Ah, I like it."

"You stay out of this," Maddie said.

She couldn't stop laughing, even if she wanted to. Whenever the three got together for one of these impromptu parties, some new truths always came out.

Maddie pointed her finger. "I mean it."

Good to know she wasn't the only drunk, talkative woman modeling sexy stuff in the dress shop in the early morning hours. She'd learned two new things about her best friends. Maddie's secret didn't surprise her, however. Everyone knew she had the hots for

Ethan Bishop but was afraid to do anything about it. No one knew why, however.

Angie's secret crush on Cass's brother came as a complete surprise, though.

Maddie stepped closer. "Now it's your turn to put on what Angie and I picked out."

Pulling her mind from her thoughts, she picked up her glass and wandered to the wine. After refilling it, she raised the bottle. Both drained their glasses and lifted them. She filled them to the brim before setting the almost-empty bottle on the counter and walking back to the fitting rooms. Taking a long sip, then a second one, she set the glass on a low shelf inside the dressing room and sighed. "How many bottles of wine have we consumed anyway?"

"Enough." Angie pressed her into the room. "Stop changing the subject and get into that room."

"Here. This one's for you."

A slight slur muddled Maddie's words. She handed the bright-red, shockingly sheer negligee to her and stumbled back a step. The matching panties didn't look capable of hiding the delicate area it was supposedly designed to cover. "Where's the rest?"

"You can't refuse." Maddie pushed her farther into the dressing room. "I put on that tight yellow bustier and Angie modeled that black leather thingy. Now it's your turn."

"I've tried on a few of them." Cass pleaded. "In fact, I tried on more than either of you combined."

"Yes," Angie whispered. "But you haven't tried on any of the more revealing samples. Fair is fair, Cass. We picked this one especially for you."

"Put it on, now." Maddie pulled the curtain shut,

shaking it roughly. "Now, Cass."

"So bossy."

"You know it." Words slurring with a laugh, she wiggled the curtain again. "Need any help?"

"You stay out there."

Both giggled again.

Cass shook her head and glanced into the three-way mirror. She took a drink and set the glass onto the wooden seat. Letting the scrunched material flow from her tight grip, she placed it in front of the more sensible, light-blue T-shirt type nighty and twisted her body left and right. She had to agree with Angie. Red did look good on her.

"No, really, do you need any help?" Maddie slurred.

"No."

"Are you sure?" She added. "I could always go and get *Jack.*"

Oh, thank you very much. The drunker she got, the more she wanted to model for him. "I really need to stop drinking."

"Did you say something?"

Maddie's hearty voice startled her. She shook her head at her reaction. "No."

"Didn't think so."

"Now quit stalling and put on that negligee," Angie said.

The curtain wiggled again. The thick material stopped moving a second before a burst of giggles rang out into the air. Two sets of voices—one outrageous and loud, the other demurer and gentler, but both badly slurred—called out her name. If she didn't do as they said, both would rush in to help her. "Okay, okay."

"If it looks good," Maddie said. "I might let you borrow it for your date with Jack."

She stripped the T-shirt from her body and dropped the silky material over her head. It hugged lightly against her curves, bringing to life her generous lines, sienna skin, and rich black hair. She twirled around and studied her image from every direction, for once not finding anything wrong.

"Almost done?" Angie asked.

She tore her bikini panties off and replaced them with a wisp of cloth. "Wow."

The curtain opened.

She twisted, enjoying the silk rubbing warm against her upper thigh. "So, what do you think?"

"Jack wouldn't stand a chance." Angie whistled. "I don't think there's a man alive who would be able to say no."

Cass didn't care about any other man.

Maddie snatched the wine bottle from the counter and refilled all three glasses. "Do you want to keep it?"

"Maybe," Cass said. "But not on our first date."

"Good." Maddie handed her a refilled glass. "I'm glad you're finally admitting you're going on a date."

Oh, brother, when will I learn?

****

Unexpected ringing woke Jack from a deep sleep. He rubbed cobwebs from his eyes and stretched his arms high into the air before checking the digital clock near his bed. The phone gave out another clanging sound, and he reached past the clock for it. "This had better be good. It's almost two in the morning."

"Jack?"

"Who else would it be?" He wasn't acting at all

professionally, but he couldn't find the strength to care now. "Do you need a vet?"

"Oh, no. Sorry for the late call," the voice said. "But I think you'll be glad when you hear what I have to tell you."

He rubbed his eyes again and swung his legs off the bed. "You might want to start with your name."

"Oh, sorry," he said. "It's Hank. Hank Wayne."

Hank? The PI? Jack yanked his head high. "Tell me you found out something about Billy."

He's alive."

Jack shot off the bed. "Are you sure about this?"

"I talked to William Rodgers' daughter a few hours ago. Seems she was directed to the wrong room when she first showed up at the hospital after her father's accident. She told me the person in the bed was a young man who'd been admitted a few days before. And get this, she told me he'd lost his memory."

"What?" He stepped toward the window and glanced out. "Oh, man, I can't believe I forgot that. Dad told me. So, that's why he's never gotten in touch with his family."

"No one from the rodeo remembered anything about Billy's family," he said. "Seems he never talked about them. I've got a copy of the emergency form everyone filled out, but it has only you and your father listed."

"That doesn't make any sense," Jack said. "I was there when he filled it out. He put his parents' information on it."

"No, it only has yours and your father's," Hank said. "The next-of-kin portion isn't filled out."

"I don't understand."

"Me, either."

Jack let it go. "What else did you find out?"

"One of the nurses told me he'd left without permission the same day the other man had his surgery. That man died a few hours later."

Was Jack still sleeping? Was this all a dream?

"But I think I might have found a lead. Another nurse told me he'd gotten close to one of his nurses and her husband. The person I talked to thinks he might have started working for the nurse's company, Wholesome Natural Products. The nurse owned it with her husband and brother."

"That name sounds familiar," Jack said. "Cass or one of her friends might have mentioned it."

"Oh, really?"

"No, wait. I remember where I heard that name before." Jack exhaled and stepped away from the window. The roughness of the hardwood floor woke him completely. He wasn't dreaming. This was all real. "The man who showed up at my meeting with Cass about the Martinson building is part of that company. Mr. White. Daniel.

Crunching gravel sounded in the quiet room. He stepped back toward the window and glanced outside. A well-tuned engine growled up the little hill curving toward his front door and stopped.

A small man exited the passenger door and stepped to the porch, stopping and turning toward the vehicle.

Barely heard words flowed to him.

"Jack? What's going on?"

No, it can't be. That's the man from the diner.

A tall form eased out of the driver's side, stretching out strong to his full height.

Billy. "He's here, Hank."

"Who?"

Billy moved around the truck.

"Is it Billy? Are you telling me your friend just showed up at your house?"

The two men disappeared from his view a few seconds before the doorbell chimed. "Call me back, Hank."

"Don't you dare hang up."

He ended the call. Another door chime sounded at the same time he landed at the bottom of the stairs. He raced toward the door and swung it open, surprising the smaller man back a step. "Billy?"

"Hey, Jack." A sad grin lined his mouth. "But my name isn't Billy Rogers anymore. My name is Peter Morgan now. Pete. I legally changed my name."

"I don't care what your name is. I'm just glad you're here." Warmth spread through his entire body. He reached out and grabbed his hand, shaking it hard. "Man, you don't know how good it is to see you."

A more mature Billy half-grinned. "Yeah, I think I do."

"Damn." Jack slammed his left hand against his shoulder. "Cass and your mom will be so happy to see you're not dead."

"Dead?" He raised both hands and then let them fall. "Mom thinks I'm dead?"

"Come on in." His phone rang then. "I need to get this call, and then we'll talk."

"Everyone thinks Pete's dead?" Daniel followed him into the room. "I wonder how that happened."

He waved his hand toward Daniel, then accepted the call. "Hank?"

"Fontaine, you better tell me what's going on, or…"

The PI's loud angry voice echoed through the phone. "No need to do any more investigating, Hank."

"He's there?"

"Yes." Jack grinned. "He's standing right beside me."

"Wow," he said. "I'm in Greenfield now. I want to meet this guy before I tell our ladies."

"Sounds good, Hank."

"I can't wait to tell Janessa and her daughter."

Neither could Jack.

And people say miracles never happened anymore.

Chapter Twenty-Two

Pete went through the living room and sank into the one and only chair.

Even with all the furniture and things Jack had moved to the ranch the day before, he still had nothing to place in his living room.

He sank deeper into the chair, head hanging down. "Mom thinks I'm dead?"

Since he'd heard about the accident, Jack had been living with this same type of defeat. A different feeling raced through him now. A different type of guilt threatened to bury his relief. Cass's brother might be alive, but he still had lost three years of his life.

"Why would anyone believe I was dead?"

Jack shook away his deeper feelings and glanced at the smaller man still standing at the door. "I'm sorry I don't have any place to sit out here. I haven't brought any new living room furniture yet."

"I'm fine." Daniel crossed his arms at his waist. "I sit too much as it is."

"I knew I'd find you here." Pete leaped from the seat and roamed around the room. "Place looks a lot different, though. Less home-like somehow. Emptier."

"You should've seen it when I first moved in." Jack stepped toward the hallway leading to the kitchen and then stopped. "What you see is an improvement, believe me. I've been cleaning and fixing things like a crazy man for the last couple of weeks."

Pete glanced around him. "So, you only just recently moved back?"

He nodded.

"Did your dad move back to Greenfield with you?"

He took a deep breath and then let it out slowly. "Dad's gone."

"His heart?" He leaned forward. "You mentioned to me once he was having problems."

Jack could only nod.

"I'm sorry to hear about that." Pete stepped closer and grabbed his shoulder. "He was a good man."

"Yes." He glanced at the older man standing quiet by the entryway door. "Would the two of you like some coffee? I'll be glad to make it."

Pete looked at Daniel, and then shrugged. "Might be a good idea. We both have a lot to say."

Jack suspected he might be right. He needed to explain why he hadn't been with Billy when he needed him the most, and why he let a woman cause such a problem between them. A woman so opposite of the one he'd always wanted but couldn't have until now, maybe.

"Lead the way, Jack," Pete said. "I want to hear all about Drea and my mom and Dad."

More importantly, he needed to tell him about his father's death. Billy—Pete—would never have the chance to make things right with his father. Jack would need to find a gentle way to break the news. Was there an easy way to tell a man his father was gone?

"Speaking of my sister," Pete said. "I won't stop you from dating her."

A cocky grin curved his mouth. Some things

haven't changed. "What?"

"Hopefully, she'll still want to be with you."

Like a bull crashing headfirst against him, the truth rocked him backward.

"Drea had a major thing for you back then."

Wow, has he always loved the woman? Is that the reason he'd only got with wilder women? Women everyone said were no good. Mostly blondes or red-headed women with tainted reputations and questionable morals who didn't expect more than just sex? Was that why he could never settle down? Because he'd already found his one and only love?

"Jack?"

He shook his questions away. "Let's make that coffee, Billy."

"I'm Pete now." He stood straighter. "That cocky Billy guy is long gone."

"Okay, Pete." Jack focused his attention on his old friend. "Yeah, you do seem different now."

"I am."

Jack glanced from him to the quiet older man and nodded. "Follow me." He led the way into the dim kitchen, switching on the light. "Have a seat at the table. By the time the coffee's done, Hank should be here."

"Hank?" Pete settled in a chair facing him, placing his arms onto the table. "Who is he?"

"A PI your mother hired. Seems only four people in town knew you were supposed to be dead." Grabbing the pot from the machine, he turned on the water faucet. "Well, three and me."

"My sister." Pete frowned. "But who were the other two?"

"Well, actually three more," Jack measured the coffee into the filter and added water to the machine. He closed the top and pressed *Start* before twisting toward him. "A friend of Cass's saw you in a rodeo and asked her if you might be related. He showed her the newspaper article about your accident. She told your father."

His only reaction was a narrowing of the eyes.

Daniel looked at him while pulling out one of the chairs and sitting. "Who were the other two?"

"Cass also told her two best friends," he added. "Maddie and—"

"Angie, right?"

"Yes."

Daniel's mouth dropped open. "You remember their names?"

Pete relaxed in his seat. "I'm wondering how I could have forgotten them, especially Angie." He quieted for a moment before shaking his head and gazing up at Jack. "She used to follow me around like my sister followed you."

Jack had forgotten that, or maybe he hadn't noticed at all. Hard remembering anything, with his sweet sister flushing every time he got near her. Cass disappeared every time he came too close. He'd intentionally focused his attention on her, just so he could experience that innocent blush.

"You're still interested in my sister, aren't you?"

Pete's words froze him at the counter, but he didn't comment.

"I hope you are." He leaned forward. "My sister was probably one of the reasons you set up your practice in Greenfield, because you knew she would still be here. She had no desire to leave home. All she'd ever talked about was working in that bookstore."

No, that wasn't true. He'd decided on this town because this was the place where his mom's ashes were buried. The one place he could truly call home. None of the other areas he'd lived in stayed with him like Greenfield. No other place ever had him feeling like he belonged. He'd kept in touch with Mr. and Mrs. Speyer, grabbing at the chance to buy this ranch when they'd offered it. Almost every penny he'd managed to save during his semi-successful rodeo career went into securing the ranch and opening his vet clinic.

But Billy was also right. Pete…was right. Hadn't telling Cass about his part in her brother's supposed death been one of his reasons for returning? Hadn't wanting her forgiveness for his part in him leaving Greenfield in the first place been on his mind? He cleared his thoughts and rummaged through his cupboard for three coffee cups. He set two on the table, leaving the third on the counter beside the coffeemaker. "I drink mine black."

"So do the two of us," Pete said.

Yeah, he remembered that about Billy. *No, he's Pete now. I need to start thinking of him that way.* "Yeah, good and strong."

"Like mud." Pete grinned.

His grin showed over bright, shining eyes. Then both the grin and expressive look changed to one of blankness. Pete was hurting. Jack hadn't a clue how hard it must be for his old friend to suddenly remember over twenty years in a few hours.

"I thought everyone liked strong coffee until I meant Daniel and Ed, my other partner."

Pete twisted toward Daniel. "Daniel here makes the weakest coffee."

Yes, this attitude he remembered. Billy might have changed his name, but he was still the same man.

Daniel shrugged. "Not everyone likes it as strong as you do, Pete."

"Jack and his father do," he said. "Or his father did. So does my dad. My mom and sister like to sweeten it with that flavored creamer stuff."

He needed to tell Pete about his father's death now. An awkward silence settled in the room, except for the gurgling liquid dripping into the glass pot. It sputtered a few times, and then went silent. He reached for the pot and filled his cup before twisting and filling the two other cups on the table, leaving Daniel's half empty. He placed the pot back into the machine and got a chilled bottle of water from the refrigerator. "Figured you might want to water it down."

"He will." Pete lifted his cup and took a drink "Great."

"Thank you." Daniel cracked open the top and poured water into the cup. "I have to drink Pete's coffee this way."

Silence once again filled the room.

"Your father used to talk a lot about retiring here." Pete sat forward in his seat, setting down his half-filled cup. "That's why I figured you would be at this ranch. The two of you talked about this place a lot, and about the people of this town, especially the Speyeres and my sister."

"We did?"

"Both of you talked about the ranch and its old owners." Pete said. "Only you talked about Drea."

"I don't remember mentioning her all that much." He slouched against the counter, wrapping his fingers around the thick mug. The rich coffee scent lifted from the cup. "Maybe a few times after you first showed up, but not much after that."

Pete arched his brows. "I thought I was the one who'd lost his memory."

Thankfully, a pair of headlights brightened the kitchen. Jack moved toward the window and glanced out. "That must be Hank." No one said a word as he moved out of the kitchen, walking quickly to the front door.

Hank almost fell into the living room. He caught his hand on the door to stop his forward progress, straightening before slamming the door behind him. "Where is he?"

Jack pointed toward the kitchen.

"Janessa will be so happy," he said. "I can't wait to tell her."

"*Pete* is in the kitchen."

His eyes widened and then narrowed. "He's not Billy anymore."

"He goes by Pete now."

"So, he did lose his memory then."

Jack nodded.

"Does he know about his father?"

Jack groaned and shook his head.

"What about my father?" Pete stood tall and firm near the kitchen doorway. "Jack?"

Damn, he should've remembered about his friend's curiosity. "Billy?"

"Pete." He scowled. "I told you Billy's gone."

"No," Daniel said lightly. "You might want to

forget him, but you can't anymore."

Pete glanced at his friend. "I wish we never came to Greenfield. If I never came to this town and saw that diner and bookstore, I would've never remembered…that phone call. I would've never remembered the last argument with my dad. What I said to him, and what he said to me."

"It's better to—"

"But that doesn't matter anymore." Bitterness edged over Pete's anger and sadness. "What matters right now is…my father."

"He's—"

"We need coffee." Jack glared at the PI. "I think it might be best if we went back into the kitchen."

"No."

His old friend's tone sharpened, fists clamping hard against his thigh. The old Billy stood in front of him now.

"I need to know about my father," he whispered. "I heard some…rumors I didn't want to believe."

Jack glanced over at Hank and saw him shrug. He didn't want to be the bearer of bad news. Shouldn't Cass or his mom be the one to tell him of his father's death?

"So, those rumors are true."

A hard hand landed on his shoulder. Jack turned toward Pete. He'd never seen him so unsure and sad.

"Your Dad isn't the only one…gone, is he?"

Tears clouded his vision. Jack's grief rose to attack him.

"I need to know the truth."

He swallowed dryness. "No, he isn't."

Silence echoed in the room, and then Pete gasped

out a forceful breath and sank against the nearest wall, sliding down to the floor. "No, no." He covered his face with his hands and moaned low in his throat, fighting the tears. "No."

Daniel walked toward him and placed his hand on the top of his head before releasing him and standing straight. "When?"

"Last year," Jack said softly. "Two years ago, he had a heart attack, but he survived that. Last November he had another one."

"And there was nothing the doctors could do?" Daniel asked.

He forced his gaze off his friend to the older man standing beside him. "No, he was too weak."

"He's...gone." Wetness shone on his skin when he looked up. "I will never be able to say...I'm sorry. I'll never...see...him again."

Jack heaved in one loud breath after another, fighting the tears threatening to fall. Seeing his friend's crumpled form against the wall, face buried deep in his hands, brought back the pain of his own loss. The world had lost two good men last year. Two men with so much still to give. Both just a few years past fifty, with plans and dreams left unfinished. "I'm sorry." Totally inadequate words. Yet, Jack could think of no others. "I'm so sorry."

A low moan of pain was the only response.

"Dad did want to return to Greenfield," Jack whispered. "He wanted to live on this farm and start a vet clinic. He wanted to play with a grandchild or two."

"And he never...got that chance," Pete said. "My father wanted the same thing."

"Yes."

Hank stepped closer to the two at the wall. "I've never met your father, but I do know your mom and sister. You still have family."

Pete dragged in a deep breath, released it, and stood from his crouch. He stood tall and gazed at the PI. "Do I?"

"Yes," Jack said. "And no matter what might have happened in the past, they will be overjoyed to see you again."

"No matter what happened." Pete lowered his glance. "I'm not so sure of that."

"They love you." Jack placed his hands on both of his slumped shoulders. "And you need them now." Pete's shoulders sagged under his hands. "And they need you."

"Not now." He shook his head. "I'm not ready."

"Are you sure?" Daniel stepped around him and stopped beside the quiet private investigator. "It'll be good to see them. They think you're dead."

"Cass does," Hank said. "But Janessa believes you haven't returned because of your…father's attitude. That once you found out he was…gone, you would come home."

He turned his attention onto Hank. "Did my mom tell you about my last phone call?"

"No." Hank shrugged. "Tell me about it."

"The only time I called home." Pete sighed, and then glanced over at Jack. "I called right after you made me put Mom's and Dad's names on the release form."

"You called them?"

"Mom answered," he said. "She was so happy to hear from me. So happy that when she called for Dad, I didn't hang up like I…like I wanted." The words trembled and slurred. "Like I…should have."

"You argued?"

"Yes, Jack, we argued."

A ragged edge lined his voice. Jack heard his own pain in that sound.

"I never talked with him again. The next day, I filled out a new emergency contact form, leaving the next-of-kin section blank."

"So, that's why the hospital never notified Janessa?" Hank stood tall.

Something in Pete's look must have alarmed Jack. Hank's hint of interest in his mom might be the last thing he needed to hear now.

"Or your sister and father," Hank quickly added.

Pete nodded, "I left it blank."

"You shouldn't have done that." Jack glanced back and forth between the two uneasy men. "If Cass or your parents were notified, the last three years would've never happened."

Breath rumbled from Pete's throat. "Then I would've never met Sarah, Daniel, or my other partner, Ed. They are my family now."

"And I'm glad, too, Pete," Daniel said lightly. "But you have a real family. You have a mother and sister who've never given up on you. You need to talk to them."

Pete jerked away. "Not now."

"Then when?" Daniel raised his right hand toward him. "They need to know you're alive."

"Soon." He studied Daniel before focusing back on Jack "I just need a day or two to get my head around Dad's death. Maybe see his grave."

Jack nodded. "One day. I'll give you time to say

your peace at his grave."

"Thanks."

"You can stay here tonight," he said. "Both of you can."

"I appreciate you including me." Daniel smiled. "It's nice."

Unexpected warmth filled him. "Don't be so sure of that, Daniel. The two of you will have to share a bedroom. One will be sleeping on a sofa, and the other on a twin bed I found in my parents' collection of stuff."

"That'll be fine, Jack." Daniel nodded. "I'll take the sofa."

Should he tell Pete about Cass coming to see that collection tomorrow night?

No, tomorrow morning would be soon enough for that.

Chapter Twenty-Three

Cass had taken the sexy red negligee early this morning, and then hidden it in her dresser drawer, under a pile of brightly colored panties and bras and more sensible T-shirt sleepwear. She stared at the drawer now, groaning and placing her hands on her forehead. *Oh, why did I drink so much wine last night?* Before Saturday in San Antonio, the last time was at The Corral when she'd left so foolishly with Johnny. Six months before that occasion, she'd drunk at Maddie's birthday party.

Tonight, she planned on sticking with coffee. Sexy negligees and wine were a waste on a first date anyway, if you wanted a second one. With Johnny it didn't matter, but Jack was a different story. With Jack, she wanted more.

Cass moved past her unmade bed, lowering her look from the early afternoon sunlight beaming through her window. She rubbed her fingers over her forehead and moaned. *Really do need to cut back on the wine.*

Ring-ring-ring.

The phone, clanging like a church bell, echoed inside her head. Next time Angie and Maddie asked if she wanted to get a few bottles of wine, she planned on saying *no*.

Ring-ring-ring.

"I'm coming." She snatched up the noisemaker

before it could pierce her brain a third time. "Hello."

"Cass?"

Who else would it be? She silenced her irritation. "Yes."

"You sound rough."

Her heart sped at the teasing voice. "Jack?"

"Did I wake you?"

"No." She glanced over at the digital clock on her nightstand. "It's after ten."

"Well, I thought you might have slept in. Seeing that it's Saturday, and I noticed you weren't downstairs in the bookstore."

"Mom is there today." A grin sounded clear in his tone. She settled on the bed easily, cupping her cheek into her hand. "She's planning out the final design of the shelves with two of our employees. We need to get the bookstore up and running again before Memorial Day. We can't just rely on website sales." She rubbed her forehead gently, easing the ache a bit. "I can hear them downstairs, moving stuff around. I might go down later and help."

"Have anything heavy you need lifted?"

Peace flowed through her. "Are you offering to help?"

"Sure."

Quickly, a bit too quickly. *What are you up to now, Jack Fontaine?*

"Then you and your mom can come to my place and check out my mom's treasures this afternoon."

Disappointment fought against the renewed ache in her head.

"I know I promised to make you dinner tonight," he said. "Unfortunately, something…came up."

After all the trouble Maddie and Angie had convincing her it was a date, the man had no right changing his mind. It *was* their first date. Something wasn't right. Cass could sense it in his careful words and disappointed tone. She jerked up to her feet and instantly regretted it. She rubbed her pounding forehead. "Please tell me your change in plans doesn't have anything to do with Gary."

"Gary?"

Puzzlement sounded clear in his voice.

"No, he has nothing to do with this."

She wanted to believe him. "Are you sure?"

"Look," he said softly. "This has nothing to do with Gary or the Martinson building."

"I think it does."

"No, it doesn't."

"He doesn't like we're thinking about leasing it together." She covered her eyes with her hands, swallowing nothing. "You told him what we talked about, didn't you?" No answer came to her question. "Jack?"

"Does this mean you want to be a joint owner of the building? You haven't even seen any of the stuff I pulled out of storage yet."

Carefully, gently, his words sounded almost fearful. His careful reaction told her she'd made the right decision.

"Have you decided on it yet?"

"Yes."

"Good."

Yes, Cass had decided right. After explaining the situation to her fifteen minutes ago, she had received Mom's agreement Jack could keep his mother's dream alive, and she could expand the bookstore while Mom handled the coffee shop and lectures.

Everyone wins.

"Look, Cass, Gary really doesn't have anything to do with my canceling our date tonight." He swallowed hard. "I have…guests staying at the ranch now."

"Guests?"

"Old friends from…my rodeo days," he said quickly. "Visiting for a few days."

She relaxed slightly at his words. "You don't want me to meet your old friends?"

"Not yet," he said. "Soon, I promise."

If there was no trust, how could two people hope to be in a relationship? If she refused to believe him in such a small thing, how could she ever hope to gain his love? And she wanted him to love her as she loved him. She'd always loved him.

"Instead of dinner," he said suddenly. "Maybe I could make you and your mother lunch. How does that sound?"

Dinner alone with Jack could wait. Once the two started working together, they would have plenty of time. "I'll have to ask Mom first, but I think we can make it."

"Can you find out now?"

A hint of guardedness lowered his voice. Cass froze in place.

"I must leave here. I mean, Greenfield, by one, one-thirty at the latest."

"I'm sure it'll be fine."

"Could you come around eleven?"

If she wanted his love, first she needed to show him her trust. "Eleven, it is."

"I'll see you then."

"Yes." The line went dead the same moment Mom's gleeful laughter rang out loud and clear downstairs, followed by a gruff male voice. Only one male since Dad's death ever made her laugh so freely. Leeriness fought inside Cass with the happiness the private investigator's presence gave her. Hopefully, Mom would still feel the same when he finally told her the truth about Billy.

Hopefully, Mom would still feel the same way about her.

****

Three hours later, Cass stood in the doorway of one of Jack's bedrooms. "Your parents did have a lot of stuff."

"I told you so." Jack leaned into the door frame, placing his hands flat on one of the plastic storage containers. "And this isn't all of it."

"There's more?" Mom glanced at her before looking at Jack. "It's all stored here?"

"Yes." He stepped back toward the opened door. "The house has four bedrooms."

"Four?" Janessa shook her head. "You have stuff in all those rooms."

"Pretty much," he said. "Except for the one I use."

"Wow." Janessa placed her right hand on one of the nearest plastic containers. "I can't wait to see what's in these storage boxes."

"These containers are filled with mostly small items and clothing," Jack added. "Bigger pieces, like old-fashioned furniture and devices from the past, are in the other rooms. I even found an old, crank telephone and a large radio from the 1940s. I doubt they work, but they look nice."

Cass scanned around the small bedroom, searching over the neatly stacked storage containers from floor to within a foot of the ceiling. Only a foot or so in front of the door stood free of any boxes.

"I can't wait to search through all the rooms," Mom said. "Like Christmas."

"Mom?"

"She's right," Jack said. "I'm looking forward to checking the stuff out, too."

Cass peered over her shoulder at a smirking Jack.

Hank leaned into the hall wall beyond, shaking his head.

This man would be good for Mom, if only he wasn't a private investigator.

Time's up, Cass. You need to tell Mom today.

"I think we should sell some of this in the bookstore," Mom said. "Don't you think that would be a good idea, Cass? Collectables from the 1940s would fit well in the overall look of the town. Most of the buildings were built during that time frame."

"If the stuff is nice, it'll fit well." Her chest tightened, breath slowing. Could she truly tell Mom about Billy? Did she really want to take away that smile? "We'll discuss it later."

"We could use that old telephone and radio as decorations for the lecture area," she added. "They would look good in there."

"Maybe."

"I could look through the rooms now, with the help of one or two of our younger employees."

"Mom, all this stuff belongs to Jack." She cleared her throat and raised her hand. "You shouldn't be making those kinds of decisions."

"Once Mr. Martinson signs the co-lease agreement," Jack said. "And Mr. Cobert and Gary finish writing up our working contract, all of this will belong to Fontaine-Rogers, Inc. I have no problem with your mother looking through the containers."

"Rogers-Fontaine," Mom said.

"That's right." Cass looked behind her. "Two against one, we win."

Deep male laughter roared. "Looks like you're outnumbered, Jack."

"Yes, it does look that way." Jack settled his hand flat on her back. "But, hopefully, not for long."

Cass twisted to the man. "And what do you mean by that?"

No smirk lifted the corners of his mouth now. Yet, what did shine from his eyes stopped her breath. "Jack, what do you mean?"

"In time," he said gently. "You'll find out in time."

"Jack?" Mom turned and stepped toward the intense man. "Cass might be an adult, but she's still my baby girl. I won't allow another man to hurt her."

"That will never happen, Janessa." He stood tall, tightening his hands at his sides. "Nothing has ever been able to change my feelings for your daughter."

"Good."

Jack had just shown he cared in front of the one person she loved more than anything. He could never take it back now. In time, he would release the words she most wanted to hear.

Mom stepped through the door and grabbed Hank's arm. "Come and help me with lunch."

"Wow." Hank stumbled a step, righting his stance.

"Do I have a choice?"

Mom had never been so obvious before. "Want my help, Mom?"

"No, honey." Wrapping an arm around the man's waist, she grinned. "Hank and I have everything under control."

Cass stepped out of the crowded room and a few feet down the hall before firm arms enveloped her waist from behind.

"I like your mother and Hank, but I wish they weren't here today."

"Really?" Cocking her head backward, she studied him. "Then you shouldn't have changed our plans at the last minute. I was really looking forward to having dinner with you tonight."

He brushed his lips over her cheek. "I'm glad to hear that."

"I'm not complaining, though." She twisted around in his loosening arms, pressing her body against his firm front. "Mom dragged Hank away so we could be alone up here. She likes you."

Jack lowered his gaze and shifted to his left. Something was different about this man today, but she couldn't quite put her finger on it. Freedom, a lightness that wasn't a part of him only yesterday, shimmered in the air. Like a heavy weight had been lifted from his shoulders.

"Honey."

A whispered breath warmed her ear.

"I promise to make dinner next weekend."

If only she could find closure to her own problem, then she could find the same type of peace. Yet, telling Mom would wipe away her new-found smile, and she didn't want that to happen.

He pushed her gently away from his warm body.

She barely noticed. Only one thing stayed in her mind, the lie she'd told Mom. Or rather, the truth she'd left unsaid.

Oh, Dad, why did I listen?

"Something came up. Someone."

She twisted around. "Have you ever hidden something important from your dad?"

He stepped back, eyes widening. "Hidden something?"

"Something you knew he should know, but you just didn't have the strength to tell him."

"My dad and I never kept things from each other." He studied her intently. "Why are you asking?"

The weight of her lie settled hard on her shoulders, sending her sliding down the wall to the floor. "I should've told Mom years ago. I shouldn't have listened to Dad." She pushed away his hands. "I understood his reasoning for hiding Billy's death, but I should've told her, too. For three years, she's believed a lie. One that led her to Hank."

"Billy's death?"

"I need to tell her the truth." She looked at him. "Yet, how do I do that? She's just beginning to come back to life. If I tell her now, it'll turn her back into the person she was after Dad's death. To that quiet, closed-up woman again."

He pulled away. "No, you can't tell her."

She glared. "Mom is not a weak person, Jack."

"I know." Crouching, he gathered her into his arms and stood easily.

She tried to fight.

He tightened his hold. "All I'm saying is now might not be the right time."

"Then when is, Jack?" Slamming her dangling arms into his thigh, she wiggled until he released his hold slightly. She leaned back and stared, tears wetting down her cheekbones. "I need to tell her today. I'm sure Hank's found out the truth, but for some reason, he hasn't told her yet."

"He cares about her."

"Today." She wiped at her tears, took in a long breath, and stepped back. "I'll tell her today."

****

Oh, if only Jack hadn't promised her brother time to get everything together. If only he hadn't promised to stay quiet until Pete was ready to let his family know he was alive.

"Yes, today," Cass repeated. "I should be the one to tell her, not Hank."

The sweet, warm girl he'd liked a decade ago was suddenly replaced by the more professional woman he loved now. Tomorrow, Pete had promised he'd go and see his family. Jack needed to find a way to keep the mother and daughter apart until then.

"Lunch is ready," Janessa yelled up the stairs. "You two better come down before Hank eats it all."

Hank? Yes, he would ask the older man to take Janessa away for the day.

"Leave some for Cass and Jack." A scraping sound echoed up the stairs, followed by a high-pitched cry. "Hank, what are you doing?"

"Take a guess?" Hank said. "I'm sure you can figure it out."

"Stop it."

Jack grinned. The unmistakable sound of female laughter told him Janessa wasn't being truthful.

"We're not alone here," Janessa said. "Hank?"

Yes, he doubted he'd have a problem getting Hank to help him.

Gruff male laughter followed another laughing half-hearted protest, shadowed by an unexpected breathless silence.

"Mom will need his support when I tell her."

Maybe Hank had the right idea. He wasn't sure what was going on between the two older people, but he could make a logical guess. Every time he looked in the man's direction this afternoon, he'd been staring at Janessa. The man didn't even bother hiding his interest.

"Let's go eat," Cass said. "Then Mom and I will go to Dad's grave."

No, she couldn't do that. His heartbeat quickened in his chest. He needed to keep the two separated until he could talk to Hank. *Think, Fontaine.*

"I'm hungry."

If all else fails…

"Me, too." Traveling his hands around her waist, he gathered her into his arms. "But not necessarily for food."

"Jack?" Her eyes widened, a slight grin moving over her lips. "What are you doing?"

"Hey, why should your mom and Hank have all the fun?" He brushed his lips along the edge of her jaw over to her chin, feeling her resistance melt away. He lifted his mouth from hers. "Want me to show you what I think they might be doing?" Like he'd hoped, Cass shook her head and peered up at him.

"This isn't stopping me from doing what I need to

do."

"Not trying to do that." His lips touched hers, sending his heart pounding against his chest. Her breath whispered warm when he lifted slightly away. "Just want to kiss you."

"Then kiss me." Desperation sounded in her voice. "Please."

"No, not like this." He jerked his head back. "No."

"Yes, like this." She captured his mouth, wrapping her arms tight around his waist. Her tongue teased over his bottom lip before sliding easy inside his opened mouth, attacking his with a low moan.

He needed to stop this, now. "Your mother is downstairs."

As if walking out of a fog, she froze in his arms. "Oh, what am I doing?"

"Wrong time," he whispered. "For that type of kiss."

"I shouldn't have done that."

"Done what?"

She backed away. "The one and only time I've ever acted so…forward, the man was gone the next morning."

"And you thought you were pregnant, right?" he asked.

"How did you know that?" She backed away, stiff. Then she nodded and relaxed. "Small towns, right?"

He just shrugged.

"Of course," she said. "Well, anyway, I promised Angie and Maddie I'd never do that again."

"Do what?" No matter how hard he tried, he couldn't hide the beginning of his grin. Thankfully, she hadn't noticed his reaction. "Have sex?"

"Of course not." She pressed on his chest. "They would never ask that of me, and I certainly wouldn't have agreed."

A snort blasted from his mouth before he could clamp it shut. Her eyes flashed heat.

"Oh, you think getting pregnant by a one-night stand is amusing."

"No." He swallowed down his laughter. "Okay, maybe a little."

"Stop laughing."

"I'm not laughing."

He touched her face lightly. "And you're not pregnant."

"Well," she sputtered. "No, I'm not. But for a couple weeks, I feared I was."

He fought his grin.

"And, if I was, I had no idea how to let Johnny in on the secret."

His eyes narrowed. "So, the loser's name was Johnny?"

She studied him for a long moment before turning and moving toward the staircase. "I'm not getting into that predicament again."

"Good." He followed her to the stairs. "And, for your information, I don't do one-night stands anymore."

"Wonderful." Placing her hands on her hips, she twisted toward him. "Because when I sleep with you, I expect you to be there in the morning."

When, not *if*? His laughter fled. Did she even realize what she said? Damn, but he loved this woman. That man who'd left her sleeping alone the day after had no clue what he'd passed up.

"If you're not willing to do that," she said. "Then you might as well leave now."

"Honey?"

She stopped halfway on the stairs and peeked up.

"When you and I sleep together." He set the tip of his index finger against the side of her nose. "Or rather, when you and I make love, I won't make the same mistake that other guy did."

"Promise?" The hall light flashed in her eyes, and then she smiled. "You do promise?"

"As long as you're next to me when I wake up," he whispered. "I'll be next to you."

"Oh, there you are," Hank said. "It's safe to come down now."

Jack turned in time to catch the man enveloping Janessa and walking her back into the kitchen. Bright, warm laughter flowed out of the room.

"I'm glad Mom found someone new." Cass moved to the bottom of the stairs. "I just wish he wasn't a PI."

"Things have a way of working out, honey."

"You think so?"

"Trust me."

She led him downstairs and through the living room area. Then, she stopped suddenly at the kitchen door and turned.

No glare darkened her eyes now. No frustration or desperation lowered her mouth into a frown. Peace flowed from her, something like hope warmed in her look.

"I don't know why, but I do trust you."

Warmth filled his entire body, settling close to his heart. "Good."

She pushed at the kitchen door, and then froze

again. She studied her hands before nodding and glancing at him. "Maybe I'm just being a coward, but I think I'll wait to tell Mom."

Yes, no doubt about it. Everything would work out.

Chapter Twenty-Four

Her mouth dried the second Cass wandered into the kitchen, but she ignored it at the sight of Mom's sparkling eyes. She'd known about Billy's death for three years, so a few more days wouldn't do any more damage. If she kept repeating that, maybe she'd start believing it.

"Come on in," Mom said. "Everything's ready."

"Thanks, Mom."

A large platter filled with assorted luncheon meats and cheeses sat in the center of the table. A bag of sliced whole wheat bread next to it. Another smaller plate held cut-up pieces of tomatoes and onions with a small bowl of shredded lettuce and an opened big jar of salad dressing, with the knife still inside it, sitting next to the bread. A smaller jar of mustard sat next to that. A colorful bowl of fruit sat on the far side of the table, close to the edge. Apples, oranges, and grapes sat beside a few bananas.

"Looks good," Jack offered. "I'm starving."

"Sit down. I'll get you some iced tea." Mom grabbed a pitcher from the table and poured it into two glasses. "Here."

"Need to put your own sugar in it," Hank grumbled. "Janessa doesn't like sweet stuff, it seems."

"No problem." Jack took the glass and stepped toward the counter, snatching up the sugar container.

"Better to do it yourself."

"Exactly." Janessa handed her a glass before settling back into her chair. "Too much sugar is not good."

"I know, Mom."

"I know *you* know, honey." She winked. "Unfortunately, other people don't."

Another grumble sounded in the room.

Jack pulled out a chair across from Janessa's. He sat. Taking a long drink of his tea, he grinned at the older man.

Hank only shook his head, picked up his sandwich, and took a big bite.

Cass took a sip of her tea.

Jack focused on his glass, not looking her way.

Her dad had acted the same way whenever her mom was upset. She glanced across the table and grinned. "You look happy, Mom."

"I am, honey."

Cass sneaked a look at the still-grumbling older man. "I'm glad."

"Are you really?" Intensity shined from her look. "It's only been a little over a year."

"It's been long enough, Mom." Mom's smile beamed, warming her face with its unexpected delight. Maybe her father had been right. Her dad had a hard time showing his feelings, but she'd known he loved her. He'd always done what he thought was best. Even for Billy. She might not have gotten everything she'd wanted, but she always had everything she needed. Her father had a hard time saying the words, but she'd never doubted he loved her until after Billy left town.

Sudden understanding settled inside her as one

memory after another flowed through her mind into her heart. Her father rarely said *I love you* to any of his family. He was always there, though. Whenever she needed him, he was there.

"What are you thinking about, honey?"

How could she have forgotten that? "I miss Dad."

Tears glistened in her eyes. "Do you really?"

"Yes."

"I'm glad."

"Of course, she's missing her father." Hank placed his half-finished sandwich onto his plate. "Why wouldn't she miss him?"

Jack had the same questioning look on his face. She didn't answer his unspoken question, though. Mom understood the puzzling conversation, and that was enough. Just as her mom was moving forward, she was slowly letting go of the misunderstanding she'd experienced with her father.

"Hank, least you can do is put on more vegetables," Janessa said. "Eating too much processed meat isn't healthy."

"I told you." Hank looked over his sandwich. "I like meat."

"That's obvious." She let out an exasperated sigh. "But you also need to balance it by eating fruits and vegetables."

Cass had to smile at her statement. How many times had she heard her tell Dad the same thing?

"I put some on this one." Hank lifted the overloaded mess in one hand, peeling the top piece of bread away from the side. "See."

Yes, a small piece of onion, lettuce, and a little bit of tomato. But that was not even remotely enough to do any good.

"There's some on it." Jack reached over and grabbed the bread, took out two slices, and offered the package. "Seems like more than enough."

"Right," the other man agreed. "And I promise I'll eat an apple or something."

Janessa glanced over at her, then at Hank, then back at her again. "Just like your father."

Hank muttered a few choice words before taking a large bite.

"I remember." Cass took a piece of ham and provolone cheese from the platter. "But I don't remember Dad ever grumbling like Hank."

"He never did." Her mom glanced over at the older man. "He knew I only wanted the best for him."

"When I need my mom," Hank said. "All I need do is go visit her in Florida."

A very unladylike snort rose in the air, surprising Cass as much as upsetting her mom.

Jack fought a grin.

Hank's smile widened around his chewing mouth.

Pink rose high in Mom's cheekbones, spreading lightly over her entire face.

Was she blushing?

"I don't remember Mom doing that." Hank studied her reaction with wide-open intense eyes. "But I like it."

"Like what?" Jack asked. "The snort or the blush?"

"Both," Hank said softly. "But personally, I like the blush better. I like I can still embarrass a gorgeous woman."

Mom glanced down at the table. "Hank, that'll be enough of that."

Yes, she was blushing.

"Yeah, it's nice, isn't it?" Jack asked.

Until Jack wiggled his eyebrows, Cass hadn't even realized Mom wasn't the only one flushing.

Jack winked. "Like mother, like daughter."

****

The rest of the weekend went by quickly, too quickly to talk to Mom about Billy. Every time Cass picked up the phone, she slammed it down without even dialing. Telling Mom over the phone wasn't the right way to go anyway. Unfortunately, one thing after another kept her from visiting her until Sunday night, and then no one was at the house.

Now on Monday morning, she was still weighed down by three years of guilt.

The chime over the store's entrance rang out. She leaped out of her chair and moved toward her office door. Instead of Janessa, Lucy came through the neatly spaced, unfilled shelves in the main room. The place looked so much larger without the mess of books and unopened boxes and coffee shop equipment lying all around the floor.

Cass stepped into the sunlight beaming through the clean front window. All she needed was to restock the shelves and the place would be ready to reopen on Memorial Day.

"Good morning, Cass." Lucy stopped at the door and grinned. "This place looks a lot different than it did the last time I was here."

"Mom and some of my younger employees cleaned all weekend," she said. "Jack and Hank moved all the books to the storage room and the tables and chairs into the other building." She froze at her words. "Oh, I hope that was okay. We signed the lease with Mr. Martinson, but we still haven't set up the new corporation with your father and Gary."

"Fontaine-Rogers, you mean?" Lucy grinned. "Or have you and your mother convinced Jack it should be Rogers-Fontaine?"

"We decided to go alphabetically."

"Good way to go." Her grin widened. "I might be a traitor to the female species, but I like the first one better anyway."

"Don't tell Mom this." Cass leaned in closer to the other woman. "But so do I."

Lucy made a zipping motion over her lips.

"I just made some coffee," she said. "Would you like a cup?"

"That sounds good." Lucy stepped toward the office door. "I got up late this morning and didn't have time to make any."

Cass nodded, and then moved back into her office. She waved a hand toward the seats in front of her desk before grabbing a second cup out of the cabinet below the coffeemaker. "I like favored cream in mine."

"French vanilla?"

"One of my favorites."

"Mine, too."

Cass poured two cups and spooned some creamer into one. She waited for Lucy to place a briefcase on the other chair before handing her the small bottle and a spoon. Grabbing the hot cups, she wandered around her desk and set one in front of Lucy before settling down in her seat.

"French vanilla creamer." She sighed and stirred a spoonful into her coffee. "One of my guilty pleasures."

All Cass did was grin. The barely there hint of vanilla rose in the air.

"Never smoked or did drugs, and stopped drinking my senior year of college," Lucy admitted. "And I haven't had sex in…"—she looked up into the air—"seven months." She took a sip of her coffee, held it, and then swallowed. "I'm allowed at least one bad habit."

"Seven months, is it?"

Her lips pinched at the ends. "Now, how did I know you would comment on that?"

"It just seems like a long time." She couldn't tell if Lucy was angry or if she was only joking. "If you want to hear the truth, it's been a while for me, too."

"Yes, maybe." Her grin softened the edges of her mouth. "But, at least, you have someone more than willing to fix that problem."

Yes, I do.

"For me, there is no one." Lucy shook her head. "Greenfield is such a small town."

Cass could feel her pain. "There are a lot of men in the world, so you shouldn't give up yet."

Lucy only shrugged and took another sip of her coffee. Setting the cup on the desk, she picked up her briefcase and opened it. "Gary and Jack will be here soon, so I guess I should get all Dad's paperwork ready."

She sat straight in her seat, clutching the cup tight in her right hand. "I can't wait to get this corporation started."

"I can tell." Lucy handed her a set of papers. "Dad placed all the information in the agreement about your new venture. While we're waiting for Jack and Gary, you should look through it. I think he got everything right, but just in case…"

"All right." She placed her cup to the side of her desk and took the legal papers. "I read it at your father's office, but I should look it over again."

"Yes," Lucy said. "Dad discussed the agreement last you saw him. All you really need is to make sure all the information pertaining to Fontaine-Rogers is correct." She looked up suddenly. "Oh, Gary lengthened the period for either of you to opt out if you want from three days to five. Other than that, everything else is the same."

"No, I don't think I'll be changing my mind." Cass set the thick packet of pages on the desk and glanced at the first page. "It's a good thing we didn't decide on the other name."

Lucy shrugged. "The first time you mentioned setting up the company, you used his last name first."

She jerked her head back. "I did?"

"Yes."

"I don't remember that." She flipped to the next page, skimming through the entire document. "Everything looks correct."

"Good." Lucy snatched her cup and settled into her seat. "Now, we just need to wait on Jack."

"You know something?"

She looked over her cup.

"When I first found out someone else was interested in the building, I thought I would have a fight on my hands." Cass looked out of the office door into the bright, new-looking store. "It wasn't as bad as I thought it would be."

"No, it went easy on my end, too." Lucy sipped the

liquid and then sighed. "But I doubt it'll stay as easy, once you and Jack start deciding on what to do with the building."

Cass had a taste of that just the other day about the upstairs apartment. She wanted to rent it out. He wanted to decorate it with some of his mother's old furniture and charge people to see it.

Stubborn guy.

"Gary told me today he's insisting on turning the upstairs into some kind of 1940s apartment." Lucy set her cup down. "Like a small museum."

She gazed at the forgotten cup near the document. "Not just that apartment, but the back room, also. He thinks it'll be better."

"It's different." Lucy gazed past her shoulder and then back to her face. "Those quotes you got for redoing the upstairs to modernize it seems on the high end."

"But we will be earning rent every month." Cass shook her head, soft hair flipping against her cheekbones. "And I'm using some of the money Dad left me to pay for the bulk of the cost."

"After you sign the agreement, all that money will belong to Fontaine-Rogers." Tone neutral, she took a drink of her coffee. "All three of you will have a say in how it's spent."

Yes, Cass understood that. "The contractor I want didn't have the lowest bid, and Jack thinks we should go with the lowest bidder."

The chime over the door interrupted her comment.

"That must be your new partner and his lawyer now."

Gary wandered a few feet into the room. "Wow,

this place looks so different."

"Amazing what a bit of elbow grease can do." Jack moved through the room, stopping at the office door. "Cass's mother worked me like a dog all weekend."

"Hank helped," Cass said. "So did Jenny and Patrick."

"Right?" An eyebrow arched upward over his smirk. "If you call what those two kids were doing helping, then they helped."

"Well, they're kids." Cass fought down her own grin. "And they like each other. Did you really expect them to work all that hard?"

"No." Jack shrugged. "But I didn't expect your mother and Hank to start acting the same way."

Neither had Cass.

"Where did Janessa meet that man anyway?" Lucy asked.

"San Antonio," Jack added simply. "He's a private investigator."

"I need to get to the city more often." Lucy set her cup down and rearranged the papers. "All the decent guys in Greenfield are taken or have their sights set on someone else."

"Let's get on with business." Gary moved to stand beside Lucy. "I have an appointment at eleven today."

"Yes," Lucy said. "Dad went through the agreement with Cass last week, and she agreed to it. Today, she looked it over again and told me all the information about Fontaine-Rogers is correct. Cass is ready to sign now." Standing from her chair, she faced Gary. "Is your client ready?"

"More than ready." Jack slammed down into the same chair. "Give me that document, Gary, and a pen."

Gary grinned and opened his briefcase, pulling out another set of papers. He set it and a pen down on the desk.

Lucy handed her a pen at the same time.

They signed the documents together. Then they switched the documents and signed again, placing the pens on top.

Swallowing down any lingering misgivings about the venture, she glanced up at a grinning Jack. "There, done."

"And Fontaine-Rogers is born." Jack gathered up her pages with his and handed them to Gary and Lucy. "Now, the fun begins."

Thirty-five minutes after Jack left, she sat alone at her desk. Nothing was finalized about the upstairs apartment, but she wasn't too unhappy.

Cass really shouldn't allow him to distract her from every disagreement in such a high-handed way, though.

If only he wasn't such a good kisser.

Chapter Twenty-Five

Two hours later, Jack parked near the front porch of his house and exited his truck. He moved toward the steps and nodded at Pete.

"Hey, Jack." He stood, a pleasant grin lifting away his sad frown. "Looks like everything went well."

"Fontaine-Rogers, LLC is official." Jack tamped down his excitement. "Now, the hard part begins." A soft laugh echoed from Pete's throat. A sad sound, maybe, but at least it was something. "Cass and I have been arguing about the apartment since signing the agreement," Jack admitted, with a grin. "But I do enjoy quarreling with your sister."

"If I remember her correctly, you'll probably regret going into business with her. She likes to have her way. She must have driven...Dad crazy." A bittersweet look played over his features. "Or maybe they drove each other crazy. They are so much alike."

He shook his head. "You're remembering more and more?"

"Everything," he whispered. "Too fast, too quickly."

Jack couldn't even imagine what his old friend was going through. He hadn't a clue what to say, so he only settled on the steps. No one could help him, anyway. He needed to find his way through his returning memories in his own way and time.

"It's funny. The one thing I wanted during the last three years was to regain my memory, but now…" He stepped into the yard and glanced toward the old barn. "I don't like what I'm remembering."

"You're thinking about the way you fought with your dad, aren't you?" A range of different emotions stole across his face, ones Jack couldn't quite catch. Hard guilt finally settled into his features, mixed with the look of overwhelming sadness.

"My dad must have thought I hated him." He crossed his arms around his waist and looked at the ground. "I loved him, Jack. I really loved my dad."

"He knew that."

Pete didn't move from his place.

"Did you visit his grave yet?"

"Not yet." He quickly turned toward him, lifting his arms and then letting them drop. "I just need a little more time."

"You had the whole weekend, Pete."

"I'll go today," he said. "I promise."

Was he afraid? But why would he be frightened? The man he'd met a decade ago hadn't been afraid of anything, and he seemed even stronger now. "You have changed." He stayed quiet for so long Jack suspected he hadn't heard him.

"I'm a much better man now." He stood tall. "Much better."

Jack rose from the porch step and moved toward him. "You're different, not necessarily better. The Billy I knew was a good guy."

"A good guy wouldn't have put his family through what I put them through." His shoulders hunched, head hanging down. "I'm not good."

Jack wished he knew what to say to help him.

"He would've made things right with them before it was…too late."

"Your mom and sister are still here, Pete." He shot from the steps. Pete needed to visit his father's grave, and he would make sure he did it today. Jack raced toward his truck and opened the door, beckoning for him to get inside the vehicle. "I'm taking you to the cemetery. Now."

Pete froze in place and then squared his shoulders and moved to the truck. "You're right."

"It helps, Pete." Jack waited at the passenger door. "The first place I went when I arrived in Greenfield was my mother's grave."

He peered his way. "And it helped you?"

"Yes."

Pete slipped into the truck and slammed the door.

Jack backed the truck out of the drive and headed toward the main road. Fifteen quiet minutes later, he slowed at the entrance of the well-maintained cemetery on the far side of town. "You ready?"

He nodded.

"Good."

The warm sun shone brightly through the windshield when he turned onto the grounds and slowed to a crawl. Curving around the backside of the cemetery, he drove down a single-car lane and pulled to the side at its halfway point. He stopped behind a small vehicle and opened his door. The passenger side door opened at the same time he spied the owner of the car near one of the graves—and froze.

****

Cassie and her mom turned at the same time.

Janessa reached her arms out and fell hard to the ground.

Cass stood frozen in place.

"Mom? Drea?" Pete reached the stricken woman.

Warmth rushed back into Jack's limbs. He opened the door and slid from his seat, studying the three.

Janessa cried out Pete's birth name and reached up toward him.

Pete pulled her off the ground gently, settled her onto her feet, and then stood away.

Cass moved in beside their mother. She looked at Jack, hard painful shock widened her eyes. Sadness mixing with disappointed anger. She sighed and glanced back at her brother, a soft smile lifting her lips.

"It's you," Janessa said. "It's really you."

"Yes, Mom."

She sprang forward and wrapped her arms around her tall son.

Cass stood frozen in her original place, looking toward the ground rather than at the two in front of her.

Jack lifted his right hand and then dropped it. This was something she needed to get through on her own.

"I was beginning…" Janessa started.

"Dad's…"

"He's gone." She pulled slightly away. "Last year."

"I'll never…get the chance to tell him…I'm sorry."

The older woman didn't say anything, only continued to study him.

Total forgiveness widened her eyes when she looked in Jack's direction, mixed with a layer of bewilderment and confusion. So many questions raced across her face. She didn't ask any of them.

"Can you ever…forgive me?" Pete touched her

face and then dropped his hand. "I don't…"

"Forgive you?" Mom settled her look on her son. "You've done nothing to forgive, Billy."

"Maybe I've done nothing to you." His voice echoed rough with unshed tears. "But I did hurt…Dad. And I'm sorry."

"He'll understand, honey." Janessa touched his face lightly. "You can still talk to him."

"He's gone." He swallowed. "I can never tell…him how…I feel."

Janessa cupped her hands lightly on his cheeks and glanced back at her quiet daughter.

Cass looked directly at Jack, with an unreadable expression flushing over her.

He lowered his head. He deserved it. Her brother was alive, and he hadn't told her.

"Cass and I talk to him all the time."

Cass moved beside Janessa and reached out for her lean brother.

He wrapped one arm around each woman, a sad-happy smile softening his mouth.

Cass stepped back. "I'm so glad you're home."

Jack backed away until the front of his truck stopped him. He didn't belong here now, experiencing this family's reunion.

Cass had mentioned the two of them had visited the site a few days ago, so no one should've been here today. Yet, maybe their being here was for the best. Pete needed to let his family know he was still alive, and Cass and Janessa needed to find out what had happened three years ago.

Shaking away his awkwardness, he eased open the truck door and slipped inside. He never took his gaze off the three. Only Cass glanced his way when the diesel engine roared to life.

She moved from the others and walked toward him. The sadness and tears were gone now, only disappointment and anger darkening her features. She sighed and jerked around, not looking as he drove down the dirt path to the main road.

He gazed into the rearview mirror, spying the mother and son still facing the grave, arms wrapped around each other's waist. Yet, all he could focus on was Cass's defeated form frozen on the opposite side of her family.

But why should she feel so down when everything was well again? Her brother had returned home, and she now leased the Martinson building to expand her business, so why such a long face? Why did she look as though her world had just imploded? "What is wrong, Cass?"

He slowed the truck and pulled it to the side of the road, not taking his gaze off her.

She looked toward the road and then walked toward the exit of the graveyard. A minute later, she slipped inside the truck, still not saying a word.

"Are you okay?"

She sighed low. "You...lied."

"What?" He jerked his head toward her. "I've never—"

"No, I don't want to hear any more lies." She glared, wiping her unshed tears. "When did you know?"

He clamped his hands on the steering wheel. "Cass, I—"

"Just answer my question." A wet glare shined from her green eyes, wetting down her face. "When did you find out Billy was…alive? Or did you always know?"

"It's not what you think," he said. "Hank told—"

"Hank?" She twisted in her seat, back straight and hands tight. "Even that PI knew?"

"Cass." He raised his right hand.

She stiffened and backed away. "Why did that PI know?"

He dropped the hand onto the seat between them. "I don't understand why—"

"That's right." Her hands fisted in her lap. "You don't understand."

"Cass?"

"I don't want to hear it." Grasping at the door handle, she crashed the door open and collapsed out of the truck. Her shoulder sagged low as she dragged in loud, deep breaths. "We should've never signed that document." She tightened her back and turned toward him. "I refuse to work with someone who hid something so important."

No, she can't be serious about dissolving our hard-fought agreement. "I didn't hide anything, Cass," he said. "Pete—"

"Pete?" Tears slid down her cheeks.

He lifted his hand again, only to drop it back onto the seat.

"He changed his name. Why would he do that?"

Opening his door, he raced around the truck.

She raised both hands and stopped his forward momentum.

He halted a few feet from her, clamped hands falling to his side. "He lost his memory."

"Yet, he remembered you." She backed a few more

feet, squeezing her arms around her waist. She caught her breath. "You knew he was alive, Jack. You've probably known all along, since…" She widened her eyes. "You knew when we all went to the buffet in San Antonio. Both you and Hank knew then."

Jack held his breath and then let it out. "He asked me—"

"I told you how bad I felt not telling my mother." Tears rolled freely down her cheeks now. "And, still, you refused to tell me he wasn't dead. You refused."

"Cass, it's not like that."

"Shut up, Jack." She dragged in one hard breath after another. She stood straight and tall, back stiff with clamped hands. "Just shut up."

He closed his eyes tight and then opened them. "Let me explain."

She lowered her head and backed from the truck, not stopping until she was halfway up the dirt path. "I don't want to talk, Jack. I don't want to see you again."

"What are you saying?" He jerked straight. "Cass?"

"Never again." She raced into the cemetery and slipped inside her car, pulling onto the path leading to the roadway.

Janessa called her name.

Pete raced toward the vehicle.

It sped down the path and out of the cemetery.

A hard hand clamped on his shoulder an indeterminate time later, a softer one landed on his back a second after. "What did you say to her?"

"I didn't say anything, Pete." One of the reasons he'd returned to Greenfield was to apologize for his part in her brother moving away; now, he had another reason to be sorry. He had suspected her brother might still be alive—and he hadn't told her.

Chapter Twenty-Six

"Your brother is alive?" Angie leaned toward the desk, pushing at the tablet. "You've seen him?"

"Yes, at my father's grave." Cass slipped from the office chair and moved around her desk, settling into the visitor seat next to Angie. "I still can't believe it."

"Billy's alive?"

"This is good news." Maddie jerked from the door and backed into the main store area. She stopped near the center bookshelf and glanced at Cass. "Why the long face?"

Cass sighed and sat back, forcing her body to relax by taking one breath after another. Maddie and Angie had accepted her news better than she'd expected. At first, they had looked dumbfounded and then disbelieving. They only seemed as shocked as she was when she turned and watched her brother get out of Jack's truck now.

He'd known all along he was alive, and he hadn't told her. Even after knowing how upset she was about keeping it from Mom, he still hadn't let her in on the secret. How could she trust the man after his lies? How could she possibly own a business with him? She didn't even want to think of that now.

Picking up a pen, she wrote a reminder to call Lucy's father. Cass needed to get out of the agreement. No way could she work with someone she couldn't trust. More importantly, someone who didn't trust her. If he didn't think it important enough to tell her Billy was alive, what else would he hide? She couldn't risk it.

"After all, he did lose his memory, you said." Maddie raised both hands and slapped them to her thighs. "That's probably why no one from the hospital let you know he'd been in an accident. No one knew how to get ahold of you."

Maddie could be right, but that still didn't change her mind about working with Jack. He'd known about Billy all along, and he didn't see the need to tell her. Is that why he'd distracted her before going down to the kitchen that day? Is that why he kissed her?

"Billy's alive." A sweet smile hovered over Angie's mouth. "He's really alive."

"He changed his name to Pete." Cass shook her head. "I don't know if I'll ever get used to that name."

"He changed his name?" Angie leaned toward her. "Why would he do that?"

The ding of her front door rang loud in the sudden silence. She clamped her hands on the desk, inhaling in a focused breath.

"Billy?" Maddie ran through the reorganized store area, reaching her hands out toward him. "Wow, you look good for a dead guy."

Billy's—no. Pete's deep laughter burst out. "How do you know I'm not a ghost?"

"Because you can't hug a spirit," she mumbled. "And I can hug you."

Mom's lilting laughter rang out, free and unrestricted.

Cass liked the hum of it. Tears flowed down her face, both happy and sad ones.

"You need to let my son go, Maddie. You're suffocating him."

All Maddie did was snort.

Angie glanced at her before sighing and drifting toward the office door. She arranged her signature model smile and walked into the main store area.

Cass followed her out the office door in time to see her brother's stunned reaction.

A beaming smile warmed Mom's features a few steps from Billy... No, he's Pete now.

"Hello, Billy." Angie stopped near the grinning Maddie. "I thought you—"

"You thought I was dead," he said gently. "Jack told me."

Cass let out a soft sigh, but it was still loud enough to reach the others in the room. Four faces turned her way, showing different reactions. The bell dinged over the door again, drawing her attention to the entrance.

Jack wandered in.

"You have a lot of nerve showing up here," Maddie said. "Cass is mad."

"I know." He took a step closer. "That's why I'm here. To find out exactly why."

"Why?" *How can you say that with a straight face?* "You know why, Jack."

"No, I don't." He ran his hands through his hair. "Not really."

She swallowed her harsh words.

"We need to talk."

"No." She raised her hands in front of her and backed into the office. "I have nothing to say."

"Drea, I think you should talk to him." Pete disconnected from Maddie's side hug and moved to stand beside Angie. "I made him promise not to tell you."

"Yes, listen to your brother, Cassandra." Mom stepped past the three younger people, stopping a foot behind Jack. "A promise is a promise, after all."

"That doesn't matter." She refused to look her way, traveling around the desk. "I need to call my lawyer."

"Why?" Jack moved into her office, not stopping until he stood in front of her desk. "Are you changing your mind...about Fontaine-Rogers?"

"Yes." Weak knees landed her hard into the chair. "I can't do business—"

"Cass?" Maddie yelled a bit louder than necessary. "Angie and I are taking your brother to get some coffee. We'll see you later."

"No." She jerked off the chair and raced toward the front area. The chime on the door rang loud, right before a slamming sounded clear in the air. She entered a silent room. "No."

"Cassandra." Mom stood with both hands on her hips in front of the large front window. "What are you doing?"

A heaviness weighed down her body. Her heart hurt. "I can't talk now, Mom."

Janessa studied her for a long moment before nodding. "I'll be up in your apartment when you can."

This time, the entrance door closed with a soft thump.

A slight movement brought Cass's gaze to the silent man standing in the middle of the room. Nothing showed on his closed features now, except for narrowed eyes and a deep frown. "I need to think, Jack." She twisted toward the office door. "Please, just leave."

****

Jack watched her shoulders sag, head bowed low. He saw her pain but didn't understand it. Why was she getting so upset? Shouldn't she be happy seeing her brother alive and well? Shouldn't she be happy for Janessa? Sure, he didn't let her know her brother was alive, but that shouldn't make her so upset. Something more had to be bothering her.

"You need to go," she said softly. "I'm reopening my store on Wednesday, and I still have a few things to do."

"What about the other building?" He moved closer, raising his right hand to lift her chin.

She backed away.

He dropped his arm. "What about the coffee shop and my mother's thrift shop?"

"I...changed my mind about that."

"You're serious? You want out of our deal?"

She stiffened for a second.

Shining wet eyes stared hard at him, a fleeting confused, torn look moved through them before blankness arose.

"Yes."

This had something to do with their conversation at the cemetery. Could she truly be upset he didn't tell her about Billy? Did she really believe he'd lied?

"You...don't trust me, Jack," she whispered. "Just like my...father."

Her father? What did her father have to do with it? "I do trust you, Cass."

"No," she said. "If you did, you would've told me about Billy."

"He didn't want anyone to know." He fought to

keep his words light. "I promised your brother I wouldn't tell you or your mother until he had the chance to visit your father's grave. I promised him time to process his grief a bit."

She crossed her arms tight around her waist. "And yet you told Hank."

"Hank told me, Cass." His voice hardened. He didn't try to soften it this time. "I didn't know anything about the mix-up at the hospital until that PI called me a few weeks ago."

"A few weeks ago?" Another tear traced down her cheek. She swiped it away with more force than necessary. "You knew Billy was still alive for weeks?"

Seeing her pain froze him in place. "No, I didn't."

"So, now you're still being untruthful with me?" She twisted away. "Just leave, Jack."

"I'm not lying." He dragged in a needed breath. "I am not."

"Go."

The pain and anger in that one simple word brought emotions to the surface. Confusion, anxiety, and disbelief at her attitude. His entire body tensed, heart booming quick and fast in his chest. Could she truly believe he would ever be untruthful? That he could be that awful toward someone he'd always loved? He always loved. The beat of his heart slowed. He relaxed in the door frame.

"Just go." Her voice trembled with unshed tears. "I don't have anything more to say."

She needed time to think through the situation with Pete's sudden appearance. Jack would give her that time.

"Lucy's father will be calling your lawyer," she

said. "I think we shouldn't work together."

No way was he allowing her to change their deal. "I don't agree."

Her shoulders sagged under another exhaled breath. "You need to leave, Jack."

No, that was the last thing he needed to do.

"You need to leave now." She did turn then, unshed tears flashing in her glance. "I want you to go."

He clutched his hands tight. He so wanted to wipe away her tears, but the action would not be appreciated now. He'll give her time. "I'll leave…for now."

She didn't say a word.

He exited the office and wandered through the empty store area, stepping through the front entrance and turning toward the diner. Soft voices echoed when he entered the bright, warm building and noticed his old friend. Ignoring the glares from the two women sitting with him, he settled into a booth a few tables away.

Less than a minute later, Pete slid a cup of coffee across the table before settling into the opposite seat with his half-filled mug. He gulped down a swallow of the dark liquid and studied him closely. "You look like crap."

No smile lined his mouth now. No echo of familiar laughter. Instead, a host of questions burned in his eyes, questions he wasn't sure he had an answer to now. "Thank you for not asking why." Jack glanced across the table. "Even though I'm sure you probably can take a good guess."

Pete nodded. "You always were interested in my sister."

Jack would never deny that truth.

"And she seems interested in you." Pete peeked

past him toward the table. "That is according to Maddie and…according to her friends."

"Still can't say her name, can you?"

He jerked his look back. "What?"

"Angie," he said. "Her name is still Angie."

"With a different last name," he whispered. "She's not free anymore."

Doesn't he know? Didn't her more verbal friend let him know she was divorced?

"But, we're not talking about me." Slamming his hand onto the table, he leaned close. "We're talking about you and my sister, and I want to see both of you happy."

He shook his head. "She's mad at me for not telling her I knew you were alive."

"She's just being stubborn."

He didn't think so. "She thinks I'm lying. She thinks I don't trust her like your father."

"Like Dad?" He sat straighter. "She said that?"

"Yes." He studied his cup as if the answers were there. "She still has some hang-ups about him."

"I'm not sure why." Pete sank back into the booth, pushing his cup away. "She was always Dad's favorite."

"That's not true."

"Maybe not."

He closed his eyes and then opened them wide. Unmistakable pain darkened his eyes.

"But I'll never know now, will I? I lost my chance over a decade ago."

Would he ever let that go? "He loved you, Pete."

"Yeah, that's what Mom's been telling me." He studied the rough surface of the table before shaking his head and glancing up "But, as I said before, we're not talking about me."

"No, we were talking about Angie."

Pete glared. "You need to go back and talk with Cass until she hears reason."

"She needs time," Jack said. "Tomorrow is soon enough."

"I've waited too long." He focused his attention on the table behind him. "I'm not allowing my best friend to make the same mistakes."

"Pete?"

"Go now, Jack." His gaze focused on the table again. "Before it's too late."

Was it too late?

Or could he somehow convince Cass he wasn't like her father? He saw her as a forever partner and friend— a woman to complete his life.

"You're right, Pete." He sat tall. "I'm not willing to let her win."

Chapter Twenty-Seven

The second Jack left the building, Cass locked the bookstore and turned off the ringer on her phone. Stubborn, yes, but she needed time to think through her problem before she went upstairs. Did she want to give up her chance to expand the lecture series? She'd been living with the idea for years. Was she truly allowing her stupid, stubborn attitude to put that desire on hold?

Her head was saying yes, but her heart... That organ that was so in love with the man was being obstinate. Yet, for the hundredth time since locking down her store, she refused to listen. She refused to acknowledge the truth.

He didn't trust her, just like Dad. She couldn't love another man who didn't believe in her. "I don't love him."

"Then why are you acting this way?"

She jerked forward, placing her hand on her chest. "Mom? When did you come inside? How? I locked the door."

"Just now." She settled into one of the seats in front of her desk. "And for how, I have a key, remember?"

A long, drawn-out silence yelled with unspoken words. "I can't talk with you now. I need to think."

"There is nothing to think about, honey." Calmness relaxed her and tempered her voice. "Because I'm not allowing you to stop Fontaine-Rogers."

"Mom?"

"You want me to be a part of the bookstore, so I have a say in what happens." She pointed toward the wall behind her. "You still want that building, right?"

"Of course, I still want it." *Now, Mom wants to be involved with the business. Now, when everything was going wrong.* "Why are you acting this way? Why do you suddenly care about the bookstore? You never did before."

Her eyes widened. "You don't think I cared?"

She shrugged. "You only care about it now because Billy's back. Just like Dad wanted you to."

Her eyes darkened; her face flushed.

Rarely did she see her mom so upset.

"You need to find a way to get past your feelings for your father, Cassandra Maria Rogers. Holding onto bad things isn't good for anyone."

"He never wanted you involved in the bookstore." She clamped her fingers to the edge of her desk. "Now, you want to get involved. Now that Dad is…gone."

"You don't think… I was always involved with the business." She took a deep breath, letting it out slowly. "After you were born, I decided—I decided, not your father—to put my family first. You and your brother and father were more important."

She heard the truth. Mom had never lied to her. Maybe, she didn't want to completely accept it because that might mean she was all wrong about her father. And Cass wasn't ready to let that belief go. "I thought…"

"And he didn't want to decide for you or Billy, either." She relaxed in her seat, taking in a long, deep breath. "He's Pete now, isn't he? I need to remember that."

"You're wrong about me and Billy, Mom. Dad had our lives all planned out. Well, at least he had Billy's." She glanced down at her desk. "He always expected him to take over the business one day."

"Because he's our oldest, honey."

"No, it was because he's a male."

Mom considered her comment before bursting out into a gleeful laugh. "You really believe that? You believe your father was a chauvinist?"

"Yes." She stood straight. "Yes, I did."

She reached over and grabbed her wrist. "I can't believe you think so lowly of your father."

"He treated you like..." She pulled away from Mom's grasp and took a deep breath, letting it out on a rush of words. "Three years ago, a friend of mine from college asked if I had a brother named Billy. He showed me a newspaper article about his car accident. Later, my friend heard the man in the accident died." Swallowing one breath after another, she calmed. "Dad told me you were too weak to accept it. That the news would destroy you."

She frowned and then grinned, tears glistening in her eyes. "Yet, he's alive."

Yes, he was alive.

"So, what does this have to do with Jack and the business partnership?"

"He knew Billy was alive." Why was Mom so accepting of this? Why wasn't she more upset? "Even after I told him he was dead and I needed to tell you before Hank did, he stopped me from doing it. He...kissed me."

Her smile softened. "Was it nice?"

"Yes." She jerked forward and sighed. "But that's not the point, Mom. The point is he didn't tell me. He knew for months."

"His name is legally Peter Morgan now, honey," she said. "You'll need to call him that."

"That won't be easy." Cass let out a breath. "But it's something we all need to do."

A gentle grin warmed her. "Tell me, honey, what would have happened if you told me about his death?"

Cass didn't know how to answer her.

"I fainted dead away when I saw your brother," she said. "Imagine how hard I would have fallen if you'd told me he was dead." She cupped her fingers around her wrist again. "It seems Jack did both of us a favor."

Yes, Cass was beginning to see that.

"Just the same as your father did three years ago." She frowned and leaned forward. "He was thinking of me."

"Yes." Peace flowed through her suddenly, leaving her feeling warm, and safe. Real. For three years, Cass had been worried about how Mom would react to her secret, and yet, only gentleness and love shined in her eyes. "So, you're not angry?"

"Not about this." She tightened her hold on her wrists. "But, I am upset about you breaking up your brand-new partnership with that man you claim to love so much."

"No, I said I didn't love him."

All Mom did was sit back and smile.

"I don't love him, Mom."

Her smile just deepened.

And that grin told Cass everything. Moms sense

truth in their children sometimes, right?

Maybe Cass should listen to her mother.

****

Mom had left the building two hours ago; still her last words rang out clear. Cass still saw her last knowing smile. "I don't love him, Mom. You're wrong."

Yes, you do.

Her heart whispered the sentiment. Her mind stayed silent this time.

And you loved Dad, too.

Tears rolled from the corner of her eyes down her cheek. She wasn't sure why.

Yes, you do.

Yes, she was crying because everything had changed...for the better. But also, for the worst. Her brother wasn't the same man he was when he left Greenfield, but that didn't mean he wasn't a part of her family anymore. *Pete* would always be her brother. He'd changed his name, but he was still family.

And Dad had died before he had the chance to make things right...to tell him he was sorry for everything. Pete deserved the time to process that loss, didn't he?

Was that the reason the younger Jack stayed so clear in her mind a decade later? She'd loved him because he was so sensitive to others. Simple as that. Was she about to lose the man because of her unresolved issues with her father?

"No."

She quickly closed her shop and entered the stairwell beside the store leading to her apartment. The brightness of the overhead lights flashed against the

297

chrome of the stove and sink, stirring her from her waking sleep. She covered her eyes and moved through the kitchen area into her living room, falling onto the soft sofa.

Footsteps echoed on the steps sometime later, and then a knock sounded. She wiped her eyes, not rising from the sofa.

Another knock came, louder this time.

Cass heaved in a deep breath but still didn't move from the couch.

"Cass?"

Oh, why hadn't I locked the lower door? "Go away, Jack." Silence followed her whispered acknowledgement.

Then a third knock sounded. "We need to talk."

"No." She rose from the couch and stepped toward the kitchen. "I don't have…anything to say."

"I'm not leaving this doorway until you let me inside, Cassandra Rogers."

Jack's tone told her he would have used her middle name if he'd known it. Just like her parents and Billy had done when they'd been upset with her.

The wood of the door creaked. "I'm not kidding."

She believed him. Why was she holding on to her unforgiveness anyway? Why was she still seeing her father in Jack? Mom's words rang in her mind. She'd always believed Dad didn't want her help at the bookstore. She'd been wrong. Was she also wrong about Dad wanting a man to take over? If she was older than Billy, would he still want his elder child running it?

Deep down inside rang the truth. Mom was right. Cass had misjudged him. She breathed out her bitterness over her father. Maybe not completely, but it was a beginning. A lifetime of belief needed more than a few seconds to change.

"Billy asked me—"

"His name is Pete," she whispered.

Silence.

"Dad slammed down the phone on him once." She swallowed a hard lump of pain. She might never forgive her father's attitude toward her brother all those years ago. She'd try, but she didn't know if she could. "Dad made him leave. Dad made him not want to come back. Dad caused all of it."

"Your dad didn't—"

"Yes, he did." A tear slipped down her cheek, then a second and third. Soon, a flood again flowed unchecked off her chin. She might have wanted to let the old go, but it wouldn't be easy. Not where her brother was concerned. "My brother never wanted to run the bookstore. If Dad trusted me, everything would be different."

He didn't say anything for a long moment. Only a creaking sound and a single step whispered into the sudden quietness.

"Dad made me promise not to tell Mom he was gone." Yet, Billy wasn't dead. Could Mom have known all this time? Could Dad? No, no one was notified. Neither of them could know for sure. Her parents just wished it was so. "Mom was right all along. My brother wasn't gone. She always believed he would return to Greenfield when things were safe."

"Cass, unlock the door."

Safe for him? Why was she thinking like that? Her father would never hurt him. He would've welcomed him back with open arms. Wasn't that why he wanted her to keep his death from Mom? That it was all a lie and someday he would return. And Dad was looking forward to his return.

Dad wanted him to come home.

Not because he thought Mom was a weak woman, or she was incapable of running the business, but because he was a desperate man.

"Your dad loved you."

Yes, she was beginning to remember that. Even if Mom hadn't convinced her, she sensed it to be the truth. Dad had to have noticed the changes she'd made at the bookstore, and he never complained even once. How could she have been so misguided?

A loud pounding sent her back a few steps. She inhaled a deep breath. She might have gotten things wrong about her father, but not with Jack. Jack didn't trust her enough to tell her about her brother. Even if he was thinking about Mom at the time, she could never forgive him. Even if he had promised her brother time to process Dad's death, she still... "Why don't you leave? You know I don't want to talk now."

"Tough." Knocking with a little bit less force on the door. "Look, we need to talk...about us."

She sighed. "I used to think there could be an *us*, but not anymore."

The knob rattled. She stared at the movement for a long second before letting out her breath and stepping toward the doorway. Her fingers wrapped around the twisting handle, stopping its slight rotation. Then her hand froze in place.

"Please, unlock the door."

"I know you promised my brother, but why didn't

you tell me?" Tightening her fingers around the rough door handle, she stared at the door. "Why did you want me to suffer? Hank must have suspected something was wrong. You should've told me what he thought was going on long ago." The knob relaxed in her hand a second before she heard him back away.

"I wanted to tell you, but what if Hank was wrong? We had no way of knowing then. We both thought waiting would be better."

Her hand tightened around the cool lock and twisted it open. Only despair rode her emotions when he grabbed the edge of the door and forced his way inside. Confusion and uneasiness arose as he shut the door and leaned against it. She couldn't read him now. She couldn't tell what he was feeling.

"I believed he'd died in that accident," he whispered. "I wasn't questioning things until I talked with Hank that first time."

"Yes, weeks ago." Sharp pain edged her backward into the table. "So, you did know something wasn't right when we ate at the Chinese restaurant? You and Hank knew then?"

"No, he only suspected something."

She slid along the table's smooth edge, keeping her distance from his advancing figure. No one could hold on to anger for long. With every word of their conversation, she realized her rage was dissolving. She wasn't ready to let it go. If he touched her, it'd be gone completely. "You can stay where you are, Jack."

He raised both hands and backed into the door.

"When did you meet the private investigator?" Freezing near the sofa, she looked down at her hands and then back at him. More of her anger left her at his backward movement. "Did you know him before you returned to Greenfield?"

His eyebrows arched high. "Is that what you believe? That I knew about your brother for months?"

"Yes." Cass clamped her fingers into the sofa. "I do believe it. You knew Hank before we went to the restaurant. You were calling each other by your first names."

"Because he asked me to call him that, that's why." He took a step toward her. "I told you that."

"I didn't believe you."

Not touching her and not even reaching out, he forced her into the side wall. Then he stepped back.

Fear rose sharp at his action, wiping out the last of her rage. Then confusion and something like painful regret took its place. He would never hurt her. He would never lie to her. Something in his eyes told her this truth now. Something real and truthful, something she might never see in them again, burned in his glance. If she couldn't find a way to make things right, she could lose him forever, and Cass didn't want that. Mom was right. She did love him.

"I admit I should have told you." He backed until the sofa stopped him. "I should have trusted you enough to let you know he'd shown up at my home. Especially after you told me you never said anything about it to your mother."

"I told Mom today, and she understood my reasoning," she whispered. "Or rather my dad's reasoning for asking me to withhold it."

"I'm glad," he said. "Yet, I should have told you."

"No," she whispered. A part of her wanted to hold on to her temper longer; a deeper side forced her to let it go. She didn't want to stay mad anymore. "If you promised my brother time to say goodbye, you needed to keep that promise."

His eyes widened now.

"I'm mad at Dad, not you."

His eyes widened even more. "Your dad loved you."

"I'm starting to remember that." She looked past his left shoulder. "I'm trying to focus on that truth."

"Honey?"

She gazed at him.

"I mean, Cass?"

She fought a grin. "Yes?"

He raised his right hand. "Can I move closer?"

She shrugged, and he shuffled a step closer. She lifted her hands between them. "Close enough."

"Remember when I told you Billy used to show up at the farm?"

She pressed her lips together and frowned.

"It was always after Billy and your father fought over you."

Her mouth opened slightly. "Me?"

He nodded. "They fought about you a lot."

"I never knew they did that," she said. "Why would they argue about me?"

"Simple." He whispered the words "Your dad wanted Pete to be more like you. He wanted him to enjoy working at the bookstore as much as you did." He leaned closer, placing both hands flat on the wall.

With her newfound knowledge about her father, she heard truth.

"He wanted his firstborn to run the business, not his second."

"He was old-fashioned and chauvinistic in some ways, but he wasn't a bad man." She looked past his squared shoulders. "He acted like Mom and I were incapable of being more than a wife and a daughter." She looked deep into his blue eyes. "At least, that's what I always thought until a few hours ago when Mom explained things. She chose to stop working at the bookstore. She wanted to focus on her family." A finger traced down her cheek, capturing the tears caressing down her chin.

"Your brother understood that part. He understood your mother wanted to take care of the three of you. But your brother saw your father in a different light. He told me your father wished you were the firstborn, so he would feel right leaving you the bookstore."

"No, he always wanted Pete to run the business…." She shook her head. "But I'm wrong about that, aren't I? Mom told me Dad held onto me too tightly because he was afraid I would leave like my brother."

"Maybe." He lifted her chin gently with rough fingers. "You need to talk to Pete about this, Cass."

Yes, she did.

Cass glanced at the hand still clamped into the sofa. She relaxed her fingers and stepped back.

"And you need to tell me the real reason you want to cancel our business arrangement."

She stopped near the side wall, looking everywhere but at the expressionless man. Why could she not read him now?

"You must have a reason for wanting to dissolve Fontaine-Rogers, LLC?"

Did she truly want to tear up the contract? Did she want to disappoint Mom like that? To mess with his mother's dream? Her own?

"Tell me you've changed your mind. Tell me you want to continue our agreement."

The pleading in his tone touched her. The sincerity behind it lightened her heart. She'd been so stupid and wrong. However, some things needed to change. They needed to be honest and talk to each other about everything. They needed to be open. "I need to be able to trust you, and you me."

He bit his lip. "I do trust you."

Cass believed him. "We need to always be honest with each other."

He raised both arms and slapped them on his thighs. "I've never lied, Cass."

Why was she still holding back? Had he done anything incorrect in this situation?

"Look, if you're uncomfortable sharing the Martinson building, I'll understand."

Oh, why did the man have to be so accommodating? She was the one at fault, not him. She was the one comparing him to another man. A man she was seeing in a different light. Dad wasn't a bad man and neither was Jack. They were both just, flawed, stubborn, and opinionated men.

"Cass, talk."

But, wasn't she just a flawed, stubborn, opinionated woman? Everyone said she was just like Dad. "Mom thinks I should keep the partnership going." Cass stepped closer, settling both hands on his upper arms. "She has the right to give her opinion on the issue, and she doesn't want to dissolve the partnership."

"But what about you?" He stood tall, lifting his

right hand. "Do you still want to work with me?"

The words leaped from her heart to her mouth. "Yes, I still want to work together." Real warmth and peace filled her. She tightened her fingers around his arms. "Yes, I do want that."

"Good," he said on an exhaled breath. "I'm glad."

The grin she loved so much broke over his face, brightening the room with its power. Flawed or not, Jack was the only man she wanted in her life.

"So, does this mean you're not upset anymore?"

"Maybe." Cass beamed. "We'll see."

He arched his eyebrows. "Just maybe?"

"You promise to discuss with me and Mom everything about our business from now on?" The questions needed to be asked, but she sensed his answer. His face showed her everything. "You won't hide anything from us again?"

He nodded. "I promise I'll never hide anything from the two of you again."

"Good." Cass looked away and then back. "One more thing, Mom will need the final say on what we'll sell in the coffee shop."

"I can live with that."

"Great." Her breath caught deep in her throat. "And one last thing, I want to use the contractor I chose to install the windows. Mom and I will be using Dad's money so I think we should have the final say. I will not be changing my mind. I want those new windows."

His brow arched. "All of your father's money now belongs to the LLC, honey."

"Yes, I'm aware of that." She tightened her hold on his arms. "But I still want to use it for those windows."

He stepped closer. "Oh, do you?"

"Yes, I do." The light scent of his tangy aftershave warmed her. "And we can debate about what to do with the upstairs apartment. Even though modernizing and renting it out is the best way to go."

"I don't agree, Cass. Setting up that apartment with some of the old-fashioned furniture in Mom's collection—"

"All the stuff belongs to Fontaine-Rogers, LLC now." She tapped his shoulder lightly. "Like Dad's money, your mom's collection belongs to the business also."

"Yes, the old-fashioned furniture in *our* collection is a way more unique way to go." He circled his arms around her waist. "And setting the backroom like an old-fashioned mercantile store would be a good, too."

"No way." She shook her head. "That's not happening."

His eyes darkened over a charming smile. "We'll see about that."

Cass figured she had a fight on her hands, but she could live with it. She loved fighting with this man.

Life was so much more interesting with Jack by her side.

A word about the author…

Theresa Stillwagon has been writing most of her life. Since one of her teachers praised a poem she wrote for a class assignment in the eighth grade, she's been putting words together in the hopes of seeing them in print. Not caring if anyone other than herself ever read them. Her dream came to reality in 2008 when she signed her first writing contract. She has since followed that with a dozen more. Two series and a few standalone romances.

Getting bored with life in Ohio, Theresa and her husband bought an RV and started traveling around the country with their cats, living and working in campgrounds. She enjoyed the lifestyle yet decided to give it up a half a dozen years later. She settled down in Georgia, near Savannah, with her cat. The heat in that state was too much for the three of them, so they moved back to their home state.

She's currently hard at work trying to finish a few older stories and rewriting a couple previously released ones. She's busy.

Her husband bothers her to no end, and her cat, Frankie, bites her for no apparent reason, yet she's happy.

You can reach her at her website—www.theresastillwagon.org

Other Titles by Author
One and the Same
Without Love